NEED HIM

BOYS, DADDIES, SNUGGLES AND MORE

ELOUISE EAST

CONTENTS

LIST OF CHARACTERS

Alice Mycroft, Ben's mother
Ben Mycroft, supermarket manager
Caleb Duncan, computer genius/app creator
Felix Cooper, Market Food night manager
Gareth Tremain, supermarket assistant
Lindsay Wentworth, Ben's personal assistant/friend
Martin Mycroft, Ben's father
Ollie, reader of the blog
Preston Miller, car salesman, Gareth's friend
Richard Tremain, Gareth's father
Toby, reader of the blog
Victor Welland, editor, Gareth's friend

1

GARETH

"We'd like to offer you the position if you're still interested?"

The words Gareth Tremain had needed to hear were music to his ears, and he tried not to grin like a lunatic as his shoulders relaxed. "Yes, I am. Thank you. I appreciate you taking the chance on me, regardless of my work history."

The blonde-haired woman smiled, collating the paperwork in front of her. "We believe in giving people as many chances as they're willing to use. Your extensive, though short-term, past workplaces gave high recommendations. In my experience as a recruiter, employees will stay at a company when they find what they're looking for."

Gareth raised his eyebrows. "That's..."

The woman, Ruby, laughed. "Not how everyone else thinks? Yeah, I know. It's caused several...fraught meetings between the manager and me over the years."

"I can imagine." He rested his hand on his chest. "I appreciate it, though. I won't let you down."

"Shall we take a look around, and you can familiarise yourself with the building before you start next week?"

"Sure."

They wandered down the stairs, chatting about the job and the company itself. Gareth didn't care what job he did as long as he had money coming in to pay the bills. There was nothing wrong with his past jobs. It was just his need to control things he struggled to let go of. He had hoped, when he applied for this job as a supermarket assistant, it would give him the freedom to do the job but under his own steam. He'd have to wait and see if that happened. He was too set in his ways after too many years of keeping his own head above water.

Ruby showed him through the store, pointing out the major areas he needed to be aware of. He would be mainly stocking shelves and keeping the warehouse in order, though he would be called to the checkouts when it was busy.

"Ah, here's someone I'd like to introduce you to. Ben, can I borrow you for a moment, please?"

"I do only have a moment, Ruby."

The voice was low and had a rumble as if the interruption annoyed him and he was restraining a growl. As he faced them, Gareth curbed his need to get closer. The man had black hair, shaved on the sides and longer on the top, showing several grey strands. His black-rimmed glasses, resting on a Roman nose, highlighted the green of his eyes, though did little to hide the bags underneath them. He was clean-shaven, and Gareth found himself wanting to test whether there were prickles coming through at that time of the day.

"Gareth, may I introduce Ben Mycroft, the manager of Market Foods? Ben, this is our newest recruit. Gareth starts next week."

Definitely not testing those prickles.

"Nice to meet you, Gareth." Ben gave a perfunctory smile and refocused on Ruby. "I need to get to a meeting, but please send over the current list of new employees as soon as you can. And let me know which staff are due their annual appraisal."

"Of course."

He nodded and strode off, Gareth watching his back until he disappeared around a corner.

"He's not always so abrupt. He's got a lot on his plate at the moment," Ruby said with a small smile. "Let me show you the staff areas, and I'll let you get back to your day."

The rest of the visit went by quickly, and he said his goodbyes before escaping into the heat of the summer lunchtime rush of the high street. He wore a white shirt, which he unbuttoned and removed, leaving him in a white T-shirt he'd worn for this reason. It had been warm in the meeting with Ruby, but he'd known being outside would be worse in a constricting shirt. He slung the shirt over his shoulder and made his way down the street towards The Pub—an ideal name for a pub, in Gareth's opinion—where he was meeting Preston.

Preston Miller was a forty-two-year-old man who worked in the same company he'd joined when he left school at sixteen. The car salesman might've had different roles within the company, but he had never felt the need to find somewhere new. Gareth gave him plenty of flack for it, but to be honest, it amazed him that anyone could stay in one place that long. Saying that, what Ruby had said made sense. When an employee was happy, they'd be willing to stay where they were. Why rock the sex swing when they didn't need to?

He passed by the black cast iron tables and chairs sat outside waiting for customers and pushed through the dark wooden door, the light catching against the gold trim around the frosted glass windows. The noise increased a fraction inside, conversation levels higher in the smaller area, but they were manageable.

He strode straight for the table they always tried to sit at and found Preston waiting for him.

"Hey, man. How are you?" he asked, leaning in for a back-slapping hug before sitting opposite him.

"Good, good. Did you get the job?" Preston's bushy black eyebrows raised as his deep blue eyes bore into him.

Gareth grinned. "I did. Start Monday." He laid his shirt over the back of the chair next to him.

"Nice one. I don't know how you charm all these companies to take you on. You're a menace." Preston chuckled, swiping his beer from the table and gulping the frothy brew.

Gareth shrugged. "They must know they can't survive without me."

"Yeah, sure." Preston rolled his eyes. "Hungry?"

"Starving," Gareth replied. He didn't bother opening the menu because he knew the contents by heart. Having been coming to this pub since before he was of legal age, he knew everything there was to know about the place, even though it had changed hands three times since then. The menu changed occasionally, but it didn't take him long to memorise the new contents.

"You ordering, or am I?"

"My turn, I think." He stood. "What're you having today?"

"Lasagne and chips, and can you grab me another beer?"

"Sure."

He aimed for the bar and rested his arms on the counter while he waited for the bartender to finish with their current customer. The air conditioning blew across his shoulders, cooling the sweat on his skin as he checked his phone. Nothing. He didn't know why he checked. There were only two people who would message or call him, and one of them sat across the room. The other was at work.

He placed his order and paid, carrying the beers back to the table after some small talk with the bartender.

"How did the meeting go?" Preston asked when Gareth returned to his seat.

"It was good. She showed me around the place, and I got to meet the manager." Gareth frowned.

"Not a good guy?"

Gareth scrunched up his face. "I don't know. He seemed…busy. Too busy."

"Isn't that what a manager usually is? They have plenty of work to keep them occupied."

"Yeah, I know." Gareth took a sip of his beer. "I don't know. Maybe it's nothing."

Preston leaned forward. "As you always tell me, trust—"

"Your instincts. Yes, I know." Gareth chuckled and shook his head.

They spoke about the usual crap friends talked about, continuing after their meals arrived. By the time they'd finished, it was time for Preston to return to work, and as Gareth drifted through the streets towards home, he, once again, wished he had someone other than his friends to socialise with. His father still worked all the hours of the day, as he had since Gareth's mother died when he was nine years old. Gareth had expected his dad to slow down now that he wasn't responsible for Gareth's financial situation, but if anything, the man worked harder now. He didn't know why.

But other than his father, Preston and Victor, his next-door neighbour, he had no one. The jobs he'd had were short, and he hadn't taken any friends along with his departure from the businesses—except Preston, but he was like a little to his cuddly…not letting go anytime soon.

He loved his friends, but he wanted more from life. He wanted someone to go home to. Not that he expected them to stay home; it was more a figure of speech. He wanted to know someone lived in the same house as he did and was excited for Gareth to be there, too. Problem was, he couldn't find someone for more than a few nights. His needs weren't excessive, he didn't think, but he knew he went full-on when he wanted something—or someone.

His Daddy nature wanted someone to look after, someone to cherish, someone to *need* him. Several past partners had told him he was too obsessive in his needs, too controlling. He'd tried not to be, but in the end, suppressing his nature had made things worse. For *him*. He'd gone completely the other way and had tried a non-kink relationship. He hadn't chosen the man well. His partner had been cruel and violent, hiding his physical nature behind a dazzling smile and humour that had only come to light several weeks later. Gareth had known it wasn't a good relationship after the first fist to his stomach, but he had wanted to change the man.

Gareth shook his head when he reached his house. There was no changing a man like that. After four months and too many bruises to count, Gareth had ended it, leaving the guy's place with a bruised jaw to match his ribs.

He'd locked himself inside his house for two weeks, giving himself a reality check, before emerging a new man—or rather, his original self. The same way he couldn't change that guy, he couldn't change himself. He was who he was, and he was now resigned to that fate. Be it alone or with someone.

The door lock engaged, and he strode for the kitchen, throwing his white shirt into the washing basket as he passed. His house was cooler than outside, but his throat was a desert, so he aimed for the fridge. A cold glass of milk helped lower his body temperature, and he wandered to the room he used as an office. Not that he needed an office, but the house had three bedrooms, and he didn't see the point in having them when there was only him. He knew why he'd bought a three-bedroom house, though. He was waiting for his boy.

Turning on his computer, he settled into his chair and brought up the information on the supermarket again. Since he'd been requested to return after the initial interview, he'd read through the company's details many times, wanting to be prepared to answer any questions they might throw his way about the company itself. Many companies wanted to know how much knowledge someone had about what they did, and often, penalised applicants for not having done their research. He hadn't needed to, but he found himself curious now that he'd met a couple of the staff. He clicked on the "Meet the Team" section and found photos of the major players of the company.

His gaze fell straight on the first picture. *Ben Mycroft. Manager. Had been with the company for nineteen years.* Gareth raised his eyebrows at that. Nineteen years? He must've started with the company straight out of school or college, depending on his age. Gareth had no idea what that felt like. He'd had far too many jobs between when he'd finished school and getting this latest one. He needed to find a job to stick with because soon, he'd have no more businesses to try if things didn't work out.

The only thing he had going for him was that he didn't leave the company in trouble with his departure. He always waited until they had a replacement for him and trained them where necessary. This helped persuade them to give him a better reference for new recruiters. This latest gap between jobs had been the longest he'd been without income, and he'd begun to worry he wouldn't find anything. He had some money saved, but it wouldn't have lasted more than a couple of months.

He stared at Ben's picture, the grey strands in his hair not visible in the photo as they were in person. He was also not wearing his glasses, making his green eyes appear more vibrant. What was it about the guy that sent a frisson of something along Gareth's skin? The man was good-looking, but his abrupt dismissal of him and Ruby had been unnecessary. If Ben had been his boy, he would've been spanked for that behaviour. No one should treat an employee like that, no matter what they did.

Shaking his head, Gareth exited out of the site and brought up his second love: his blog. *Boys, Daddies, Snuggles & More* had been running for several years, and each week, Gareth added a new post about the realities of being a Daddy, the expectation versus the truth, the emotional toll that being alone took on a Daddy. He didn't expect his blog to raise the roof, but he had a good number of followers, and comments flowed in whenever he posted. Some comments were sometimes a confusing mess of *"What the hell did I click on?"* but, for the most part, they were positive.

He opened up his latest draft.

When Money Matters by Daddy G

Money is a scary subject for most people. They hide the details behind closed doors, not wanting to show the depletion of their coffers or the mystical ability to duplicate coins. But, here and now, I will explain what I've come to realise. Money is scary. Having money is scary. Having no money is scary. There doesn't seem to be an in-between because when you have money, you're scared you'll lose it, and when you don't, you're scared you'll not be able to pay bills. For me, money is important for one reason only. I need money to be able to take care of my boy, to keep a roof over our heads, to keep food in our stomachs. It all boils down to needing it for my boy. And isn't that the scariest thought of all?

He read the entire article and sent it over to Victor for editing before he posted it that weekend. It was pure luck that his next-door neighbour was an editor. He hadn't known what the guy did for a living when they'd bumped into each other at the club they both frequented. Their surprise meeting at Bound had been fortuitous for many reasons. Victor was a boy looking for a Daddy, but their personalities didn't allow for a relationship between them. They were looking for different things, but it didn't stop them from becoming friends instead of the usual nods of greeting whenever they saw each other in their gardens in passing.

Gareth rubbed at his chest, the ache deepening when he thought of the gap in his life. A visit to Bound was becoming necessary, but he knew he wouldn't find what he was searching for. He never did. He had to try, though, because he refused to believe he would be alone forever. That wasn't possible. His boy was out there. He just needed to find him.

2

BEN

Ben Mycroft stifled a third yawn in as many minutes and scratched his head. The spreadsheet in front of him didn't make any more sense after his jaw cracked. He pulled his glasses off and rubbed his eyes. Sleep was what he needed, but he didn't want to set foot inside his house until it was absolutely necessary, and—he checked the clock on the computer—ten-thirty at night was not late enough to avoid his parents' questions. The time was coming when he would need to sit at the table with them for dinner because they only went a short time between updates about his life and work. After all, according to them, they were the reason he had what he had, weren't they?

Ben wasn't sure, but he knew their social standing made it necessary to keep up appearances. It was the only reason he agreed to the dinners, which were only between the three of them, thankfully. He had no siblings to help him shoulder the weight of being a vision of perfection, and the weight continually pressed down on him.

He pushed his paperwork to the side and leaned back in his chair, the squeak of it irritating him, staring out of the large windows and into the darkening sky. Summer had well and truly arrived, and with it, the lighter nights. In one way, it helped Ben get more work done because it felt like it was earlier than it was, but it also meant his parents stayed up later entertaining their guests. How they got away with paying for it all, he didn't know.

As expensive as their taste was, they did not have the money to back it up. Behind the scenes, his father, Martin Mycroft, was an investor, but he wasn't good at it. They certainly hadn't been able to afford to send Ben to university, as his student loan could attest. Somehow, though, they always scraped through their lavish lifestyle and kept their poise and standing within the community Ben wanted nothing to do with.

He stood and did a circuit of the office, then sat again, pulling the printout closer to him. He refocused on the numbers and lost himself in his job, barely remembering to turn on the light when it darkened enough to need it.

Groaning, he stretched his back out after having been bent over the papers for the last two hours. The figures looked good, and he put them in a pile to finalise the following day. He never signed off on reports late at night. He always waited until he'd rechecked them in the light of day.

He switched off the computer and grabbed his jacket from the back of his chair, slipping it onto his shoulders. Snatching his bag from the floor, he strode for the door, scratching at his rough, scruff-covered chin. He would've preferred to sleep at the office, but he'd done that enough times this past week. Too many times in a row, and people got talking. And not the good kind of talking.

Unable to stop the need, he strode for the shop floor, though he knew his assistant manager was more than capable of dealing with the supermarket during the night hours. The squeak of wire cages being emptied by the night staff, the bump of boxes being stacked and the occasional voice interrupted the quiet of the shop floor. Night shifts at the supermarket were lonely, from what Ben could tell. Employees worked on different aisles at the same time, making it nearly impossible for them to converse.

He wandered around, checking each of the aisles for problems before returning the way he came and bumping straight into an employee who had come around the end of the aisle at the same time he did.

"Sorry! I didn't see you there."

Ben frowned at the guy, not recognising him. "Who are you?"

The guy raised his eyebrows and continued folding the empty box he had in his hands before holding it against his chest. Ben had to look down slightly but immediately noticed the almost golden hue of his eye colour, along with laughter lines bracketing them.

"Gareth. Tremain. I started on Monday."

The name didn't ring any bells with Ben, but he wore a uniform and appeared to be working, so he let it go. Ben nodded, transfixed by his eyes. He couldn't remember seeing the colour before. His gaze roamed the man's face, his five o'clock shadow thicker than Ben's was but matching the colour and scruffiness of Gareth's hair—brown with streaks of grey. Gareth's forehead creased, and Ben thought it matched the deep lines beside his eyes.

"Mr Mycroft? Is everything okay?"

The man's voice broke through his daze, and he repeatedly blinked, trying to get his brain to fire on all cylinders again. A tricky feat for that time of night.

He cleared his throat. "Yes, fine, thank you. I'm heading home. Have a good night, Gareth."

The name on his lips felt strange, but he couldn't pinpoint why. He curled his lips in some semblance of a smile, nodded and hustled off, keeping his gaze ahead of him instead of over his shoulder like he wanted it to be. He must be more exhausted than he thought. He scraped his fingers through his hair and checked in with Felix before leaving him to it and heading for his car. Throwing his bag into the boot, he climbed in and set off for home, hoping his parents were in bed or at least enclosed in their room and Ben could sneak past them to his own room in the furthest part of the house.

He parked in the front of the house, lowering his beams to stop from advertising he was home, but the crunch of the gravel was loud in the stillness of the night. Grabbing everything he needed, he closed the car door quietly and aimed for the front door. The house was a three-storey detached building with six bedrooms, five bathrooms, three receiving rooms, a dining room, a large industrial-sized kitchen, a large conservatory and a triple garage. It was another reason his parents struggled for money because they refused to part with the house, though it was entirely too big for the three of them. Luckily, the house itself was paid for by Ben's grandfather, who was no longer with them. The only thing his parents had to do was keep the house afloat.

He kept his sigh to himself as he went in, locking the door behind him. Slipping off his shoes, he crept up the stairs, avoiding the steps he knew creaked. By the time he was safely behind his closed bedroom door, exhaustion had claimed him wholeheartedly. He stripped, throwing his clothes into the washing basket and, without even bothering with a shower, dropped into bed.

His phone alarm woke him not enough hours later. He rolled onto his back, groaning with the effort and feeling like he'd been in the same position as when he'd first fallen asleep. He threw a hand over his face and laid there waiting for an energy flare he knew wasn't coming. When his alarm blared again, he pulled himself upright and leaned his elbows on his knees, rubbing at his face until he couldn't stand the pressure against his skin any longer.

He blew out a breath, trudged to the shower and made the water just a shade above cold. It was the only way he knew how to get him awake and ready to go in the morning. Going through the motions of his morning routine, he let his mind wander to what needed to be done that day, but for the life of him, he couldn't remember. It might have something to do with the less than five hours of sleep he'd had.

With it being early, he knew he wouldn't see his parents and took a detour to the kitchen once he was dried and dressed to grab some fruit and a croissant, which he made quick work of while he drove back to Market Foods. As he parked the car, he stared at the building he'd made his career off.

When he'd been nearing the end of his university degree, he needed to find a placement for his final year, and Market Foods had been hiring for an assistant. He'd applied, and they agreed to take him on. He'd worked his ass off for the company and had climbed the ladder quicker than anyone else they'd ever employed, according to his previous boss. After thirteen years of working every part of the store, including all the office jobs, he'd been given the opportunity to take over as the manager when his boss had taken early retirement. Ben had jumped at the chance to prove what he was capable of.

His parents were over the moon, and although Ben had wanted the job, he wasn't as happy as they were. They threw it in everyone's faces whenever they could and made sure he was front and centre at their events, much to his consternation. Which was why he never attended unless he received specific instructions to. Unfortunately, it happened more than he wanted.

He loved his job, but something was missing in his life, and he didn't know what it was. He could do his job with his eyes closed and doubted many people could do it better, but he didn't do well with changes. When things didn't go according to plan, it irritated the hell out of him, which was a problem because things often didn't go his way, despite trying to think of every contingency. Lindsay, his assistant, was invaluable, and he refused to even contemplate her leaving. She was one of the few people who could withstand and break through his moods. If he could do the job without interacting with anyone else, he would.

Climbing out of the car, he locked it and wandered back into the store about six hours after he left it. He strode through the front doors, nodding at the security guard and drifted along the aisles, repeating his route from the night before. A voice stopped him from continuing.

"Mr Mycroft? What brings you back so soon?"

He glanced over his shoulder and got caught in the golden eyes of the new employee. What was his name again? "Good morning, Gareth. Someone has to keep this place running like clockwork."

"Don't you have underlings who can take over from you for more than a few hours? You look like you've barely slept."

Ben wrinkled his nose, wondering why Gareth was debating his sleeping habits, and glared down at him when he regained his brain function and realised the man had no right to question where he went and when. He might have sneered a little.

"I don't think that's any concern of yours, is it, Gareth?"

Gareth shrugged, those muscular arms holding onto a box as his body moved beneath the standard navy blue uniform every employee wore. "I was just trying to show some concern, but message received and understood."

He scooted around Ben and over to the cage, piling the box on top of the others. Pulling out another one, he retraced his steps, and Ben watched as he crouched, opened the box and began stacking the shelves with the bottles. Ben twitched his nose, trying to understand why his palms were clammy and his heart raced. There was something about that guy. He needed to keep an eye on him.

Ben shook his head and continued his routine, then went to find Felix.

"Good morning, Felix. How have things been?"

Felix was a stout older man whose ruddy complexion made him look three sheets to the wind. Ben knew he didn't drink on the job, but he'd been concerned when Felix had first started. The man had proven himself several times over, though. Another positive was that Felix had no complaints about working a continual night shift. His wife had passed five years previously, and they'd had no kids. Felix had told him many times that getting himself out of the house almost every day was a good thing. Gave him something to live for. Ben could've thought of better things to get up for every day, but each to their own.

"Same old, same old. Nothing to report. Shelves are being filled as they should be, and the bakery staff has already arrived and is working on getting the first loaves and cakes out of the oven within half an hour. All usual."

Ben clapped him on the shoulder. "I didn't believe you'd have it any other way. I'll be upstairs if you need me."

"Sure thing."

Ben aimed for the back of the building, pushing through the double doors to the employee area, and turned right, jogging up the stairs. Lindsay wouldn't be in for another hour, so he could check over his work from the previous evening and make sure it was all ready for her to distribute to the relevant people.

When he sat behind his desk and fired up his computer, he stared at the image that appeared. It was of a stone bridge over water, and the photographer had stood in a place where the edge of the bridge had met the water and created a perfect circle. Didn't that hit close to home? He was going round in circles. Working, sleeping, eating occasionally and drinking his weight in strawberry milkshakes, though he hid that weakness from everyone. As far as Lindsay knew, he consumed coffee, which he did a little, but not as much as the milkshake. There was a reason he had a lock on the lower drawer of his desk. No one would ever know about his drinking habit.

He stared at the picture a moment longer and clicked to log in. By the time Lindsay had arrived, Ben had a pile of documents waiting for her, and he had already polished off one glass of milkshake.

"Would you like anything from the bakery, Ben?" Lindsay asked as she stood in his doorway after their morning meeting.

"No, I'm fine, thanks."

"That's what they all say." Lindsay smirked.

As she walked away, he called her back. "I want someone to monitor the new employee, Gareth."

"Why?"

"I don't know. Just a feeling."

"Okay. I'll mention it to the team leaders."

Ben nodded and focused on his computer. He had work to do. Unfortunately, he wasn't as enthusiastic as he should be because his mind couldn't let go of the image of the flash that went across the golden eyes when Ben had shut down his concern. He shouldn't be worrying about upsetting employees when they cross boundaries they shouldn't have.

For some reason, he hated that look in the man's eyes.

3

GARETH

S ince the last time he'd spoken to the manager, Gareth had kept out of his way. Whenever he saw him approaching, he went in the opposite direction unless he had no other choice. He didn't need another tongue-lashing. Having been working there for a week, he'd heard softly spoken conversations about the man, and he'd asked questions, but most employees were closed-mouthed about him. It made Gareth more intrigued, but he kept pushing it aside. He didn't need the hassle of messing with his boss.

On his next night off, he arranged with Victor and Preston to visit Bound, and the moment he entered, his entire body relaxed. He grinned at his friends and made a beeline for the bar, ordering three bottles of water.

"God, I need this," he said, snapping his bottle open and taking a sip, all the while looking around to see if he could spot anyone who might be interested in his specific need.

"You're not the only one," Victor replied. His friend leaned his elbows back on the bar, opening his body to those who were looking his way. The boy in Victor knew the image he gave, and several men gave him a once over. Victor had the classic good looks of tall, dark and handsome with muscles that shouldn't exist with being an editor who spent much of his time on his ass. It wouldn't take him long to find someone to ease him that night.

As for Preston, the man had been in a foul mood since they'd picked him up. He'd refused to talk about it, but Gareth knew he would head for the impact play area sooner rather than later. The need to let those feelings loose would overwhelm him otherwise.

Gareth didn't see anyone who caught his eye straight away. "Let's hope there's something for everyone tonight."

"I've seen mine. I'm out," Victor said, bumping fists with Gareth and striding across the room.

"I'm not looking," Preston mumbled, turning to the bartender and requesting a whiskey.

Gareth raised his eyebrows at him, then turned to his side to study him closer. "What happened? And don't give me the 'nothing' crap. Something's got you riled. What is it?"

Preston snorted. "Life."

He threw the whiskey back the moment it landed in front of him, stopping any chance of him being able to play that night. Gareth frowned.

"Come on, man. What happened between yesterday and to-day?"

Preston pushed off the bar and faced him. "What? You mean he hasn't taken a billboard out yet?" He shook his head.

Gareth rubbed his forehead, feeling the creases. "Who? What billboard?"

Preston blew out a breath, holding his finger up for another drink. "My boss is engaged."

He said the announcement without a flicker of emotion, and Gareth wondered what it mattered that Preston's boss was getting married. Until he watched Preston rub his left pec straight over his heart as if it ached.

"You're in love with him." Not a question.

Preston swallowed hard. "I... We... I never even knew he had a girlfriend. I'm such an idiot."

Gareth winced. Crushing on your straight boss was never a good thing. "No, you're not. You have no control over who you fall for."

Preston snorted again. "If only falling was all it was." He shook his head.

"What do you mean?"

Preston dropped his head into his hands. "I've been sleeping with him for four months."

Gareth stared at his friend, making sure his face didn't show any of the surprise he felt. It was the last thing he needed. "Shit."

"He's made me into the other man, Gareth. I swore I would never be in that situation."

Gareth narrowed his eyes as heat surged through him in defence of his best friend. "That asshole is not worth it, Preston. You can do much better. It's not your fault."

"Do you know what the worst thing is?" Gareth waited. "He even looked me in the eye and smiled when he introduced her. The night after we'd been together." Preston threw back another whiskey.

"Right, man. Let's get wasted." He tapped the counter, getting the bartender's attention. "Could we keep these coming? We need to forget, please, Mr Bartender."

The bartender, who Gareth knew was called James, smiled and gave a single nod. "Your wish is my command."

"Park your ass, Preston." Gareth requested a pen and paper from James and wrote something down.

Preston waved his hand. "No, go find what you need. I'm good on my own."

"Nope, not happening." He turned back to the bartender and handed him the paper and his credit card. "When we're too drunk to stand, could you please get us a taxi back to this address?" He scooted himself onto a stool beside Preston.

"Not a problem." The bartender shoved the paper in his pocket as he slid two glasses of whiskey in front of them. "Bottoms up, gents."

Gareth clinked his glass against Preston's. "To forgetting."

"Shit yes."

They swallowed the liquid and slammed the glasses back down. Gareth had wanted to play that night, but his friend was hurting, and he would prefer to take care of him than have another empty hookup. The bartender returned his card and fixed them another drink.

"Do you want to talk about it?" Gareth asked Preston.

Preston remained quiet for a moment, then said, "Not really, but it's the least I can do when you didn't even know about the relationship."

Gareth didn't push. Words would come when he could say them, not before. When their next drink arrived, Gareth sipped it instead of guzzling it, staring at the brown liquid as he swirled it in the glass. For some reason, an image of Ben flickered through his head. The man needed to loosen up. A lot.

"As the movie script would have it, we worked late one night at the office, and one thing led to another. I honestly thought he was gay and single because there had been nothing to say otherwise." Preston swallowed another gulp. "We didn't advertise our relationship because, although the company doesn't stop inter-office relationships, they also don't push them. I was fine with not announcing us. I knew we would at some point, but it wasn't urgent for me."

Gareth wanted to punch the asshole. What was the point of keeping Preston on the side? Other than the sexual kind.

"He called a meeting this morning as soon as he came into the office. Everyone was surprised because he'd always refused to do a meeting on a Friday when employees were tired and waiting for the weekend." Preston huffed a laugh. "Barely eight hours after the last time we slept together, he had his arm around his girlfriend—fiancée—making the announcement."

"It's his loss, Preston. I know it doesn't feel like it now, but soon, you'll forget about the heartbreak and find someone else." He squeezed his shoulder.

"I know." The tone in his friend's voice showed exactly how much he agreed.

Two hours later, the bouncer bundled them into a taxi, which deposited them on Gareth's doorstep. Gareth wasn't as drunk as he expected to be, but the floor seemed to go full tilt-a-whirl on him when he tried to put the key in the door. Once he'd dragged Preston up the stairs and into the spare room, he was exhausted. He removed Preston's clothes, leaving his boxers in place, and tucked him under the covers. A glass of water and paracetamol on Preston's bedside table was the last thing Gareth did before heading for his room. He stripped and ducked under the shower spray, hoping to keep the nausea at bay. He swallowed paracetamol once he'd finished and dragged himself to bed.

As he lay on his back, Ben's face swam to the forefront of his mind again. What was it about the guy that had caught Gareth's attention? It wasn't like they had anything in common except where they worked. Ben was a workaholic—anyone could see that—and Gareth did what he needed to do and went home. The man barely smiled, and Gareth laughed enough for the both of them. From what Gareth could discern from the quiet murmurings at work, Ben was strict but fair. Gareth was strict, but only when it came to his boy.

He rubbed a hand over his face. He needed to stop thinking about him and create a plan of action to find a boy for himself. Maybe he needed to look further afield. Not long-distance or anything, but a short drive would be fine if he could find what he was looking for.

With that idea planted, he drifted off and jerked awake when a crash sounded, followed by curses.

Gareth laid a hand over his chest and calmed his heart before checking his clock and realising he'd been asleep for several hours. He dragged some joggers on and descended the stairs. When he entered the kitchen, Preston was standing barefoot amidst a spray of shattered glass.

"Stay where you are," Gareth said immediately. He jogged to the front door, slipping his bare feet into his shoes and grabbing Preston's, and returned to the kitchen.

"Sorry."

Gareth waved him away, handing over the shoes. "Don't be sorry. Just don't move. I don't want you to cut your feet."

He retrieved a brush from the cupboard under the stairs and swept the glass to the side of the room. Preston stayed where he was until Gareth told him it was clear, then he shoved his feet into his shoes and sank into a chair, cradling his head in his hands.

"Coffee?" Gareth asked.

"Please."

Silence descended between them while the kettle boiled. Gareth made the coffee in silence and placed the cup in front of Preston. He dropped into the seat next to him.

"How's your head?" he whispered.

Preston removed one hand and tilted it back and forth before cradling his cup.

Surprisingly, Gareth's head was fine. He had taken it easier than usual because of Preston's bombshell, but even then, he'd normally have a raging headache. Maybe he was still drunk. As they sat there in silence, Gareth thought through Preston's predicament. Was his boss going to expect them to carry on as they had been? Were they over and done and on to pretend nothing had happened? Could Preston continue working for him with everything that had gone on?

All questions he couldn't answer but wished he could.

"You'll be fine, Preston. I promise."

Gareth rested his hand on his best friend's back, hoping to give him a little comfort in the mess his world had become.

When Sunday rolled around, he was ready for work. He had spent the previous day with Preston and Victor, trying to cheer up the former. It hadn't worked despite the number of films they'd sat and watched. They'd both left late in the night, and Gareth had fallen asleep almost instantly—and slept for eleven hours. His body had obviously needed it.

The heat of the summer was still lingering as he entered Market Foods at eight that evening to start his shift. The night hours were perfect for him because there were fewer people who could tell him what to do and how to do it. He truly could do things his own way, as long as the items were where they should be by the morning. There were also fewer customers during the night, making him wonder why the supermarket stayed open twenty-four hours a day. It wasn't his business, though.

"Gareth, how are you doing?"

He pushed through the doors to the office so he could sign in and smile at his colleague. "I'm good, thanks. Did you have a good weekend?" He slid his employee card across the sensor and checked it flashed with his name before facing the woman.

Jane was a store assistant who spent most of her time at the checkouts or customer service desk. She was an older woman with greying hair that she said gave her the looks of a wise woman. Gareth couldn't disagree. Even though Gareth had only been there a week, he thought she and the assistant manager, Felix, would do well as a couple. He wouldn't mention it, though.

As she answered his question, footsteps sounded on the stairs, and he turned his head as Ben came into view. He immediately fixated back on Jane, nodding at her words, though he couldn't have repeated what she told him. Ben's shoes squeaked when he finished descending, and Gareth followed his progress across the floor, using that noise as an indicator of where he was. When it stopped too close for comfort, he clenched his jaw and interrupted Jane, pulling his phone from his pocket.

"Sorry, Jane. I need to get this."

She waved him away and faced Ben with a smile. Gareth pivoted in the opposite direction of his boss and put the phone to his ear, pretending to answer it. He pushed through to the staff room and over to his lockers, throwing his phone, wallet and keys into his small metal locker. After checking his watch, he sat on a seat in the corner, crossing his ankle over his knee and stared out of the window. He still had ten minutes before he had to be in the warehouse, and he needed that time to decide how he was going to interact with Ben if he needed to.

He wasn't sure why he was making such a big deal of it. It wasn't the first time he'd been brushed off. Resting his elbow on the arm of the chair, he cupped his jaw and sighed. What was it about the guy that had his words hitting closer to home than normal?

He let his mind wander, going over their interactions, few as they were, with a fine toothcomb. The man was tired and grumpy, which usually went hand in hand, but there was also something else Gareth couldn't put his finger on. It could just be that because Ben was his boss, he had to do what the man said and, as he knew better than anyone, having control was important to Gareth. While he worked at Market Foods, Ben had control over him in every aspect of his working environment. Maybe that was it.

Either way, he needed to get over it. Avoiding Ben would only work for so long, and it wasn't professional, which was something Gareth prided himself on.

He rose, brushing down the front of his uniform. He needed to grow some balls.

4

BEN

B en scrunched his nose as Gareth made his escape. He hadn't been able to speak to him properly since their last conversation the previous week. The apology he planned on giving the man was becoming harder and harder to deliver, and it meant he would have to do this in an official capacity. At least on the outside.

His conversation with Jane dragged on until she had to leave to start work, and he returned to his office. There was plenty of work still to be done, and after, he would call down to Felix and get him to send Gareth up. The man wouldn't be able to avoid a direct order from his superior.

He barely finished his first task of writing up his summary of the staff appraisals that had taken place that week before his hand was on the phone and ringing.

"Felix."

Ben cleared his throat. "Felix, could you send up Gareth, please?"

"Of course. Anything the matter?"

"No. I just want to speak about his first week."

There was a second of silence before Felix agreed, and Ben knew why. He hadn't asked to see any of the other employees when they'd been there for a week before. He didn't care what people thought of him as long as their jobs got done. The rumours surrounding him were not far off the mark, but he was never mean to anyone unless they truly deserved it. His perfectionist nature ensured he needed things to be done in the right way, and if that meant he told someone how to do it, so be it. He knew much about this business, having been in every job position within the company, that he wanted to impart his knowledge so they did things properly. After all, the fate of this particular branch was in his hands.

He unlocked his bottom desk drawer and opened the cardboard box lid. The strawberry milkshake mixture waited for him, and he pulled it free, spinning his chair around to reach for the milk from the mini-fridge behind him. The milk glugged from the carton as he filled his travel mug, and he smiled. He had no idea when he'd received his first taste of the drink, but he'd been obsessed from the minute he'd tasted it. His parents refused to entertain his obsession and served him tea or wine during the required dinner meetings. But here, where no one could see him or tell what he was drinking, he could drink it all he liked.

He replaced the milk in the fridge, spooned some mixture into the cup and whisked it together. Most people enjoyed the thicker, creamier milkshakes they could get from restaurants, but he loved the more liquid kind. Once it was ready, he replaced the mixture, spoon and whisk after giving them a clean, closed the lid and locked the drawer again. He tightened the lid to the travel mug, sipped through the hole and closed his eyes as the strawberry flavour burst onto his taste buds.

The knock at the door came seconds later, and he double-checked the lid was in place and called for Gareth to enter.

"Gareth, good. Come on in and take a seat," Ben said, scooting his chair closer to the desk and setting the mug next to his laptop.

Gareth stood tall as he wandered across the room, though Ben could sense the tension in him. He settled his slightly smaller frame in the visitor's chair and crossed his ankle over his knee. His forehead was heavily lined, and the lines around his mouth were deeper, though not from laughter this time. His scruff appeared more pronounced than usual. Had he been out the previous night or even earlier that day? Was he still drunk?

Ben realised he was staring and refocused on the paperwork in front of him. It was a blank appraisal form, but he had no intentions of going through it.

"How are you finding the work?" he finally asked.

Gareth raised his eyebrows. "It's fine. I know what I must do and when I must do it, and it gets done. It's not difficult."

The words were sharp, and Ben thought back to their previous encounters. The slight edge to Gareth's tone had been missing in those conversations. Was he angry?

"Do you have a problem with me?" Ben asked.

Gareth snorted. "I would think that would be the other way around. You seem to have taken a dislike to me from the beginning."

Ben sat back at that. "I have nothing against you."

Gareth stared at him, then shrugged. "My mistake."

"I don't," Ben insisted.

"If that's how you speak to all your staff, I'm surprised you have any left."

Ben stared at him, unused to the backtalk, as he would call it. "There is nothing wrong with the way I speak to my staff. I explain what I need to be done, and they do it. If they don't, there are consequences."

"It *is* just me, then."

Ben bit down on his bottom lip, scrunching his nose as he gazed at his paperwork. Why was he focused on Gareth? He didn't know, but something was bugging him about the man.

"Are you happy with the shifts you've been given?"

Gareth nodded. "Yeah. Neither here nor there for me. I have no one waiting for me, so I can come and go as I please."

"Must be nice," Ben murmured, eyes widening when the words escaped his mouth instead of being under his breath.

Gareth leaned forward, resting his elbows on his knees and cocking his head. "Why are you here all hours of the day and night if you have someone waiting for you at home?"

Ben swallowed and chewed his lip some more. "That doesn't concern you."

"Do you have a problem at home?"

Gareth seemed invested in Ben's answer, and whereas normally he would've brushed it off, he found he didn't want to. He brushed his hand across the front of his desk, wiping away invisible dust as he tried to regain his bearing on the conversation. He set his shoulders.

"My home life is none of your concern, as I've told you. It's nothing I can't handle."

"I'm serious. Is your partner kind to you?" Gareth's nostrils flared.

Ben's gaze met Gareth's, the golden hue shimmering with an intensity Ben couldn't understand. "I don't have a partner," he found himself saying.

Gareth raised his eyebrows. "Why do you not want to go home? Is your house too empty?"

Ben snorted. "No. Far from it, unfortunately." He shook his head to get rid of the need to bare his soul to this man he didn't know. "That's not why I brought you here."

"Do you have roommates?"

"No."

"Do you live with family?"

Ben blinked. "Yes. How did—"

"Are they kind to you?"

Ben shifted. "They're not unkind."

"Do they treat you right?"

Ben chewed his lip. "It's not all bad."

"Do they know you exist?"

The words, however intrusive, hit Ben where it hurt. But instead of folding in on himself, he glared across at Gareth. "Enough now. We're here—"

"Do you wish they saw you as a person?"

He stood. "I said, enough."

"Are you scared to go home?"

Ben stamped his foot. "Stop!"

Gareth stood, facing him on the other side of the desk. He pointed his finger at Ben, eyes narrowed. "Do not stamp your foot at me," he said. His voice sent shivers down Ben's spine. "I'm trying to understand you. Do not get upset when someone shows an interest in your life."

"You're being—"

"Did I say you could talk?"

Ben clamped his jaw and glared as hard as he could. His skin felt tight, his temperature rising like the lid of a pan of boiling water. Who gave this man the right to talk to him like this? Ben could fire him for how he behaved.

Gareth shoved his hands into his pockets and lifted his chin. "I'm going back to work. I want you to sit down, drink your strawberry drink and calm the hell down. Do not think about touching your paperwork until you have finished your drink. Nod if you understand."

Though it galled him to do so, he nodded.

"You're working too damn hard, and your emotional levels are overwhelming you. Take some time to relax and get your head on straight." He paused, running a hand through the greying, scruffy strands of his hair. "If you need me, call for me."

Ben watched Gareth stride to the door, slip out and close the door again. Why did he not fire his ass? He had every right to with how he'd been spoken to, but something held him back. That elusive understanding, just out of reach, of why he didn't want Gareth gone.

He reached for his drink, taking a sip, and paused when he remembered Gareth's words: *Drink your strawberry drink.* How had he known? No one else did. Closing his eyes, he sipped his milkshake, letting his mind clear. What Gareth said didn't matter. He didn't know Ben. He didn't know about his life. He had no clue what Ben had to put up with.

But he'd guessed right, hadn't he?

Ben scrunched his eyes tighter to stop tears from spilling and tried to clear his mind again, letting everything go except the feel of the cold, strawberry milk flowing down his throat. He breathed deeply, allowing the leather chair to cradle his body. When he finished his drink, he opened his eyes and focused on his paperwork, sliding it towards him.

Three hours later, he realised he'd finished everything he could. It was unheard of. He always left some things to be finished the following day. Staring at the piles of paper on his desk, he wrinkled his nose. Surely there was something he'd forgotten.

He shook his head as he packed everything away, locked his office and headed for the shop floor. The walkabout settled him until he saw Gareth. Pausing, they stared at each other, neither coming closer. Gareth raised his eyebrows in a question Ben understood, and he nodded in response before tearing his gaze away and finishing his rounds. He bid goodnight to Felix and drove home.

Distracted as he was, he didn't notice the lights were on in the house until he'd already opened the door. So much for a relaxing evening. As he entered the lounge, it was worse than he thought.

"Benjamin, come join us. Martha and Henry have come for a visit. We've just poured some wine." His mother, Alice, looked closer to thirty than her actual age of sixty-two, her platinum blonde hair coiffed perfectly atop her flawlessly made-up face. Her dress was in impeccable condition, swaying around her knees as she effortlessly sashayed across the room towards his father, who held out his hand for her. She perched on the arm of the chair and crossed her legs. "Don't just stand there. Pour yourself a drink. Henry was just asking us about your career. Now you're here, you can answer his questions."

Exactly what he didn't want to do, but he obediently drifted to the bar, poured himself a large glass of white wine—he hated the stuff, but it would fortify him against the coming inquisition—and sat on the chaise lounge opposite their guests.

"Well, Benjamin," He gritted his teeth at the use of his full name, "how are things up in the skies of management?" Henry asked, grinning like there was a secret club they were both in.

Ben gave a small smile. "Busy, as always. Things are going smoothly. Staff retention is higher than it has been in years. Recruitment has been increasing. Sales are up. Expenses are down. All in all, I couldn't ask for more." Except, apparently, someone to put his foot down and tell him exactly what he should be doing. He pushed the image of Gareth aside.

"Glad to hear it. Are you aiming for the area management role next?" Henry asked.

Ben's father, Martin, interrupted them. "Of course, he is. He's been in this role for long enough now. He's brought the store up to scratch, and now, it's on to bigger and better things. I can see him reaching the top soon enough."

Not if Ben could do anything about it. There was no way he wanted to take over in the upper echelons of management. If he had his way, he'd stay where he was. If he was *completely* honest with himself, he'd prefer to be demoted to store assistant again, though he knew his perfectionist tendencies would baulk at that.

Tuning back in, he heard, "—him to attend the benefit. He'll be able to meet some influential people there," Henry said, puffing out his chest.

"I agree." Martin turned to him. "Benjamin, make sure you book out that date. You'll need to attend by yourself because your mother and I will be out of town that weekend."

Ben's heart raced, and he forced himself not to shout his happiness to the rafters. "Could you please remind me again which weekend that is?"

Alice sighed. "Oh, for goodness' sake, Benjamin. You need to get your PA to work more efficiently if you haven't been reminded of the dates." She shook her head. "It's the last weekend in September. Remember? We're going for a long weekend to the Lake District. We're meeting with many independently wealthy people."

And that is the only reason they're going. To see who else they can pull into their circle and use to gain favour.

"I remember now. I apologise. There has been a lot going on at work."

The conversation turned to the events Henry and Martha were holding in the run-up to Christmas, and Benjamin stayed until his wine glass emptied. Feeling tipsy, he gave his apologies and bid everyone goodnight, trying to walk in a straight line while there was a chance his parents were scrutinising his every movement. When he closed the door behind him, he leaned against it for a moment, then dragged himself up the stairs, using the bannister to help him.

He climbed into the shower after throwing his clothes in the washing basket and stood under the spray for as long as he could stay upright. His legs threatened to bend and not keep his weight, so he dried and fell into bed. Despite his energy levels being at an all-time low, his brain couldn't stop moving like an express train. There were many things he could think about, but the one that stopped front and centre: Gareth.

He had many questions about the man and his effect on Ben. How had he known what was in his mug? How did he manage to calm Ben down when Ben hadn't realised he was spiralling? Why did Ben listen to a stranger? Why had it made him more productive than ever before? Why did he not fire the man after being spoken to like an errant child? Or, even worse, a troublesome teenager?

And last but not least, the question that scared Ben the most. Why did he want Gareth to do it again?

5

GARETH

Gareth had waited with bated breath for Felix to come and escort him from the premises. He knew he'd crossed all sorts of boundaries with Ben, but he'd seen behind Ben's façade. The man was walking a tightrope, and Gareth could see he was teetering. Whether Ben wanted to jump or if he just held too much and couldn't take it all, Gareth wasn't sure, but he refused to allow him to do so. There was something between them, no matter whether either of them agreed, and Gareth wanted to know what it was.

When Ben had stopped at the end of the aisle Gareth had been stocking, he'd stared at his boss, waiting for the summons to leave. In the silence, he'd raised his eyebrows, asking if everything was okay in the only way he dared. Ben had nodded and wandered off, leaving Gareth exhaling heavily. At least he still had a job. For how long, he didn't know because all it would take was for Ben to sleep on it and awake the following day with different feelings about the situation.

There was nothing he could do about it now. What was done was done, and all that.

Ben's situation and reactions were with him for the entire shift, and the closer he got to the end of his shift, the tenser he became,

39

expecting someone to yell at him and for him to yell back, ending his time with the company. No one did, and he didn't see Ben either. As he left, he checked the car park but didn't know which car was Ben's; therefore, he didn't know if Ben had arrived or not. It was only six-thirty in the morning, and most people would still be in bed. If there was one thing he'd learnt about Ben, though, it was that he didn't sleep much and spent far too many hours at work. Gareth would have loved to get that routine out of Ben's system, but it wasn't his place.

As much as he realised he wanted it to be.

Boys, Daddies, Snuggles and More

What do you do in Age Play? by DaddyG

Andyplays231: I've heard the term Age Play used in the club I go to, and I wanted to know what it involves. I'm new to the lifestyle and want to learn where I fit in. I'm not sure if it will be what I need or not. Thanks, DaddyG. Andy.

Well, readers, this is a question I get a lot. And my answer is simple. You do whatever you want to do. Of course, there is a more detailed breakdown of what you could do, but nothing is set in stone. You can, and most likely will, find your own way through the process.

However, because I'm such a good friend, I'll give you a few pointers to get started and see if this is something you might like to explore.

First and foremost, let me say that Age Play is when an adult regresses to a younger age than they are. It could be a baby with nappies, dummies and bottles. It could be a toddler who wants to build towers and knock them down. It could be a pre-teen or teen who becomes unruly and destroys the calm. The terms for these differ depending on the person, but they could be Babies, Littles, Middles or Boys, just for starters. If you are at all unsure, ask and respect what you're told because everyone is different.

Returning to the subject at hand, what to do in Age Play. The long-winded answer to this is that it depends on what age the boy is regressing to.

Gareth stopped and rubbed his face. He needed more sleep than what he'd got, but no matter what he'd tried, he hadn't been able to drop back off after one o'clock. Five hours of sleep was less than optimal, but at least he'd had some. It was why he was now working on his next blog post, though, admittedly, he didn't know how much sense he was making. Luckily, it wasn't needed for four days, and he had time to re-read it when he was more coherent.

He dragged his fingers through his hair and decided to grab something to eat—he had, after all, been up for three hours now. The kitchen provided the fixings for sandwiches—his favourite. It was a simple meal, but with the different types of fillings he could put in them, they were versatile. If he wanted something simple, he could have a cheese sandwich. If he wanted something more substantial, he could have a chicken, sweetcorn and mayo salad. Or a roast beef with horseradish. Or tuna salad. There was a sandwich filling suitable for every occasion as far as he was concerned.

He'd just taken a bite from his egg mayonnaise when his phone rang, and he cursed. Chewing fast, he pulled it from his pocket and paused. Market Foods was calling. He placed the sandwich on the plate and got ready to hear his dismissal.

"Hello?"

"Gareth, it's Lindsay, Ben's PA. He would like to arrange a meeting with you just before your shift tonight if you can spare the time?"

It wasn't quite what he was expecting. Surely, she wouldn't infer he would have the meeting and start his shift if he was likely to be fired, would she?

"Sure, yes. Any time in particular?"

"If you could be here for seven-thirty, that would be great."

"Yeah, okay." Half an hour. It couldn't be anything too sinister. "Can I have a clue what it's about?"

Lindsay sighed. "I don't know, to be honest, Gareth. He just asked me to make the call. I wouldn't be concerned, though. He didn't make any noise about problems with you."

"Okay. No problem. I'll be there for seven-thirty."

"Fantastic. I'll let him know. Thanks, Gareth."

He hung up and stared at the phone. If he wouldn't just end up talking to Lindsay again, he would've called and asked to speak to Ben. He remembered the way Ben had looked when he stamped his foot the previous evening. His face had mottled, and if Gareth was a betting man, he would've expected Ben to swipe everything from the desk if his temper had risen any further. It was why Gareth had put his foot down, though he'd never expected the man to acquiesce as he had.

Gareth found himself wanting Ben to be the Middle he'd always wanted to care for. A Middle who had teenage tantrums pushed boundaries and demanded attention in a variety of sneaky and inventive ways. He could see it, but he couldn't push his fantasies on the man. As far as Gareth knew, Ben could be a complete spoilt brat with his parents giving him everything he ever asked for, and that was a different type of brat.

His sandwich still tasted good, despite the competing thoughts barrelling through his head. He focused on the bite, chew, chew, swallow mechanics of eating and let his mind whirl. From experience, he knew trying to sort through the images and words before they'd settled was next to impossible. Worrying was something he tried not to do, but it wouldn't happen when his brain took over, believing there was something he needed to do to take care of someone.

Like Ben.

Did Ben even need taking care of? Gareth's instincts said he did, but he wasn't sure if it was in the same way that Gareth wanted to take care of him.

After he'd put away the dishes he'd used, he grabbed his headphones and his armband for keeping his phone safe and slipped his trainers on. It was a little warmer weather than he would usually go jogging in, but he needed the release and freedom to work through everything before he went to work that night. At least, he'd thought to put shorts on instead of joggers.

He locked the door behind him and slid the keys into his zip pocket before plugging in his headphones and choosing his playlist. He had an eclectic taste in music, but for jogging, he preferred music with a beat he could time his feet to, giving him a chance to speed up or slow down and vary how strenuous he was. The phone slid into the armband, and he stretched his legs against the wall, then set off at a slow speed, ignoring the music to begin with.

The thump of his feet against the pavement settled him in a way few things did. Being a Daddy was better, but jogging would do in a pinch. As the distance between him and his home grew, he started following the beat of the music, his legs and arms pumping, and his mind cleared. He brought forward images of Ben, remembered their interactions, noting Ben's body language and facial expressions. The attitude was hard to measure. It could be because Ben was the manager, and he'd earned the right to act how he wanted, or it could be because he wanted something he didn't understand. Someone to give him the space to act out and bring him back in again.

Or was Gareth projecting his hopes onto him?

The only way he would know is if he asked. After all, hadn't he just told his readers in his blog post to ask and respect the answer? Granted, the post hadn't gone live yet, but still.

He turned a corner and found himself almost home; he really had been lost in his thoughts. When he paused outside his house, he stretched his muscles again briefly and headed for the door, stopping when he heard his name.

"Look what I have!" Victor called from his open car window as he parked on the road outside.

"If it's anything to do with your sex life, I'm not interested." Gareth smiled and waited, hands on his hips.

Victor stuck his tongue out like the child he was and climbed from the car, holding a white bag aloft. "Chinese!"

"In which case, welcome to my humble abode." Gareth waved his hand and bowed.

"No way, mister! We're eating at mine this time. Go get yourself washed and dried. I'll be waiting."

Gareth grumbled, but he supposed it didn't matter because he would head to work soon, anyway. "All right. I'll be there soon. Don't eat my food."

He dashed up the stairs to his bedroom and jumped into the shower while the water was still cold. If Victor had the chance, he would eat both their meals before Gareth could shave. Not that Gareth shaved very often. Although he might make the effort tonight, as he'd be seeing Ben. Gareth shook his head and concentrated on washing away the sweat he'd accumulated. A hair wash, a life-threateningly quick job with the razor, and a drying frenzy, and he dressed in his work uniform and hoped he didn't make a mess of it. Kung Pao Chicken was not the easiest thing for him to eat without making a mess—nothing was, as a matter of fact—but he'd try his best. Otherwise, he'd nip home to change before going to work.

He didn't bother knocking when he arrived at Victor's house. He let himself in and hustled to the living room, where he knew Victor would be waiting.

"Finally! Where did you go for the shower? Australia?" Victor lounged on the sofa with his tie loose around his partially unbuttoned shirt, messy hair and bare feet beneath his suit trousers. The effect was…interesting. Weird but interesting.

"Yes, I did. The water is much better from there," he quipped, leaning down to take his container and a fork—he refused to use chopsticks because he'd starve, no matter how many times they showed him how to use them.

He sank into the sofa next to Victor and said, "So, what's happened?" He forked some food into his mouth, encouraging Victor to talk by just not being able to say anything himself.

Victor sighed. "The Daddy I met the other night isn't interested in more than what we had." He pushed the food around the container with his chopsticks, staring into it as if it held all the answers to the modern world's problems.

"Oh, geez. I'm sorry. There are plenty of us around, though. You'll find someone."

He sighed again. "I want to find someone now. I'm too damn impatient. I want my happily ever after now." He dropped the hands holding the container to his lap and gazed at Gareth, the sparkle usually visible in his eyes concerningly absent.

Gareth put his food back on the coffee table, did the same for Victor's and pulled him close, wrapping his arms tightly around his friend. "I know you do. It's not fair at all that you have to wait. It will be worth all the pain in the long run, though. I wish we had worked out. I truly do."

Victor snuggled his cheek into Gareth's chest and blew warm air across his body when he exhaled. "Thanks. We can't change who we are, though, can we?"

"No, which is why you'll find someone who's perfect for *you*. Give it time, and don't settle for second best. You deserve all the happiness." He pressed a kiss to Victor's head. "Do you want to go to Bound this weekend? See who we can rustle up for a happily ever after trial run?"

Victor chuckled. "Yeah, all right. I've nothing better to do."

Gareth pushed him away in mock anger. "Well, if that's how you think of our time together, I'm out of here." He went to stand but fell back laughing when Victor held onto his arms.

"You know I didn't mean it like that!"

Gareth subsided and smiled across at him. "I know. I'm only messing. Come on, eat up. You're too slim as it is."

"No, I'm not. I'm perfect." Victor pouted.

"That's right. You are. Now, we need to find that Daddy who's perfect for you."

He bid goodbye to Victor an hour later and climbed into his car, setting off for work. He had time to consider how he was going to approach Ben, but he wasn't sure the easiest way to explain what he thought Ben might need without explaining who Gareth was. He would tell him, but he wished he could explain the rest before he threw himself on the fire.

Maybe he should think about it as a blog post. Okay, he didn't have time to have a heartfelt essay ready to go, but he could explain it as he would to his readers. He hoped.

By the time he ascended the stairs to the offices, he had an idea of how to approach it, but it all depended on how receptive Ben was to his words and ideas. If he knew anything about the guy from the extremely short time he'd known him, it was that he could take offence at things and veer into tantrum land before anyone could inhale.

Hopefully, if that happened, Gareth could show Ben exactly what he was doing. Or maybe he'd fire him. Either way, they'd have an answer.

6

BEN

Ben didn't know what possessed him to ask Lindsay to arrange a meeting with Gareth. Even Lindsay had given him a strange look, but he'd ignored it, not willing to explain what he couldn't understand himself. He waited for what seemed like hours after Lindsay left for the knock on his door.

When it happened, he inhaled and called for the person on the other side to enter. The first thought that jumped to the forefront of his mind was that Gareth looked good in the navy blue store uniform. It wasn't loose enough to hide his muscles and not tight enough to be obscene, and Ben found himself wishing he'd requested the tighter versions of the clothes. The second thing he noticed was that Gareth was clean-shaven. He couldn't remember seeing him with such soft-looking, bare skin before. He focused on the sleek contours of his face until he reached Gareth's mouth—which was quirked up at one side.

Ben blinked and cleared his throat, chewing his bottom lip as he tried to regain his balance and ignore the need to fall into those arms.

"You don't need to be embarrassed," Gareth said, his voice as soft as Ben would expect someone in a library to speak. Or someone trying to tame a scared cat from behind a sofa. "You can look as much as you want."

Ben avoided his gaze. No, he really shouldn't. He tidied some paper into a pile and tapped them on the table to square them off. Carefully setting them in front of him again, he linked his fingers on top of them and braced himself to look at the man he'd asked to come. When he lifted his eyes, he was struck once more by how handsome Gareth was and couldn't find the words to explain why he was there.

Gareth appeared to understand because he sat on the edge of the chair opposite Ben and leaned his arms on his desk. "How about I go first?" he continued in that soft, alluring, calming voice. Ben nodded, and Gareth's smile was his reward. "Okay. I'm going to say some statements, and you're going to nod or shake your head for yes and no. All right?" Ben nodded. "And if you want to clarify anything as we go, you'll need to speak up."

Ben nodded and briefly wondered why he was being accommodating when, normally, he would get right up in someone's face for talking to him like that.

"Let's start with something easy. Do you like strawberry milk?"

Ben briefly closed his eyes and nodded, feeling heat creep into his cheeks.

"Nothing to be ashamed about. Everyone has at least one vice. Do you like to make sure jobs are done properly?" A nod. "Do you feel like no one can do the job as well as you can?" A hesitant nod and Ben closed his eyes, not wanting to see Gareth's expression if the questions continued as they were. "Do you like getting lost in something, so you don't have to think about anything else?" A nod and Ben lowered his head. "Are you happy?" Ben did nothing, tears filling behind his closed lids. "It's okay."

A hand covered his, and Ben held on. He didn't know why he was answering Gareth's questions, but there seemed to be something happening between them, and for the life of him, Ben couldn't stop the lorry from leaving the warehouse.

"Now for a different question. Did your parents spoil you growing up?"

Ben's eyes flew open and met Gareth's gaze straight on. "Jesus Christ, no. They were the complete opposite." It was only after he'd finished that he realised he'd spoken for the first time since Gareth had entered the room. The sound of his own voice gave him more stability and focus. He refused to let go of Gareth's hand, though. "I have been the centre of their attention for one reason only—making sure I behave as expected to shine a favourable light on them and their social standing."

Gareth squeezed Ben's hand. "I'm sorry for that."

Ben shrugged. "It is what it is."

Gareth shook his head. "You can change it. In fact, you should."

"No. Everything has been running along like clockwork since I was a kid. There's no changing the result."

"What do you mean?" Ben sighed, his free hand curling and uncurling the corner of a piece of paper, but he couldn't answer. "What are you going to lose if you step free of their 'world?'" Gareth asked after a minute.

Ben thought about it. What would he lose? "A roof over my head."

"You're the manager of this store. You can afford to rent somewhere," Gareth countered.

Ben frowned. "My parents."

"Would you? Or would they turn their attention to their own lives and find their own way to keep their social standing alive?" Ben stared at him, mouth gaping. "Anything else?"

Ben tried to come up with something else, but he had nothing. His life consisted of working, avoiding his parents, sleeping, rinse and repeat. How had he not seen that before? He had no friends, no other family, nothing outside of work. He'd sequestered himself in this role of...whatever it was. Who was he?

Gareth stood, and Ben tightened his grip to stop him from pulling away, but Gareth kept hold and rounded the desk until he was beside Ben's chair. He pulled on Ben's hand until he stood and led him to the sofa in the middle of the room. Ben's slightly taller stance was more noticeable when they were standing close. Gareth pushed Ben to sit and sat beside him, lifting his knee to the cushion to face him, always keeping hold of his hand. It seemed like the only thing that was tethering him at that moment, and Gareth seemed to understand that.

"Do you know anything about Daddies and littles and boys?" Gareth asked.

Ben frowned again. The terms seemed familiar, but he couldn't voice what it was. "Not really."

Gareth lowered his gaze to their hands, seeming to ponder over his next words, which sent butterflies soaring through his stomach.

"Well, a little is someone who likes to shake off adulthood and regress to a younger age in order to free him- or herself of the burdens of said adulthood or just because they enjoy being their 'younger' selves. Boys have a variety of meanings depending on the person—as do littles, really—and they can enjoy regressing to a young age, an older age, anything goes. Daddies are the people who take care of those littles and boys while they are in that frame of mind. The role of the Daddy is to take care of anything their charge needs."

Ben understood the idea. Now that Gareth had explained it, he remembered reading an article about it once, though he couldn't think what it had been on. Watching Gareth as he was, he saw the man swallow hard before lifting his head to meet Ben's gaze.

"There is also another type of boy that sometimes gets misunderstood. A Middle."

"Is that someone who's with two other people?"

Gareth smiled, the twinkle in his eye sparkling at him. "Not quite. A Middle is often someone who regresses to teen age. They might act up, throw tantrums, shout when things don't go their way and want attention. Things like that because it helps them. For many reasons. As I said, everyone is different in why and how they choose to be who they are inside."

"Why are you telling me this?"

"Because I'm a Daddy." Gareth waited, then said, "And I think you could be a Middle."

Ben leaned back. "I'm nothing like a teenager! I don't throw tantrums. I'm a manager of a store. I'm in charge of hundreds of staff. I keep this place running. Why would you think I'd need something like that?"

Gareth tilted his head and raised his eyebrows. "Don't move." Ben froze. "Now, take stock of where you are and how you feel. Talk it out with me."

Ben hadn't realised he'd moved, but he was standing about six feet away from the sofa, his hands clenched, his chest heaving, and his muscles tense. He didn't say anything. Just stared at Gareth as if he didn't understand it all.

"You're not a teenager, Ben, but I think you need the release. I think you need to find another way of letting all that stress steam from you without taking it out on your job or the people who work here."

"I don't!"

Gareth faced forward, resting his elbows on his knees. "When I first met you, Ruby introduced us. Do you remember?" Ben frowned and shook his head. "You greeted me and basically brushed me aside, giving Ruby a list of things to get done, then walked off. No goodbye. Nothing." Gareth held up his hand. "I know you're busy. I know you have a store to run. But being kind to those who work for you should come first." Gareth stood.

"Having a Daddy to help you will give you the space to let those feelings and emotions out where it is more suitable."

"But how would I stop myself from being this way? I never even realised I was doing it." Ben's shoulders dropped.

Gareth took a step closer. "I'm here to help if you'll let me. I'm not trying to change you, Ben. I promise. I'm just trying to help you live the best life you can."

Tears gathered in Ben's eyes, and his strength left him. His knees buckled, but Gareth caught him before he hit the floor. Arms tightened around him as they sat on the floor, and Gareth held him. The tears overflowed gently, Ben unable to stop them. He was...not numb, but like he had too much information in his head and couldn't fixate on any one piece of it. He sat there and let Gareth hold him.

After a long time, of which Ben had no idea the time, Gareth pulled back, cupping Ben's face and wiping his wet cheeks with his thumbs. "I'm sorry. I didn't mean to upset you."

Ben shook his head. "You didn't. You made me realise just how little I had to be happy about."

"God, I definitely need to apologise."

Ben chuckled. "No, you don't. You showed me I haven't been living *my* life. I've been living *their* life, and I always have. I don't know how to fix it."

Gareth's gaze roamed Ben's face. "I can help you if you want me to. Or I can find someone else." A shadow crept across Gareth's face, but it was gone before Ben could interpret it. Ben didn't want anyone else.

He gripped Gareth's sleeve. "No. I want you." He stared into Gareth's eyes. "I don't know what it is about you, but something keeps bringing me back to you. I need to know. I want to know. Everything. Anything." He paused. "Teach me?"

Gareth smiled. "I would love to. But first, you need to take some time to think about this. I've dropped a lot on you, and split-second decisions are not the best idea. Research it if you want to, and we can talk again another day."

Ben tightened his grip on him. "What if I'm already sure?"

Gareth shook his head. "You need a few days. Trust me. This is a big decision, and you need to have a clear head to make it." Ben wrinkled his nose, and Gareth ran a finger over the bridge of it, a small smile in place. "Trust a Daddy. Please, Ben."

Ben exhaled and nodded, tucking his head against Gareth's chest. He had no idea what he needed, but Gareth didn't disappoint. The man wrapped his arms around Ben and held him, making him feel secure and...cared for. That thought circled his head for a while until he had to push it aside before it drove him insane.

"I should get to work," Gareth said. "The boss might fire me if I'm too late."

The humour in his voice made Ben sit upright. He glanced at the clock. They'd been talking for about an hour, which meant Gareth *was* late.

"I'll let Felix know it was my fault," he said as he climbed unsteadily to his feet with Gareth's help.

They stood facing each other, neither touching the other, but Ben could feel Gareth all around him. The phantom touch of someone who cared. It was a strange feeling, but one Ben hoped he would feel again and again.

"You have my number. Call me if you need anything at all." Gareth stepped closer. "For tonight, I want you to go home or somewhere you can be alone. Really alone. Hide away in your bedroom if you have to. Fake an illness so everyone will stay away. Whatever you need to. Rest, relax and sleep." He lifted his hand and cupped Ben's jaw. "Please sleep."

Ben closed his eyes and nodded. "I'll try."

"I know you will."

A thumb brushed against his lips, and Ben opened his eyes, staring into Gareth's eyes. His breathing increased as he waited for something he wanted more than he could have imagined before this meeting. Despite Gareth's warning about split-second decisions, Ben surged forward, closing the distance between them. As their lips met, Ben groaned, and he opened his mouth to let Gareth's tongue invade. His hands slid around Gareth's back and gripped at his uniform while Gareth's hands held Ben's head where he wanted it.

Heat bloomed in Ben's body, flowing from the centre of him to his extremities and his groin. Gareth's tongue explored Ben's mouth, and Ben couldn't resist tangling his tongue with Gareth's. The taste of him was exquisite. He couldn't remember the last time he'd felt like this from just kissing someone. Their shared air ran out, and they pulled back, staring at each other as they panted to refill their lungs.

Gareth stared at him, a small smile in place, and pecked kisses on Ben's mouth, chin, cheeks and nose before stepping back. "I need to get to work, and you need to sleep."

"Okay." Ben nodded. "Okay," he repeated. "I'm going now."

Gareth smiled. "See you tomorrow." He held up his hand. "Let me rephrase that. See you tomorrow *evening* at the earliest."

Gareth let himself out of the office, and Ben locked his knees to stop himself from dropping to the floor. He sank into the sofa and stared at the wall. What the hell had happened here? At least, he knew Gareth was right about one thing. He needed to think everything through and see if he could research what he'd been told. That he was a snarky teenager didn't sound like a good thing, but maybe it was. He didn't know.

But as Gareth had said, he needed to sleep. Sleep first, research after.

7

GARETH

Working through the night after the meeting with Ben was harder than Gareth expected. He'd seen Ben do his usual walk-through of the store, where Ben gave him a smile and a wave, but the rest of the night was as if nothing monumental had happened. Felix hadn't been concerned that he was late; he'd known about the meeting, although he gave Gareth a strange look. It seemed Ben hadn't told anyone *why* he wanted to see him. And, if truth be told, Gareth didn't know why he'd called the meeting because he'd taken over the minute he'd walked into the room. He'd have to remember to ask why Ben wanted to see him when he next saw him.

Several colleagues tried to bring him into a conversation, but his responses must've shown he wasn't with it, and they left him alone after a while. He usually didn't mind the odd few minutes of chat, but he could barely concentrate on getting the right products on the right shelves. By the time his shift ended, he was exhausted, and not because of the physical aspect of the work.

He arrived home just as Victor was leaving his house. "Morning," he said. "You're up early."

Victor groaned, and Gareth chuckled. "This isn't early. This is hell. I hope my boss breaks a nail for getting me up at this ungodly hour."

"It's six-thirty in the morning. It's not exactly ungodly." Victor glared at him and stumbled to his car. "Do you have coffee?" he called. Victor raised his thermos. "Good. Try not to kill anyone with your words before you've drunk it!"

He laughed as Victor slammed his car door and let himself into the house. As tired as he was, he knew he wouldn't be able to sleep straight away, and, forgoing a shower until after, he changed into joggers and a T-shirt, in deference to the chilly morning air, plugged his headphones in and set his playlist going.

The rhythmic pounding of his feet as he passed house after house helped him focus his thoughts. Had he got across all the information he needed the previous evening? He hoped he'd made sense. It was much easier for him to explain things on paper—or computer—than it was by voicing them. It was one weakness he had when it came to being a Daddy. When he was a Daddy, he needed to explain things coherently, but sometimes, he struggled. It had never caused a problem in any relationship he had, but there was always a first time, and he'd hate it to happen. Hopefully, Ben would ask questions if he was unsure about anything. Either that or he would throw everything back in Gareth's face and pretend they'd never had the conversation, to begin with.

Regardless, Gareth would know where he stood.

He needed to make a list of things he had to talk through with Ben, so he didn't forget anything. Their conversation would cover a lot of minute details, and Ben deserved to have all the information he could to make the best decision for him.

It had shocked Gareth to hear about Ben's parents. He would never have guessed that had been the situation from the behaviour Ben exhibited, but it made things clearer. If the pressure had been on him since he was a child, Ben would probably not have had a decent childhood where he could've been a child. He would've been working towards his parents' goals for years before he realised it. Gareth hoped Ben could get out from beneath their weight. It wasn't doing him any good. Health-wise or anything else-wise.

And if Ben tried out this Middle lifestyle and chose Gareth as his Daddy, Gareth was all for him acting out and being snarky. In fact, he relished the idea.

His first stop was the kitchen for some water when he arrived home. The sun had come up and was already heating the air, making Gareth sweat more than usual. He never ran when the weather was too hot; it could be dangerous. After finishing a glass of water, he went straight for a shower, turning the heat down as low as he could stand it. He'd increase the heat once he'd cooled down.

Standing beneath the spray, he dropped his head forward and let it pound onto his shoulders and down his back. He rested his hands on the tiles in front of him and exhaled. As he stood there, listening to the water gurgling down the drain after pattering against the bath, where no one could see or hear him, he admitted he was scared. He didn't want to get his hopes up that Ben would be interested in anything long-term. He didn't want to hope they would find a connection that kept them together for longer than the learning period. If he did, how could he survive when it blew up in his face?

He'd been lonely long enough for his heart to jump with eagerness when he found someone he liked enough to see a future with them. Being alone differed from being lonely as far as he was concerned. Being alone just meant there was no one with him. Being lonely meant he wished there was.

Without conscious thought, his mind replayed the images, sounds, tastes, smells and feel of Ben in his arms before Gareth had left to start work. He'd not expected Ben to kiss him, and when he had, Gareth had prepared himself to push him away after a short time, but the moment he'd tasted him and heard him groan, he was lost to it. He'd wanted to strip Ben there and then and take him over his desk. How he'd found the resistance, he didn't know.

His cock filled as the images played over and over. His breathing grew heavy as he strained to keep from touching himself. Some water trickled down his chest and over his nipples and onto his cock, but it wasn't enough. He loved edging, taking himself—and others—as far as he could without touching where it was needed most.

Keeping the images at the forefront of his mind, he grabbed the shampoo and washed his hair, the suds following the path of least resistance and tickling their way down his body. When his hair was clean, he washed his body, avoiding the place he wanted to go. His cock bounced with every movement, and his eyes rolled back in his head at the need coursing through him. He washed away the soap and picked up a flannel. He folded it in half, then quarters and held it beneath the head of his cock. His breath caught when the underside of his cock touched the fabric. With the water pounding on his back, he concentrated on easing the flannel from side to side. The slightly rough texture caught on his nerve bundle, sending pinpricks of sensation along his dick to pool in his groin.

He hissed when he took it away and dropped it to the floor. In its place, he grabbed his shower toy, a hollow cylinder of silicone, which wrapped snugly around his cock as he pumped it back and forth. He dropped his head back, letting the water flow over his hair again, his free hand reaching to the side for the tiles to keep him upright. He thrust his hips faster, meeting his hand, and neared the edge.

Remembering the taste of Ben threw him over the cliff, and he sagged against the cold tiles as he spurted into the toy. He kept stroking until his stomach quivered with every touch, then pulled his toy free. The wall kept him up while he regained his breath. He faced the spray and turned the heat higher. He washed his cock and his toy, turned off the shower and padded to his bedroom, wearing only a towel. The cool air was pleasant on his skin, and he did little more than throw the towel on the floor—something he'd regret later—and dropped onto the bed.

He didn't remember tossing and turning. He didn't remember dreaming. One minute, he'd finished his shower; the next, he woke up to a pounding on his door. It took him far too long to gather the energy to put some clothes on and answer it.

He blinked at the visitor. "Dad? What's wrong?"

His father, Richard, glared at him. "I've been ringing you for five hours! Where have you been?"

Remembering his manners, he stepped back from the door, inviting his father in and shutting the door behind him. He rubbed his forehead. "I've been asleep for... What time is it?"

"Just after five o'clock."

Gareth raised his eyebrows. "I've been asleep for nine hours. Wow, I obviously needed it." He glanced at his dad. "Why have you been trying to ring me?"

Richard sighed. "I have to go to York tonight."

"How come?" He wandered to the kitchen to fill up and flick on the kettle.

"Helen is in hospital. I'm going to help with the business while she's out of commission."

Gareth swung around. "What happened to Auntie Helen?"

"She was in a car accident. She's fine, but she's broken her arm and is bruised all over. She was lucky."

"She was." Gareth blew out a breath. "Is there anything I can help with?"

"I just wanted to let you know I wouldn't be around for a few days. I don't know how long she'll need help, but there's no way she can run her landscaping business as she is."

"Yeah, definitely. Okay, I'll keep an eye on your place if you want?"

"Yes, please. I'm getting on the road now. I'll let you know when I get there, and I'll keep in touch to let you know timings and stuff like that."

"Thanks."

They didn't have the closest of relationships, but Gareth still went for a hug—or rather a backslap—before his dad left, after saying no to a coffee for the road. Gareth saw him to the door, waved and ran up the stairs to find his phone. It was still in the armband holder from when he'd been jogging. He returned to the kitchen and, although it still had some charge, plugged it in to charge fully before he went to work, and pulled up the home screen. Sixteen missed calls and twelve texts. No wonder his dad was upset. Gareth was rarely out of contact, and Richard must've been worried sick after getting the news about Helen.

As he made his tea with one sugar, he thought about Ben again. It seemed he was in his thoughts every waking minute. Had Ben done as Gareth had asked and rested and slept? He hadn't seen him that morning, at least that was something. Unless he hid in his office, in which case, Ben would need to be told about punishments.

He made some toast with marmalade and strode for his office, carrying his breakfast. The blog post awaited his finishing touch-es.

Two hours later, he was on his way to work to see if Ben was there. Well, he was going there to work, but seeing Ben was a plus. In some ways, he hoped Ben would be home already and getting some rest, but it would mean Gareth wouldn't see him. Being selfish, he wished Ben was still there and waiting for him.

He got his wish.

When Gareth stepped into the stairwell of the store, he heard Ben before he saw him.

"—what the hell you think you're playing at?"

"I didn't think it mattered. I was trying to make it more stream-lined—"

"It doesn't matter what you were trying to do. You need to follow the plan. There is a set way that things need to be done, and you messed it up. Now the night shift is going to have to redo all your 'work.'"

Gareth heard the air quotes even if they weren't gestured. He followed the voices to the staff kitchen and found Ben facing off with a man who looked like he was going to lose his lunch. Not wanting to undermine Ben's authority, he worked his way around the edge of the room until he was in Ben's line of sight and out of the man's. When Ben flicked his gaze over, Gareth made a slashing motion across his throat, telling him to stop in the only way he knew how without saying anything. Ben glared across at him, but Gareth stood his ground. He made the slashing motion again and, with his hands in front of his chest, mimed inhaling and exhaling.

Ben averted his gaze, but he saw him take a breath, the exhale heard across the room.

"I'm sor—" The man stopped when Ben glared at him.

"It's the end of your shift," Ben said with a more even tone. "Get some rest, and I'll see you when you're next in."

The man hesitated and glanced over his shoulder, but Gareth turned to the staff noticeboard before he noticed him watching.

"Yes, sir."

Gareth looked from his peripheral and saw the man leave, then they were alone. He swung around, leaning back against the wall and crossing his arms over his chest. Ben clenched and unclenched the hands resting at his sides, and Gareth gave him a moment.

"He deserved that and more," Ben bit out.

"No, he didn't."

"He moved the products on an entire aisle around! I should've fired him!"

Gareth tilted his head. "Did you explain to him why he shouldn't have done it before you yelled at him?"

Ben opened his mouth and snapped it shut again. His glare speared across the space between them.

"Maybe next time, explaining why it was wrong would be more beneficial than yelling." Gareth held up his hands. "Just my two pence, though."

He walked across to the kettle and switched it on. More tea was needed. He pulled two mugs from the cupboard and made tea for himself and coffee for Ben. When it was ready, he carried the coffee across the room and handed it to him. He hadn't moved at all.

"Relax, Ben. Lessons learnt and all that."

He returned to his tea and took it to a table by the window. Ben needed space to get his equilibrium back. He would either sit with Gareth or go to his office. Either was fine because it would be what Ben wanted, but he *needed* to realise someone had his back. And that someone was Gareth. No matter what happened or didn't happen between them.

He refused to let Ben wallow in the depths of his workload alone. They would get through it together, and with the help of others, if Ben would eventually allow it. He'd see.

When Ben slid into the seat opposite him, Gareth hid his smile in his tea.

8

BEN

Ben's body was still vibrating when he sat at the table. With effort, he set the mug down and curled his hands into fists, staring at them as they went red and white and shook. He wanted Gareth to be annoyed on his behalf, but he sat there, looking out of the window and sipping his drink as if he didn't have a care in the world. And he supposed, technically, he didn't. He only worked there. He didn't have the weight of the company on his shoulders.

The instant he thought that, he felt bad, and the fight went out of him. He slumped back in his chair and closed his eyes.

"That's better."

Gareth's voice brought Ben's attention to him. A small smile—which Ben was beginning to think, for some reason, was Gareth's version of approval—graced his lips.

"I shouldn't have snapped at him," Ben admitted.

"No, but it's understandable. He has made things difficult for you, but you could've given him the opportunity to right the wrong. It's a natural reaction to get mad when someone does something wrong." Gareth smirked. "In my case, when my boy does something wrong, he gets punished."

Ben's breath caught, the hitch audible in the quiet room. What punishments?

"Well," Gareth said, cradling his mug with both hands, and Ben realised he must've asked the question aloud. "It depends on the boy's needs. If I was caring for a little, I might give him a time out, or he might have a toy removed, or we might cancel a playdate. If he's older, he might be spanked or have to do chores he doesn't want to do. Everything in this lifestyle is fluid. It's unique to each pairing. What you and I might do would be different from you and someone else, or me and someone else."

Ben's shoulders tightened. He didn't like that idea. "What would *we* do?"

Gareth chuckled. "That conversation is for different surroundings."

Ben bit down on his lip, remembering where they were. "Thanks," he whispered.

Gareth tilted his head. "What for?"

Ben waved towards the area he'd stood in before. "Diffusing the situation. Don't think I didn't notice you also made it so he couldn't see what you were doing." He gave Gareth a wide smile he wasn't used to feeling. What had he in his life that required genuine smiles? Nothing. Until now.

Gareth covered his hands with one of his own, and Ben glanced around. "We're alone. Stop worrying. One day at a time. Or even one hour at a time if you need it. Are you going home now?"

Ben shook his head and rolled his eyes when Gareth frowned at him. "I have work to catch up on that I didn't do yesterday. I won't be here all night, though. Promise."

Gareth nodded as he stood. "Did you get some rest yesterday, at least?"

"Yes. I slept solidly for ten hours. I've never done that." His chest burned as a reminder came to him. "I have to leave early tomorrow night. I might not see you when you come in."

"It's not a bad thing to leave early."

"It is when I have to attend my parents' dinner party." Ben stared at the tabletop.

Gareth crouched beside him, placing a hand on Ben's thigh. "I'm sorry. Is there no way to get out of it?"

"Not unless I want to make my life hell." He transferred his gaze to the window, not wanting to see the pity in Gareth's eyes.

"Hey." Ben hesitated before glancing at him. "We'll figure something out. Spend today and tomorrow thinking things through. After that, we'll arrange a time to sit down and chat properly." Gareth squeezed his leg and rose. "I better get to work. Apparently, the boss cracks the whip harder than most." He winked.

Ben chuckled and said, "Gareth?" The man faced him and raised his eyebrows. "Thank you."

Gareth paused, glanced over his shoulder to the door, then stalked over to him and kissed him. Ben's brain lit up with fireworks. Kissed was the wrong word. Gareth devoured him and just as quickly pulled back, leaving them both panting. Ben stared at him while feeling returned to his body. He needed more of this man. He needed everything he could give him.

Gareth nodded as if understanding the unspoken thoughts. "Later." He exited the room, leaving Ben to regain his balance—in more ways than one.

He finished his cold coffee, staring out of the window while he tried to collate the questions he would have for Gareth when they finally met to talk about the elephant in the room. When he'd woken early that morning, he'd set himself up in bed with his laptop and researched Daddies. He hadn't been sure what he'd find, but there had been a few websites and blogs that had been full of information. The little side of things sounded like heaven—not being in charge for a while—but he knew he wouldn't be able to do that. It would be too difficult for him to let go of his independent, perfectionist tendencies. Any of the others, though, were fair game, and Gareth had spoken the truth when he'd said everyone was different. There would be no right or wrong way of doing things. He liked the freedom of that.

He rinsed his mug and put it in the dishwasher, yearning for his strawberry milkshake. Making short work of the stairs, he closed himself in his office, made a shake and leaned back in his chair as he drank it.

He had stifled his laughter at what some boys had got up to on the blog he'd read. They were purposefully naughty so their Daddy would give them attention—one of them admitted it. He chuckled at the idea. What kind of punishments were they getting? Did they enjoy them? Ben frowned. Wouldn't that defeat the object of them being punishments if the boys liked them? A question for Gareth. Undoubtedly, he would have a lot of questions for him.

The following twenty-four hours flew by, and Ben wished he could've delayed the dinner indefinitely, but his parents had insisted, and as always, Ben caved.

As he knotted his bow tie, he stared at himself in the mirror. His outward appearance hadn't changed, but he was different. He'd spent far too many hours researching and making a list of his questions for when he next saw Gareth, and there was little that interested him besides that topic. He would struggle to socialise with whoever was joining them for dinner that evening. His mother had told him, but he couldn't remember.

Ben closed his eyes and imagined a box. He opened the lid, shoved everything Gareth and Daddy related inside it and locked it. The hassle he'd get from not being "present" at the party would be worse than ignoring his newly found knowledge for a few hours.

"Benjamin, our guests will arrive soon. Come on downstairs now," his father said, knocking briskly on his door as if Ben wasn't aware of his voice.

"Yes, Father."

He stared at his reflection for one more minute and sighed, brushing a hand down his front. "Here goes nothing," he murmured.

He was right in many ways, and despite locking away those new memories, the one showing him exactly what he was doing for his parents wouldn't quit. Every time his mother introduced him to another person at a company that would benefit his parents' goals, it sank the knife deeper. Every time his father clapped him on the back and voiced his pride at what Ben had accomplished, it fell flatter. Every time Ben spoke or smiled or shook hands or nodded, his carefully locked box cracked further.

Finally, he made his excuse for needing the bathroom and climbed the stairs to his bedroom and en-suite. He refused to use the facilities downstairs—he'd made that mistake once, and his mother had ambushed him when he'd exited. This way, it would give him some quiet before he rejoined the chaos.

He locked the door to his bathroom and sank onto the closed toilet seat. His fingers linked in his lap, and he stared at the floor.

What did it matter what job he had? What did it matter as long as he had money coming in to pay the bills? How could he get himself out of this hole his parents had dug for him?

You could afford to rent somewhere.

Gareth's words came back to him in a rush, and his heart sped up. He could do it. Even if he couldn't bring himself to stop attending these dinner parties, he could move out. It would give him somewhere just for him. Somewhere to sit and figure out what *he* wanted. A renewed sense of urgency filled him, and he pulled out his phone, searching for properties to rent. He didn't need anything big—there was only one of him, after all.

Despite the time of night, he was able to book through the online system to view some properties in two days. They were one-

or two-bedroom apartments, which would suit him perfectly. He would visit them and see which suited him best.

He cursed when he saw the time. He'd been in the bathroom for half an hour. Shrugging, he left the room and went back to the guests—he could always pretend he'd eaten something that didn't agree with him if anyone asked. Or maybe saying he'd received a phone call might be better. Withholding a grin, he thought Gareth might appreciate the first version more.

"Sweetheart! I'd been wondering where you'd snuck off to. Have I introduced you to Nate?" She leaned closer and lowered her voice, but not as much as Ben wished she had. "He's gay."

Ben sighed but smiled. Another set-up. How quaint. He held out his hand to the older man, who had streaks of white at his temples, making him look older than his face alone advertised. "Nice to meet you, Nate."

"And you, too, Ben. Your mother has told me a lot about you." Nate's voice was calm with an edge of humour, which Ben appreciated, but the idea that this was someone his parents approved of sank like a stone in his stomach.

He smiled. "I'm sure she has. Whereas I've not had the pleasure." He bit back his sigh. Nothing new here.

The night continued in the same vein, and although he was "allowed" to carry a glass of whiskey around with him, his parents had always forbidden him to drink it because they didn't want him getting drunk around the guests. As if he would. As one guest, the owner of a five-star restaurant, drivelled on about something related to the best accounting software, he reconsidered his stance on listening to his parents' rules. He was bloody forty-one years old.

At that thought, he swallowed the entire glass in one gulp, wincing when it burnt his throat. He drank alcohol, just not very often, and he wouldn't have any more to drink that night because he *would* get drunk, but he needed something to take the edge off this never-ending night.

Five hours after the party started, they permitted Ben to leave, and he did without a backwards glance. The first thing he did was lock his bedroom door and jump into the shower. The parties always made him feel unclean like he was masquerading as someone he wasn't, but that night, he felt it more keenly than ever. He scrubbed until his skin bloomed a dark shade of red, towelled off and slid on some pyjamas. Even though the air was warm, he couldn't bring himself to be naked in bed when his parents were in the house. He could never tell when they would expect him to get up, and it made things easier for him if he was at least partially dressed.

Grabbing his laptop, he settled into bed and powered it on. He needed to research more before he spoke with Gareth the following day, and Ben had a tingling in his stomach that made him giddy. He was excited about something for the first time in a long time.

The next day at work was a nightmare of epic proportions. A delivery had not arrived because the lorry had broken down, meaning the store was short of stock on some popular items. Two staff members had to be sent home because of illness. Ben had attended three meetings, and a customer had knocked over a tower of cuddly toys, sending them sprawling across several aisles and checkout desks.

Ben was short-tempered and ready to kill if something else went wrong. Even Lindsay was keeping her distance. She barely said goodbye when she left at five-thirty that afternoon. He focused on the paperwork, trying to ignore everything else, but he couldn't. He debated leaving and speaking with Gareth another day, but something kept him in his seat until there was a knock on his door.

"Come in," he said, leaning back in his chair.

His heart gave a hard beat when Gareth opened the door, but the man's smile sent a wave of electricity through his body. Not the good kind. He twisted the pen in his hand, rolling it around and around, faster and faster.

"You need to go," he bit out.

Gareth's smile remained in place, but the tightening of his face assured Ben he'd heard. "Why?"

"I'm not in the right frame of mind for this discussion. We can postpone it for another day."

Gareth narrowed his eyes. "What happened?"

"It doesn't matter what happened. Get to work. I'll let you know when we can do this." Ben rested his forearms on the desk and picked up some paper as if he was reading it.

Silence filled the office, but Ben knew Gareth hadn't left. He could feel his gaze on him, burning through the top of his bent head.

"Leave," he demanded.

No sound.

Ben stood so fast that his chair flew back and banged against the wall. "I said go!" He flung his arm towards the door.

Gareth crossed his arms over his chest and stared at him, saying nothing, doing nothing.

"Why the hell aren't you leaving? I'm calling security." Though he made no move to do it.

Gareth stepped closer, the move making Ben flinch, until he reached the opposite side of Ben's desk. He leaned his palms on the table, stared into Ben's eyes and, with a firm voice, said, "Sit. Down."

Ben sat.

9

GARETH

Gareth stared across the desk at Ben, brooking no argument with his words or body language. He'd heard about the problems from his colleague before he'd even climbed the stairs. Two other staff members had told him to keep his distance from Ben. He'd known the minute he stepped into the room that Ben would be in a combative frame of mind. To get through to him, Gareth needed to take charge.

"First rule, take a breath before you say something you might regret. Second rule, take another breath before you speak. Nod your head if you understand?" Ben nodded. Just one small bob of his head, but Gareth understood the significance. "Good. Now. You've had a bad day. I get that. You have the weight of this company on your shoulders. I get that. You are responsible for a lot of people. I get that. But when it's just you and me in a room together, I deserve better than this angry, childish temper tantrum. You're tired, frazzled, worn down. I know. People will not respond to you if you stamp your feet and yell at them. They will cower, they will do as you ask, but they will not like you. Regardless of what anyone says, you need your employees to like you because if they don't, they won't stay, and that makes your life even more difficult. What a vicious circle."

He stood upright and shoved his hands into his pockets, a move designed to make him seem gentler and more approachable. He didn't say another word, just let his previous speech sink in with Ben, whose eyes had dropped to the desk. Giving him time to understand exactly what he was trying to say. After a couple of minutes, he murmured, "Shall we try again?"

Ben peered up at him and nodded.

Gareth pivoted and exited the room, closing the door behind him. He gave Ben a minute before he knocked again, allowing him those few seconds to get his bearings and figure out his next move. When his knuckles rapped on the door, Ben's voice was softer.

"Come in."

Gareth entered with a smile. "Good evening. I've heard you've had a tricky day. Is there anything I can do to help?"

Ben stared up at him, his bottom lip hidden between his teeth, his nose wrinkled, and his eyes full of unshed tears. "I think some of it can wait until tomorrow. There's nothing I can do now, but thank you for asking."

Gareth smiled and nodded. "Have you had enough to drink today?" He rounded the desk and crouched beside Ben, putting his hand on top of Ben's clenched fist. He rubbed at the knuckles, trying to ease the tension running through him. "Ben?"

"Sorry, what?"

"I asked if you've had enough to drink today? You must've been busy, but have you taken care of yourself?"

Ben blinked at him, knocking a few of the tears loose. Gareth wiped them away with the pad of his thumb while Ben regrouped. "Um, no, probably not."

"Can I make you your strawberry drink?"

Ben paused, then nodded. "It's in the bottom drawer," he whispered.

Gareth squeezed his hand and let go, rocking back on his heels so he could open the drawer. Inside was a box, and he lifted the lid. Nestled inside was a carton of strawberry milk powder.

"Milk?"

Ben swung his chair around and opened a door that blended with the decoration, showcasing a small fridge filled with milk. Gareth withheld his smile and took a carton, shutting the door again.

"Which cup do you use?" Ben held out the thermos. "Hidden in plain sight." Gareth winked, and Ben's bottom lip disappeared again.

Gareth made up the milkshake, screwed on the lid and handed it to Ben.

"Come on. Let's sit on the sofa." Ben checked the clock on the wall. "We're good. I came in early," Gareth said, guessing what Ben's worry was.

Gareth sat on the sofa and patted the seat beside him. They wouldn't be side by side because Gareth lifted his leg onto the cushion to sit face to face instead. When Ben sat, Gareth rested his elbow on the back of the sofa and his head in his palm.

"Drink up."

"Don't you want a drink?" Ben asked, sipping tentatively.

"I'm good." Gareth watched him drink a bit more and asked, "What questions do you have?"

Ben made a move to get up, but Gareth stayed him with his hand on his forearm. "I've left my list over there," Ben said.

"You don't need it yet. Try to remember. We can check if we've missed anything on it later."

Ben sat back, resting the hands cradling his thermos on his lap and staring at them. "What made you know you were a Daddy?"

"Right for the jugular, eh?" He winked at Ben's darkening cheeks. "I knew I enjoyed taking care of others, and I like the control of knowing how things will go because I'm the one doing it. I found a club that had members with various kinks and saw a Daddy and little there. The moment I saw it, it clicked."

Ben was silent for a minute, and Gareth wished he could read minds. "How will I know?"

Gareth smiled. "You try it. You'll know deep inside when you find what you hadn't realised you'd been missing. It'll feel right."

"You said I act out because I'm tired?"

Gareth exhaled. "I don't think that helps. When people's energy levels flag, they can become short-tempered and grumpy. Personally, I have nothing against tantrums. It's just where they happen that can be an issue."

"You mean like here?"

Gareth nodded. "As I mentioned yesterday, yelling at your staff will get them to do the job, but ultimately, they will leave the company because no one wants to work for an asshole." He chuckled. "By learning to handle the issues in a different way, you can retain your staff for longer."

"What if I can't keep it inside?"

"Well, if the problem is that you can't keep it inside until you get home, you might need to take yourself away from the store for an hour or call me to help. Usually, I would help you keep everything inside until you get home, and you can let it out in the comfort of your space. Have you ever heard a parent say that their kids are little angels for everyone else and little shits for them?" Ben nodded. "It's a similar scenario. They have taught those kids well because they behave while they are out of the house. When they get home, they're in their comfortable place, a place they feel relaxed and calm, and they can let their emotions leak out because they know their parents have their backs. That's why parents get the short end of the stick most times. It's because their kids trust them."

"I never thought about it like that before."

"That's how I see a Daddy and Middle relationship. The Daddy helping the Middle to learn the boundaries of their emotions." Gareth frowned. "I don't know if I've explained that properly."

"No, I understand. Is that how our relationship would work?" Ben wrinkled his nose, and Gareth barely stopped himself from rubbing his finger across it.

"It would work however we wanted it to. I would suggest us finding somewhere to talk in a more relaxed manner and see what happens."

"How can we do that? We work different hours?" Ben rested his head against the sofa.

"We talk about it and find ways around it. Maybe you could finish a little earlier some days, and we could spend time before I have to start work? We'd figure it out if it's something you want."

Ben faced him. "It is. There's something about you, Gareth. I felt the pull the moment I met you." He laughed. "Okay, not the exact moment. Maybe the second time."

Gareth smiled, enjoying Ben's lighthearted moment. "I know the feeling. How about you come over this weekend? I don't work Friday or Saturday, remember?" Ben opened his mouth, then bit his bottom lip. "You don't have to, Ben. This goes at your pace."

"It's not that. I do want this, but I'm viewing some properties tomorrow."

Gareth sat forward, grasping Ben's hand. "That's great news!"

"I'm scared," Ben whispered.

Gareth squeezed his hand. "Do you want me to come with you?"

"You'll be sleeping."

That wasn't a no. "It's okay. I don't mind. I don't want to force my presence on you, though."

Ben exhaled heavily. "I would love you to be there. Thank you. I've arranged them from three o'clock because I have meetings all morning."

"Perfect. I'll still get some sleep. Text me the addresses, and I can meet you. Or I can pick you up if you'd like?"

Ben shook his head. "No. I'll meet you there. No point in coming here and going away again."

"All right." Gareth checked his watch. "I need to get to work." He didn't make a move to leave. He cupped Ben's jaw. "You're stunning," he whispered.

Ben's bottom lip disappeared, and Gareth used his thumb to pull it from between his teeth. He leaned closer, sipping that lip between his own and soothing it, and fitted their mouths together in a soft kiss. It didn't last long because Gareth didn't trust himself not to get carried away the moment he got his hands on Ben. When he pulled away, Ben's eyelids fluttered open, his hand flexing against the fabric of Gareth's shirt.

Gareth kept his voice low, not wanting to break the spell they were under just yet. "What I want you to do tonight is rest, but also think about what you would or would not want from a relationship. We need to be on the same page. Depending on how much time we have between or after the viewings tomorrow, we can talk in more detail."

"All right." Ben rested his head against Gareth's chest and inhaled, relaxing against him. And Gareth didn't want to move, but he refused to be late again. That was one way to get the rumour mills started if they weren't already.

He brushed a hand down Ben's back and gently pulled back. He cupped his face. "I'll see you later." He pecked his lips and stood, making sure Ben was taking his own weight first. "Finish your milk, then get to work." He winked. "Not for too long, though."

"I won't."

"And don't forget to eat."

Ben smiled. "I won't."

Unable to resist, he leaned down and kissed him again before pivoting and striding out of the office before he did something they'd regret. He jogged down the stairs and clocked in before heading straight onto the shop floor. Throwing himself into his work, he barely felt the hours passing him by. The only time it registered was when Ben walked past his aisle and smiled at him. After that, he concentrated on the stock rotation he had to do and not much else.

When his break arrived, Felix had to come and remind him to take it.

"Sorry. I'm a little out of it tonight." Gareth chuckled, rubbing a hand over his face.

Felix chuckled. "I can see that. Everything okay?"

Gareth nodded. "Yeah. I'm good."

Felix slapped his back. "Go on with you. Fifteen minutes for a cuppa might do you some good."

Gareth grinned and left his work where it was and grabbed a cup of tea, sitting by the window and staring out into the night sky. He tried his hardest not to think about Ben and their situation, but it was forefront in his mind every minute of the day. To try to distract himself, he checked his phone and saw a message from Preston sent not long ago, and he took a chance and rang him, hoping he wasn't waking him.

"Hey," Preston said.

"Hey. How are you doing?" They'd had a few conversations since the previous weekend but hadn't seen each other in person.

Preston snorted in his ear. "I'm perfect." The sarcastic tone was not lost on Gareth.

"What happened?"

"Nothing. That's the problem. Not a single thing has changed, except that he's not talking to me about anything but work. He refuses to answer any questions I ask him, and it's driving me insane. I'm thinking of leaving."

"What! No, Preston. Don't let him do that to you. You've earned everything you have in that company. You've been with them for years."

"I can't handle it anymore, Gareth. I thought I had it all, and it was ripped from my hands without any provocation. I don't know how to heal from that without removing myself from the equation."

"Don't make any rash decisions, Preston. Come out with Victor and me this weekend. We can go to Bound and get shit-faced again."

Preston sighed. "I don't know if I can be bothered. I've lost any excitement about my life at the minute."

"I hope that's not a euphemism for something else. If you even think of leaving this world, Preston, I will bring you back and kick your ass."

That brought a small chuckle. "No, I wasn't thinking that. I meant I have to drag myself out of bed to go to work. I'm happy to get out of bed if I can just stay at home and do nothing."

Gareth's heart calmed. "Good. And sometimes, it's good to just do nothing. It gives your brain a chance to catch up with everything. If you don't want to come out with us, let us come to you."

Preston was quiet for a minute, and Gareth had to check he hadn't lost the connection. "No, let's go out. Maybe I can find someone to take my mind off it for a few hours."

"All right. Good. I'll call you tomorrow and sort the details." Preston made a hum of agreement. "And Preston? Call me any time, day or night, if you need me, okay?"

"I will. Thanks, Gaz."

Gareth grimaced. "Fuck off, Prez."

They laughed and rang off. Gareth finished his tea and headed back for work. Why couldn't everyone's lives be plain sailing? Why did people have to suffer?

10

BEN

B en couldn't keep his excitement contained the following day. During the meetings, he was fidgety and lacked the usual concentration he had, not that anyone commented on it. The final meeting was with his team leaders, and he could barely remember what information he had to pass on to them. Finally, the meeting ended, and everyone filed out. When the last person closed the door behind them, Ben made himself a milkshake, logged off his computer and grabbed his bag before saying good-bye to a stunned Lindsay and handing over control to Darren, his daytime assistant manager.

By the time he arrived at the first property, he was half an hour early. He flicked through his phone a few times and decided to see if there were any other properties available. A knock on his window made him jump, but he smiled when he saw Gareth. He scrambled to get out of the car and stood before him, hands clenching around his phone.

"Hi," he said, feeling stupid.

Gareth grinned. "Hi. Are you excited?"

"Very. And still scared."

Gareth took his hand. "It's understandable. This is a big step for you. You'll be fine."

Ben glanced at the property and found the estate agent waiting for them at the door. "Okay. I'm ready."

Gareth squeezed his hand, and his heart calmed. He could do this. He didn't have to be reduced to being a status symbol by his parents. He could be independent.

They joined the estate agent, introduced themselves, and headed for the third floor. When the woman entered, they followed, and Ben's excitement returned. Gareth squeezed his hand again and asked the estate agent a question about the property. Ben heard the conversation but focused on what he could see and how the place felt. The large windows gave plenty of light into the open-plan space, and he could see himself living there.

"What about the local area? What amenities are there?" Gareth asked.

Ben answered, "There are plenty of shops nearby and a pub. I saw a small cafe down the street, too."

Gareth smiled at him and turned back to the estate agent, who gave them more information about their surroundings. Ben frowned at Gareth. Why was he asking the estate agent when Ben had given him the answer? The same thing happened the next time Ben answered one of Gareth's questions. Once the woman had finished talking, Gareth sidled up to him.

"Ben, let the estate agent answer the questions, please," he whispered. "I want to know what information she has."

Ben didn't answer but nodded. What difference did it make if the information Gareth asked for came from him or the woman? Did Gareth not trust Ben's knowledge? He moved away to the windows and took in the view. He could mainly see the buildings opposite and nothing else. He worked his way through the apartment, finding a small bathroom with only a shower and no bath. That wouldn't do. Ben loved his baths.

When it was time to leave, Ben said he'd think about it, and they exited the building. Ben strode for his car, unlocking it, only pausing when his hand was on the handle.

"Are you coming to the next one?" he asked, not sure if he wanted the answer to be yes or no.

"If you still want me there."

Despite what happened, he found he still needed Gareth's support and nodded, climbing into his car. His excitement had dimmed, but he still wanted out of his parents' house, so he had no choice but to go through with the viewings.

He parked at the next one, meeting a different estate agent this time. They waited until Gareth joined them a couple of minutes later and entered the property. During that visit, Ben made sure he was quiet unless they asked a specific question and showed himself around while Gareth and the man spoke. The bedroom appeared smaller than the pictures showed, and he wasn't sure he'd be happy with it. Although he supposed he would be working most of the time, and he would use a bedroom for sleeping and not much else, so it probably didn't matter how big it was.

When they finished the visit, they said goodbye to the man, and Gareth grabbed Ben's arm, guiding him to Gareth's car. Gareth opened the passenger door.

"Get in."

Ben did, though he didn't know why. Gareth shut the door and rounded the car to the driver's side. Once he was situated, he told Ben to put his seatbelt on and started the car.

"Where are we going?" Ben asked when he did what Gareth had asked.

"You'll see."

Gareth drove for several long minutes, and Ben didn't start up a conversation. He was too wound up, and after their conversations in the days prior to this, he knew he would lash out if he said anything. He was trying not to do that, even though he believed Gareth deserved it after shutting him down during the viewings.

Gareth parked in a large car park, and Ben gazed around. "Where are we?"

"A bowling alley."

"Why?"

"To chill out."

Gareth switched the car off and climbed out, Ben following suit. "I'm not exactly dressed for this," Ben said.

"Take off your jacket and tie, and you'll be fine."

"I also don't know how," he admitted.

"I'll teach you." Gareth held out his hand. "Come on."

Ben removed his jacket and tie, leaving them on the back seat of Gareth's car, and threaded his hand into Gareth's. The bowling alley was busier than Ben had expected. He hadn't realised people still enjoyed the sport. Gareth paid for them to have one game, and they changed their shoes, Ben wrinkling his nose at the smell.

Gareth chuckled. "Just don't think about them."

They found their lane, and Gareth showed Ben how to choose the right ball. Ben found a blue one, which didn't feel too heavy, and set it on the stand.

"Right, are you ready?" Gareth asked, a small smile in place.

Ben rolled his eyes. "Would it make a difference if I said no?"

"Of course, but unless you try, you won't know if you like it." Gareth waved his hand. "You go first. I'll show you how."

They went through the motions of holding the ball, where to stand, how to bring the ball back and send it sprawling down the lane. Ben thought it seemed easy enough, but when he tried, the ball went straight into the gutter.

"Good try. For this next ball, try keeping your arm a little straighter when you bring it forward. It takes a bit of practice sometimes."

Ben gritted his teeth and threw the second ball. The same thing happened, although it got a little further down before it sank into the gutter. Ben slapped his hands on his hips and stormed to the seats. When he sat, he crossed his arms over his chest and glared at Gareth.

"It's not a problem. I'll help you next time. Watch me and see how I keep my arm. I'll do it slowly so you can see it better."

Ben watched, mesmerised by the movements of Gareth's body as he walked forward and swung his arm back and forward. The ball went sailing down the lane in a straight line, smashing into the pins and sending most of them flying. Ben chewed his bottom lip, wishing he was somewhere else. On Ben's next go, Gareth settled behind him, moving his arms for him.

"When you bring your arm forward, keep your elbow locked and try to keep your wrist straight. It takes practise."

Gareth stepped back, and Ben followed his instructions. At least, he thought he did. The ball didn't agree. Ben tried again, and a similar thing happened. He firmed his jaw and glared at the floor as Gareth took his go. This continued in the same vein for a few tries until Ben had enough.

"I can't do it. You do it. I'll watch."

"Let's get something to eat. It's almost dinner," Gareth said. He led the way to the attached cafe and sat Ben down. "Wait here. I'll be back in a minute."

While Gareth was gone, Ben checked his phone. He didn't know why he did because no one would be messaging him. He shoved it back in his pocket and tapped his fingers on the top of the table. He could feel a buzzing under his skin as if he needed to keep moving and working, but Gareth's words kept him in his seat. Why was he willing to do what Gareth wanted all of a sudden? It was as if he had no will of his own.

Before he could take that thought any further, Gareth returned with two cheeseburgers, fries and fizzy drinks.

"Eat up," Gareth said, tucking into his fries.

Ben grabbed the ketchup and drenched his fries before sticking some in his mouth. The cheeseburger called him, but he always ate the fries first because he hated it when they got cold. Cold fries were disgusting. Once the fries were gone, he grabbed his burger two-handed and demolished it.

"How are you feeling?" Gareth asked when he was halfway through his burger.

Ben finished his mouthful, thinking about the question. "Calmer than I was," he admitted.

"Good. Can you tell me what happened?"

Ben put the burger down and had a drink before answering, "Why wouldn't you believe me when I was answering the questions in the apartments?"

Gareth leaned forward, resting his arms on the table. "It wasn't that I didn't believe you. I trust your information, but we needed to see if the estate agent knew about the area."

"Why?"

"An estate agent is there to sell a property, but they might not have all the information, or they might give false information if they believe it will help sell it. I wanted to make sure they were reliable to deal with. Why would you want to give your money to people who don't respect those they sell to?"

Gareth went back to eating, leaving Ben with his thoughts again. What Gareth had said was true, and didn't that make Ben feel like an ass?

"Why do I do this?"

Gareth rested a hand on Ben's nape and squeezed. "I think you're used to not being in control of your life that your mind prefers to fight to get that control back." Gareth frowned. "I'm not very good at explaining things, but you lash out because it's one way of making people do what you want them to. You push them aside to give yourself more breathing room and because you don't want them to be like your parents. I'm not a therapist, but that's just my guess."

Ben leaned back, dislodging Gareth's hand, and stared at him. "I'm sorry."

Gareth smiled. "I don't mind. This is part of being a Daddy that I like. Dealing with unruly behaviours," he winked, "is my forte."

"I don't even realise I'm doing it," Ben said.

"It's a learned response now, I think. You're used to doing it that you don't acknowledge it anymore. It's something we can work on."

Ben smiled and finished his burger, the silence more comfortable this time.

"I have to go home and get ready now," Gareth said.

Ben nodded. "I could do with finishing a few things at work, too."

"I'll see you tomorrow?" Ben scrunched his nose, not knowing if to vocalise his thoughts or not. "Tell me what you're thinking?" Gareth said.

Ben bit his lip. "Can I see your house?" He refused to look up, not wanting to see whatever expression was on Gareth's face.

"Of course, you can. Let me drive you back to your car, and you can follow me home."

Ben's entire body relaxed, and tears filled his eyes, but he blinked them back. "Thank you. For everything."

Gareth pressed a kiss to the side of his head. "We're just getting started, sweetheart."

Ben gripped Gareth's hand as they entered Gareth's home. He hadn't been sure what to expect, but it wasn't a three-bedroom house filled with everything a person could need. He wandered from room to room, Gareth not stopping him, and found little trinkets that made him smile. After he'd seen everything downstairs, he stepped towards Gareth, hooking his fingers in the belt hoops of Gareth's khaki shorts. Gareth rested his hands on Ben's shoulders.

"Are you okay?"

Ben smiled. "I'm perfect."

Gareth cupped Ben's cheek. "You are."

Ben leaned forward, closing the distance between them. At the first brush of their lips, fire raced through Ben's body. He closed the distance between their bodies and wrapped his arms around Gareth's back, clenching his fists around the material of his T-shirt. Their lips and tongues explored slowly, maddeningly, until Ben needed more. He whimpered, and Gareth pulled back, chuckling.

"Not today, but if you want to, you can join me in the shower?"

"You're no fun." Ben pouted.

Gareth pressed their lips together. "Maybe not today, no. Another day, I will be."

Gareth kept hold of Ben's hands and tugged him towards the stairs. He only caught a cursory glance of the bedroom before Gareth dragged him into the bathroom—probably knowing Ben would get sidetracked by the sight of the bed. The bathroom was to die for. A large tub with a shower head over the top enclosed with a long glass panel on one side of the bath was the focal point.

"Wow," Ben said.

"I know. It was something I had installed when I first moved in. Nothing better than sharing a bath with someone." Gareth winked, switched the shower on and grabbed the hem of his T-shirt, yanking it over his head. Ben momentarily forgot how to breathe when it revealed the mountains and valleys of Gareth's stomach. "Are you joining me or just watching because either is fine with me?"

Ben blinked at him, trying to understand his words, and when they finally sank in, he pulled his shirt from his trousers, undid the first few buttons and dragged it over his head. He, again, paused when Gareth dropped his trousers, leaving him in black briefs that left not much to the imagination.

"Oh, my god," Ben whispered, hands shaking.

Gareth chuckled. "Get undressed, Ben. You can explore this as much as you want in the shower." Gareth dropped his briefs, revealing a dick at half-mast, and climbed into the bath and under the spray. Ben stared for a moment before he remembered he only had a short amount of time before Gareth left. He made quick work of his clothes and climbed in with the man who was making his head spin.

"I can't remember the last time I felt like this about someone," he said, standing before Gareth in all his glory and not the least bit worried about Gareth's reaction for the first time ever.

Gareth's mouth curved, and he pulled Ben into his arms. "Same."

They stayed wrapped around each other for a few long minutes, then Gareth started washing Ben, making him smell like Gareth, which Ben secretly loved. Gareth turned him away and washed his hair, Ben's eyes closing as the feeling of being cared for soaked into him. How had he ever been without this? He washed the soap and shampoo from Ben's body before focusing on himself until Ben took over. He needed to have his hands on the man. His Daddy.

"Daddy," Ben whispered.

Gareth's smile grew. "Yes, sweetheart?"

"It doesn't sound strange at all. I thought it might."

"I'm glad." Gareth kissed him softly. "One step or one hour at a time. Okay?"

"Yes...Daddy."

Gareth rewarded him with another kiss, this one taking his breath until his head spun. He couldn't get enough of this. What would happen if he let himself fall into this new world? He couldn't wait to find out.

11

GARETH

Gareth's boy was impatient, but he couldn't blame him. He was the same. He thought he had the strength to keep things slow, but the moment he took Ben's mouth, he was lost.

"Okay, I won't make you wait, but we're not having sex. I want to make you incoherent for our first time. Tonight, we can have this."

Gareth punctuated his words by wrapping his hand around both their cocks. He wanted to remember every aspect of their time together, but his head spun with lust, clouding his vision with an open-mouthed Ben, eyes closed and a look of ecstasy on his face. Ben's fingers dug into Gareth's sides as Gareth increased the pressure and speed. Hurtling towards his release, he bit down on Ben's earlobe and whispered, "Come."

Ben keened, and his release briefly painted Gareth's stomach before the water washed it away. The image sent Gareth over the edge with only a couple more strokes. He let go of their cocks and slid his arm around Ben's waist, pulling him close. The water cocooned them from everything, and Gareth didn't want to move, so he didn't until the water cooled. He had a large water tank in the attic, but even that would eventually run out of hot water.

Switching off the shower, he rested Ben against the tiles, receiving a hiss and an arch of the man's back, and brought a towel to him, drying him off and wrapping him in it. He grabbed a second towel for himself and guided Ben into his bedroom, settling him on the bed. While Ben waited, Gareth collected the clothes they'd strewn across the bathroom and brought them to the bed.

"How are you feeling?" he asked when Ben just watched him.

Ben smiled and ducked his head. "Good."

"Just good?" Gareth blew out a breath. "I'm not doing my job properly."

Ben chuckled. "I think you did your job perfectly." His cheeks darkened, and his lip disappeared between his teeth as it usually did when he felt uncomfortable.

Gareth dropped a brief kiss on his cheek and chose some clothes from his wardrobe.

"Where are you going tonight?" Ben asked.

Gareth glanced over his shoulder with a smile. "We're going to Bound." Ben frowned. "It's a kink club."

"Oh, I didn't know we had any of those here."

"It's on the outskirts of town on one of the industrial estates. The place looks huge from the outside, but it's not that big. Can you imagine the outcry if it became too visible to some of the people in this place?" Gareth chuckled.

Ben snorted. "My parents being two of them."

Gareth threw his towel to the side and pulled on his briefs, then his dark wash jeans. Shirtless, he strode to Ben and knelt before him, sliding his arms around his towel-encased hips and pushing himself between his legs.

"It doesn't matter what they think, Ben. All that matters is what you think. What you believe. What you *want*. It's your life."

Ben sighed. "I know. It's difficult to let go of."

"One day, one hour," he reminded him. Gareth kissed him. "Get dressed. You're far too tempting like this."

Ben smiled and dropped the towel, making Gareth groan when the blemish-free skin came into view. Gareth kissed down the column of Ben's neck, continuing to his chest until he circled his nipples. Ben's answering moan was like a match to paper, and Gareth laved each bud with his tongue, wishing he could get closer. Ben's fingers threaded into his hair, and Gareth could feel Ben's arousal against his chest. He gave each one a last lick and kissed his way back up to Ben's mouth, taking it in a desperation he hadn't felt in a long time.

"Get dressed, menace," he said when he finally pulled away.

Ben flopped onto his back and closed his eyes. "I'm not sure I can move after that." The towel that had been wrapped around him pooled at his waist, doing nothing to hide his rigid shaft.

Gareth grinned and faced his wardrobe again. "Patience is a virtue." He took a dark blue shirt from a hanger and slipped it on. He turned to Ben as he buttoned it. "It will give you something to look forward to. If you're coming over tomorrow, that is?"

Ben rose until he leaned back on his hands, his body arched and displayed for Gareth's perusal. With a smile, Ben pushed the towel from his groin, revealing his deep red shaft, standing proud, and wrapped his hand around it. A groan tore from his lips, and Gareth paused, wishing he could take what was on display. He narrowed his eyes.

"I know what you're doing, Ben. Remove your hand." He paused. "Now!" Ben's eyes shot open, and he froze. "Let go now." Ben uncurled his hand with a whimper. "Get dressed."

Ben stood, and Gareth tensed. Would Ben do as he said, or would he walk? Gareth had a lot more to teach Ben, but it was never too early to learn who was in charge. He watched Ben dress as he finished buttoning his shirt. When the man was fully dressed, he had a pout on his face.

Gareth withheld his smile and stopped in front of him, covering his dick with his palm. "This is mine now. You have to wait until I tell you to come. No taking care of it yourself, thinking I won't know because I will."

Ben's nose crinkled even as he glared at him. "That's hardly fair."

Gareth removed his hand. "Who said anything about fair? I'm your Daddy. You do as I say." Gareth waited for Ben to baulk at the words, but if anything, Ben's shoulders relaxed.

"Yes...Daddy." Ben winced.

"You don't have to call me Daddy if it's uncomfortable for you."

Ben shook his head. "No, it's not that." He bit his lip. "My cock jerks every time I say it," he whispered.

Gareth smiled and pulled Ben into his arms, rubbing his back. "As long as it makes you happy. If anything ever doesn't, let me know straight away."

When they were ready, he took Ben's hand, and they descended the stairs. He already had his phone and wallet in his pockets, so he grabbed his keys, and they exited the house, locking it behind them.

"Hey! I thought you would've gone already."

Gareth smiled at Victor and squeezed Ben's hand. "I'm running a little behind."

Victor grinned, eyeing Ben. "I can understand why."

Gareth felt Ben stiffen beside him, and he glanced across at him. "Easy to be side-tracked by this one."

Ben's cheeks coloured, and his lip disappeared again. Gareth narrowed his eyes. He knew, there and then, he needed to add a punishment for biting that lip. It was far too distracting. He could still sense the tension in Ben, and he nudged his arm until Ben peered at him.

"Victor, this is Ben, my..." He frowned at Ben, having not discussed how he wanted to be described to people.

"His boy," Ben stated, narrowing his eyes at Victor.

Gareth smiled, pleased Ben had taken the initiative. "And my boss." Ben closed his eyes, and Gareth chuckled. "Ben, this is Victor, my next-door neighbour and loosely classed as a friend."

Victor gasped at the words. "How dare you?" Victor ruined it by laughing and waving his hand in front of him. "Okay, that's probably true." He sobered and stared at Ben. "We're far too different to be of any good to each other, Ben, so don't worry about me trying to take him from you. I'm trying to find my own Daddy."

Victor couldn't have said anything better than that because everything about Ben relaxed at that moment. Gareth hadn't realised that was what Ben had been worried about. He'd put it down to meeting someone new and telling them about their relationship.

Gareth tilted his head, staring at Ben. "Do you want to come with us?"

Ben stared back, his nose wrinkling. "I don't know."

"You can. I can get you a guest pass for tonight, and if it's something you like, we can get you a membership."

Ben licked his lips, dropping his eyes, and Gareth let him have a minute. He turned back to Victor. "Are you heading there now?"

"Yeah. I'll catch up with Preston and keep him company until you get there." He wandered to his car. "Nice to meet you, Ben!"

Ben didn't seem to hear, and Victor drove off. Gareth knew he wouldn't be offended. He stepped in front of Ben. "Everything okay in there?" he said, tapping the side of Ben's forehead.

"Will there be other people like us?"

Gareth nodded. "Plenty. Daddy kink is popular."

"Is that all this is?" Gareth frowned, and Ben continued, "A kink? I thought it was more."

Gareth understood at that point. He slid his arms around Ben's waist. "It's called a kink, but it's more a collective name for everything that's involved. It's up to the people within that relationship to define what it means for them. Some people want it only on the weekends at the club. Some people want it all day, every day. It's up to us to decide what's right for us."

Ben's eyes glistened, and Gareth pecked him on the lips. "I'd like to come with you."

Gareth smiled. "Then you shall. Do you want some clothes to change into?"

Ben glanced down at his suit with a smile. "I think getting changed is a good idea, but I have a bag in my car."

Gareth frowned. "Why?"

Ben bit his lip. "I need them sometimes at work."

They re-entered Gareth's house once Ben had grabbed his bag from the boot of his car, and within minutes, Ben returned dressed in jeans and a polo shirt.

"Is this okay?"

"Perfect. You wouldn't usually wear them for work, though."

Ben sighed. "I sleep at work occasionally. It means I don't have to go home."

Gareth enveloped Ben in his arms and held him. "No more, okay? If you need to get away, come here. I don't want you sleeping at work."

"All right."

They climbed into Gareth's car, and he aimed for the club. He explained what Ben should expect when they got there, and in true form, they set Ben up with a guest pass within minutes. Gareth kept hold of Ben's hand as they entered the main club area. It was a cross between a pub and a club in looks, thankfully without the strobe lighting, and had plenty of seats. They found Preston and Victor at the bar, and Gareth wound his arm around Ben's waist, not wanting to lose him.

"Preston, how are you?" Gareth asked, seeing the dark circles beneath his friend's eyes.

Preston smiled ruefully. "I've been better." He glanced at Ben and raised his eyebrows.

Gareth grinned. "Preston, this is Ben, my boy."

Preston held out his hand. "Nice to meet you, Ben. How the hell can you put up with this guy?" He thumbed towards Gareth.

Ben chuckled. "He's growing on me."

They laughed when Gareth poked his fingers into Ben's side, making him giggle and squirm.

"Ooh, ticklish. That's going to be fun to explore," Victor said with a wink.

Gareth ignored him. "What would you like to drink?" he asked Ben.

Ben studied the bar, his forehead and nose creasing. When he hadn't answered a few minutes later, Gareth nudged him.

"Are you okay?"

Ben nodded, then shook his head. "I have no idea what half these drinks are," he admitted.

"What do you usually drink?"

"I don't." Ben tilted his head. "Well, I usually have a glass of whiskey, but it's just window dressing. I'm not allowed to drink it. Even though I did the last time." Ben's eyes took on a faraway look, and Gareth tightened his hold.

"How about we have something non-alcoholic, and you'll be able to look around and ask questions without the alcohol being involved?"

Ben chuckled. "I might need it to ask the question."

Gareth smiled. "No, you don't. Never be ashamed or embarrassed about asking questions. Any of us will answer for you."

"He's right," Preston said, resting his chin in his palm and his elbow on the counter. "Unless you ask questions, you don't know the answer, and that, around here, could cause problems."

Ben frowned. "Problems?"

Victor piped up, "There are certain aspects of the club that require protocols to be followed. You learn them as you go, but if we're here to help, it can stop issues before they begin."

Ben nodded. "Okay, always ask before I do or say anything. Gotcha."

Gareth chuckled. "It's nothing sinister, but it's always best to check when you're new to the scene." He placed a drink order with the bartender. "Once we have the drinks, shall we find a booth? It might be easier to see everything from there."

Preston gave a thumbs up. "I'm all for it." He threw back the whiskey he had and held up his hands to the bartender.

As much as Gareth needed to keep an eye on Ben, he also needed to watch Preston. There was no way he was leaving the guy alone when he was drinking heavily again.

"He'll be fine with us," Ben whispered in his ear. Gareth raised his eyebrows at him, and Ben shrugged. "You seem concerned, and he seems sad."

Gareth kissed him. "Thank you. I'll explain later."

"No need. He's your friend. That's all I need to know."

Gareth cupped Ben's jaw and took his mouth harder, unable to vocalise how much that meant to him. A throat clearing had Gareth pulling away, and he glanced at Preston, who held out two drinks.

"Get a booth, and you can do that without him falling over."

Victor snorted, and Gareth laughed. "On it."

He took the drinks, gave one to Ben, and threaded their fingers together once more. Glancing around the room, he could see a couple of booths free and led the way, keeping Ben close to him. They weaved through the crowd and slid into the seats to the side of the room, a perfect vantage point for Ben. Victor slid in beside Ben and Preston beside Gareth. Victor began explaining some things to Ben, pointing out areas of the club and what they could see. Gareth rested back and glanced at Preston.

"How are you really?"

Preston blew out a breath. "Pissed off, emotional, pissed off, etc."

"Any more developments?"

"No. Still treating me the same."

"Asshole," Gareth said. "Have you thought any more about leaving the job?"

Preston shook his head. "I just don't know if I can take it anymore. Seeing him every day and not being able to touch him had been hard enough when I knew I could in the evenings, but now..."

"We need to grab him and lock him up," Victor said. "Set him on the St Andrew's cross, and you can torture him until he gives you information."

Gareth chuckled, but he saw the flare in Preston's eyes. "It might be worthwhile, but you'd have to be sure he wouldn't have you arrested afterwards."

12

BEN

"Arrested?" Ben said, his heart raced at the implications. "Why would he be arrested?"

Gareth placed a hand on Ben's arm. "I'm joking, Ben. A little."

That didn't help him settle.

"What he means is that locking someone into the cross without their express permission is frowned upon, unfortunately," Victor said. "I'm sure we can make him want it, though." He winked at Preston, who chuckled.

Ben relaxed now he realised they wouldn't be arrested for just being here. Stupid thought though it was, it was something he'd never thought about before. The club was nicer than he'd imagined. He hadn't had much to go on, but he was impressed. His gaze stopped on a stage towards the back of the room. It held the St Andrew's Cross they'd been talking about, and Ben tried to imagine himself on it. He'd never been tied up before, and he wasn't sure if it was something he'd like.

"Look, there's a Daddy and little." Victor nudged his arm, and Ben refocused on the couple Victor pointed out.

They were both of a similar age from what Ben could tell—although he was rubbish with guessing ages, so he could be completely wrong—and if Victor hadn't pointed them out, there was no way he would've guessed. At least until one of them...softened before Ben's eyes. He couldn't explain it any better. The man leant his head on the other man's shoulder and closed his eyes, his body relaxing into the hold. The other man began swaying gently from side to side while continuing his conversation with their companions. After a minute, the Daddy lifted the little into his arms and carried him to a corner where Ben could see some large beanbags, plastic boxes and small tables. He set the little into a beanbag, covered him with a blanket and settled beside him, crossing his ankles.

"I bet some of the other littles will join them in a minute," Victor said. "Once a Daddy starts reading, all the littles congregate for storytime. It's adorable."

"You're just as adorable," Preston said. "I'm surprised you're not over there already."

Victor rolled his eyes. "I'm teaching."

Ben raised his eyebrows. "I didn't know you were a little. You can join them if you want to. I'm okay here."

Victor waved him away. "I'm good. It would probably do me some good to have a break from the monotony of trying to find a Daddy. It's soul-crushing some days."

"Why is it hard?" Ben asked.

"Why is it difficult to find a relationship in the first place?" Preston said. "There's nothing different here, and people still need to have something in common besides the kink to make the relationship stick."

Preston's eyes clouded over, and he sat back and downed his drink. Ben glanced at Gareth, who gave a small smile, though he seemed sad. Ben squeezed Gareth's hand.

"I think I need a refill. Anyone else?" Preston asked.

Ben raised his hand. "Could I have a whiskey, please?"

"Are you sure?" Gareth asked.

Ben nodded. "I've had it before, just rarely. I doubt I could hold more than one or two." He would stay with one drink because he *knew* he couldn't handle more than one. Although the idea of not being able to drive home at the end of the night was enticing.

"Okay. I'll have another lemonade, please, Preston."

Preston disappeared, and Victor resumed pointing out what they could see in the club; all the while, Gareth played with Ben's fingers, sending shivers, goosebumps and fire through his veins. His cock—which had gone down on the journey to the club—rose to the occasion again, and Ben fidgeted in his seat. He could barely understand what Victor told him.

Discreetly, he rested his hand against his groin to ease the pressure while trying to listen to Victor. Ben snapped his head around when Gareth smacked the hand he held. Gareth raised his eyebrows, and Ben frowned, then glared when he realised he'd been doing what Gareth had asked him not to. He removed his hand, trying to pull his other from Gareth's hand, but Gareth wouldn't let him and instead pulled him towards him.

Gareth wrapped an arm over Ben's shoulder and across his chest, nibbling on his earlobe. "What did I tell you about touching what's mine?"

"What did you expect when you're turning me on?" Ben hissed.

"I expect you to do as you're told. No matter how difficult it may be."

"You should punish him," Victor said with far more glee than Ben thought he should have.

"Punish who?" Preston asked when he placed the tray of drinks on the table.

"Ben. He was touching himself." Victor winked at Ben.

Preston grimaced. "You're heading into troublesome territory if Gareth had told you not to," he told Ben.

Ben tensed. "Well, he should keep his hands to himself if he doesn't want me to get horny." His eyes widened before he finished the last word, but everyone at the table heard.

"Ooh, Ben, what did you do?" Victor covered his eyes with his hands, though a smile graced his mouth.

Ben frowned. "What?"

Preston chuckled and stared at Ben while speaking to Gareth. "Gareth, have you told Ben how much you like edging yet?"

Gareth's chest vibrated with his laughter. "Not yet, but he's going to find out sooner rather than later."

Ben swallowed. "Edging?" He knew what it was and knew there was no hope in him ever being able to hold back an orgasm, no matter the consequences.

Gareth nuzzled Ben's neck. "Uh-huh. My favourite pastime. I can make it last...*hours*."

Ben inhaled through his nose as his eyelids fluttered closed at the imagery. A tingle of heat swept through him. How could anyone withstand such torture?

"Or spank him," Victor supplied. "He'd feel it for days."

Ben opened his eyes and glared at him. "I thought we were becoming friends?"

"Oh, we are." Victor smiled. "But I'm all for helping with punishments."

"Victor likes to misbehave," Preston said.

Ben stared at Victor, remembering what he'd read about in the forums about those boys who misbehaved on purpose to get attention or be punished. He hadn't seen the allure of it until then. To have Gareth's undivided attention...

A hand covered his cock, and he bit off a hiss and instead checked around the table to see if anyone was watching. Preston and Victor were talking, but Ben knew they were aware by the curled corners of their mouths. Ben wasn't sure if knowing people could see aided his arousal or diminished it.

"This is mine, Ben. I get to decide when you come, where you come, how you come and how long you come. And it won't be right now."

Gareth's hand left his groin, and it was all Ben could do to stop himself from putting his own hand in its place. He leaned back against Gareth, breathing deeply to get rid of the arousal pulsing through him. His three companions chatted while Ben floated. He couldn't believe someone like Gareth wanted him.

"Do you want to dance, Ben?"

He opened his eyes, seeing Victor grinning at him. He glanced at the dance floor, where several other people let loose, and grinned. "It's been ages since I have." He went to move, then paused and peered at Gareth. "Can I?"

Gareth smiled and kissed him. "Have fun. But not too much."

Ben leaned forward again, taking Gareth's mouth, and knowing he could was a heady feeling. "Thank you."

Gareth pecked his forehead, and Ben followed Victor, who was already swaying his hips to the beat. As Ben had told them, it had been many years since he'd danced. It wasn't allowed at the dinner parties—and he could just imagine the coronary his parents would have if he just bust a move in the middle of the evening—and he hadn't been out in years. The last time would have been a work Christmas party, and that didn't go down well.

Victor grabbed his hands, and Ben set his inhibitions free. He forgot about everything except where he was at that moment. Victor moved closer and closer until they were plastered to each other, grinding and sending Ben's arousal sky high. It wasn't enough to get him off, thankfully, but it set his blood boiling that Gareth could see him. They spent many long minutes dancing until Ben needed a drink. He dragged Victor with him to the bar and ordered another whiskey, having finished his previous one before he started dancing.

"Are you sure that's a good idea?" Victor asked, doubling their order.

Ben grinned. "I'm sure one more won't matter. I'm drinking water between them."

Victor held his hands up. "I'm not trying to persuade you otherwise, but you might want to check in with your Daddy."

"Says the boy who aims to misbehave."

They shared a laugh, and Ben paid for the drinks before downing his, the burn coating his throat and setting fire to his stomach. He hissed as he put the glass back on the counter.

"Woah, slow down, cowboy."

Ben grinned again, feeling lighter than he'd felt in...as long as he could remember. He didn't want this feeling to end, and it was all thanks to the man sitting at the table, watching his every move. A sense of belonging waved through him, and he ordered a fresh round of drinks for everyone this time. When the bartender handed them to him, he carried them to the booth table Gareth and Preston were still sitting at. He sidled into the seat, sliding as close as he could get to Gareth, who lifted a hand over his shoulder and pulled him even closer. Ben closed his eyes and settled his head on Gareth's shoulder, soaking in the contentment.

The conversation carried on around him until Gareth squeezed his shoulder and held a glass to his lips. "Do you want a drink?"

Ben opened his mouth to admit he'd already had one when a sip of the liquid landed on his tongue. Instead, he took a mouthful, closing his eyes again as the warmth spread through him.

"I think you might want to slow up on the drink, Gareth," Victor said.

Ben snorted, and Gareth's arms tightened.

"Why?" Gareth asked.

"Because he already had another one at the bar."

Ben's comfortable cushion tensed, and Gareth set him upright. "Did you?"

Ben licked his lips and pulled his bottom lip between his teeth. "Yes," he said quietly, studying his hands rather than facing Gareth.

"Look at me." Ben inhaled and lifted his gaze. "Why didn't you tell me?"

Ben shrugged, not entirely sure. He had wanted to take a leaf out of Victor's book at the time, but now he couldn't find the same level of need he'd had while waiting for that drink.

"I think it's time we went home," Gareth said. "Do you want to stay over tonight, Preston?"

Ben's heart cracked as the words hit home. Why would Gareth ask that unless he was done with Ben and wanted Preston's company instead?

Preston shook his head. "I'll be fine. There's nothing I can do about my situation. Even if I decide to quit my job, as you rightly said, I will still have to work the notice period unless I want it mentioned on my reference that I didn't give any."

"Are you sure?" Gareth asked.

"Perfectly. Go sort your boy out." Preston sent a small smile Ben's way.

Ben couldn't return it. Had Gareth had enough of him already? Were they finished before they'd even begun?

Hands cupped his face, pulling him towards Gareth. "Hey, hey. Breathe for me, Ben. Just breathe."

He stared at Gareth, wondering why he asked that, when he took a lungful of air and oxygen refuelled his body. Gareth wiped his thumbs against Ben's cheeks, coming away wet. Why was he crying?

"That's it. Keep breathing for me. Focus on me. Good boy."

At that, Ben's mind rebelled, and he frowned, pushing Gareth away. He tried to scramble over Victor to get out of the booth and ended up almost face planting. If Victor hadn't moved at the same time and caught him, he would've been eating tiles.

"Ben, wait!" Gareth called, but Ben was already shrugging Victor off and heading for the exit. He didn't need Gareth talking him down. He didn't need Gareth giving him attention when he had Preston or Victor waiting for him whenever he wanted them. It was obvious they cared deeply about each other. How could Ben compete with that?

He left the club without a goodbye to anyone and strode through the car park. He hadn't brought anything with him other than his wallet and phone, and those were in his pocket. There would be a taxi rank somewhere, and if not, he'd walk to Gareth's house to collect his car.

As he passed the entrance to the car park, hands grabbed him and spun him, pressing him against the wall. He opened his mouth to scream when it registered that it was Gareth moments before Gareth's mouth took his own.

At first, Ben squirmed and pushed against Gareth, then he sank into the kiss and gripped Gareth's neck. It didn't last long, just long enough for Ben to relax. Once his body eased, Gareth pulled back, resting their foreheads together.

"Don't ever run from me like that again. You scared the crap out of me." Ben pushed at him, but Gareth kept hold. "Tell me what went through your mind back there."

"No. Let me go."

Gareth let go, and Ben froze, not expecting him to listen.

"I won't ever hold you against your will, Ben." Gareth stared at him. "I'm concerned because I did something to upset you, and I don't know what it was."

"Why do you need me when you have Preston and Victor? Are you creating a harem or something?"

Gareth chuckled and rubbed the back of his neck. "No. We truly are just friends. I promise you. I've never slept with Preston or

Victor. We found out early on in our friendship that none of us were compatible. Preston is having a hard time at the minute, and I honestly don't think he should be alone. He doesn't want to impose on anyone, though. We're friends."

The words were sincere, even Ben could tell that, but it didn't stop the ache in his chest telling him that Gareth wasn't his.

"Talk to me."

Ben opened his mouth. "Why do you want me when you can have someone better?" It wasn't what he'd planned to say.

"Oh, Ben. I'm getting the impression that there is no one better for me. You're it." Gareth stepped closer, though he did it slowly enough that Ben knew he could stop if he told him to. When he cupped Ben's face like he had in the club, he waited until Ben gazed straight into his eyes. "You challenge me in ways I could never expect, yet you remind me I need to go slow, that you need to learn, that you're young in lifestyle terms. I have so much I want to show you and teach you, and I can't wait. If you let me, you won't regret it. I promise."

Ben chewed his lip, and Gareth pulled it from between his teeth and rubbed his thumb against it. Without breaking their gaze, Ben nodded. "Please," he whispered.

13

GARETH

Gareth dropped his mouth to Ben's and tasted him, whiskey and all. He'd explain why it was important for Ben to tell Gareth how much he'd drunk later, but for now, he needed to reassure his boy. Wrapping his arms around Ben and holding him tightly, Gareth poured everything he could into the kiss before pulling back.

"Let's go home," he said.

"Your place?" Ben raised his eyebrows.

Gareth nodded. "We can decide what we're going to do from there."

"Okay."

Gareth led Ben towards the car, helping him settle in the front seat before driving them back to his house.

"I really like Victor and Preston."

Gareth smiled over at him and threaded their fingers together. "I'm glad. They liked you, too. I could tell."

"They probably thought I was an idiot." Ben turned his face to the window, avoiding Gareth's gaze.

"Not at all. What we have is new, Ben. It'll take time to get our balance and figure out what we're doing. As I told you before, we choose how our relationship goes. No one else."

Ben was quiet for a moment, and Gareth left him to his thoughts. He wanted nothing more than to have his arms cocooning Ben all night—no sex intended—but he wasn't sure if it was too soon.

"I'm definitely not made for being a little," Ben murmured.

"How did you figure that out?"

"I don't find the idea of playing with toys or colouring or wearing nappies and stuff like that. I like being taken care of, but not to that extent." He sent Gareth a small smile. "I think you might be right about the Middle thing."

"You have the temperament to go with it."

Ben scoffed. "You mean surly, aggressive with huge mood swings?"

Gareth smiled. "Not at all. You've had so much of your life mapped out for you that you've not had the chance to let go and live. With me, you can do that. I'll only stop you if you're a danger to yourself or others, and if that happens, we'll deal with it through punishments. It's the quickest way for you to learn."

They reached home, and Gareth unlocked the house and guided Ben to the kitchen. "First stop is a big glass of water and some paracetamol. I guarantee you'll need it."

"I feel fine."

"At the minute." Gareth stared at him until Ben nodded.

Gareth ran the cold tap for a second before filling a glass. Hands slid around his waist, searching, and Gareth's breath caught when Ben cupped his cock.

"Ben..." Gareth warned. "All we're doing tonight is sleeping. You've had too much to drink."

"I'm fine. I promise." Ben's lips pressed against Gareth's neck. "I want you."

Gareth twisted in Ben's arms and held the tablets and glass between them so Ben couldn't reach his mouth.

"I told you, I'm fine."

"And I'm telling you that you need to take these, and we'll get some sleep." He tried to keep his voice level because Ben's hands were still groping him. Not that he minded, but he needed Ben on an even keel to have a proper discussion before they got all sexed up, and partially drunk was not the best choice.

"Maybe this will change your mind."

Ben dropped to his knees and rested his face against Gareth's groin. The sight gave Gareth a moment's pause, but he lifted Ben's face with the hand holding the tablets and said, "It's not happening, Ben."

He held out the tablets when Ben huffed and sat back on his heels. Ben snatched them and threw them in his mouth, chasing them with a gulp of water.

"Better?" Ben rolled his eyes. "Now, can I do what I planned to do?"

Gareth shook his head. "Nope. Let's get to bed."

Ben threw his hands in the air. "All I want to do is fuck! I don't want to sleep."

"You'll thank me in the morning."

"I'm not even drink. Um, drunk," Ben said while Gareth led him up the stairs to the bedroom.

"I can tell." Gareth was known for his sarcasm.

"At least we're heading in the right direction."

Ben began undressing before they'd even reached Gareth's bedroom door, and Gareth picked up each item of clothing as Ben dropped it. It wasn't something he would do in the future, but they hadn't confirmed any rules; therefore, he couldn't punish him for it. Yet.

Ben sprawled across the bed as soon as they reached it, and Gareth laid his clothes on a chair. Despite Ben's insistence that they were going to fuck, he knew all it would take was for the comfortable bed to surround Ben, and he'd be out for the count.

He quickly stripped the covers from beneath Ben and manoeu-vred him into a better position.

Ben held out his arms. "Come here."

Gareth leaned down and kissed him, avoiding his arms. "I just need the bathroom. I'll be back in a minute."

"Be quick. I need you."

Gareth dropped another kiss on his lips and covered him be-fore heading for the bathroom. Under normal circumstances, he would've persuaded Ben to shower before bed, but he wasn't above using the laws of a comfortable bed to help Gareth get his own way. By the time he'd finished and walked back into the bedroom, Ben's little snores were audible. Gareth grinned at the look of innocence on his slack face as he undressed. He put on some clean briefs and climbed in beside him, wrapping his arms around the man he hoped would be in his life for the foreseeable future.

Gareth woke as a hand clenched his hip. The bruising grip shot him to wakefulness, and he immediately took in the scene. Ben's hand was gripping his hip, and he was rubbing his ass against Gareth's morning wood. Under normal circumstances, he wouldn't mind being woken that way, but Ben was misbehaving, and Gareth needed to teach his boy a lesson.

He slid his hand around Ben's waist and down to his cock, encircling the hard shaft. Ben shuddered and groaned, rolling his head back to rest against Gareth's shoulder. Gareth stroked him twice and tightened his grip around the base. Ben gasped, eyelids flying wide.

"What...?" Ben frowned, an icy glint entering his eyes. "Well, *that* wasn't nice."

Gareth lowered his mouth to Ben's ear. "Neither was taking something you hadn't been given permission to."

"Oh, come on!"

"Who does this belong to?" Gareth squeezed, and Ben exhaled heavily.

"You." The tone was anything but conciliatory.

"Who?" Gareth tilted his head and raised his eyebrows, keeping eye contact.

Ben licked his lips. "You, Daddy."

"So why are you trying to get off when I've not given you permission?"

"Please? I'm... I need..."

"You don't know what you need, boy. That's why I'm here." Gareth let go, and Ben whimpered. "Now, roll onto your back and hands above your head."

Ben did as asked, and Gareth straddled him, making sure he braced himself on his hands and knees so their bodies didn't touch where he knew Ben needed them to. Ben tried lifting his hips, but Gareth used one hand to press them back to the bed, then returned his hand to the bed.

"Behave, or you'll understand the meaning of my edging record."

Ben's eyes flared. Maybe it was something he would enjoy, in which case, Gareth needed a different threat. Gareth leaned down and captured Ben's lips, taking things slow and easy—a gentle good morning kiss instead of a frantic, need-filled one. Ben's hands tangled in Gareth's hair, and Gareth pulled back, staring at Ben until he replaced his hands above his head. Then, and only then, did Gareth kiss him again. When Ben's hips brushed against Gareth's groin, Gareth pulled back again, staring until Ben gave a bitten-off curse and rested his hips again. Ben was a fast learner, and though he squirmed, his first attempt at taking orders went well.

After several minutes of this, with the result being Ben slack and relaxed, Gareth dropped his weight to Ben, covering him with his body. Gareth was as hard as Ben was, if not more, and they both needed a release.

"This is our first time together," Gareth whispered against Ben's ear. "I want this to last, but I want us both to remember it. We only get one first time together, and I want this to be your *best* first time."

That probably didn't express exactly what Gareth was trying to say, but he hoped he got his point across.

"I want you however I can have you," Ben said, eyes locked onto Gareth's.

"You have me, Ben. You already have me."

Gareth quickly grabbed the lube and a condom from the bedside table and dropped them beside him. He pressed their lips together, harder, deeper than the previous times. He couldn't get enough of his taste, and now he knew where they were heading, his arousal skyrocketed. Already, he could feel their precome mixing and sliding between them as their cocks thrust against each other, making Gareth feel like he was a teenager again and could come just like this. Usually, he had more restraint. He lost a portion of his control when Ben was around, and that was dangerous. But for their first time, he could allow it. He *would* allow it.

He kissed across Ben's jaw, nipping at his earlobe before descending the column of his neck and down his chest to his nipples. Ben was highly sensitive, and it didn't take long for him to be writhing beneath him as Gareth licked, sucked and bit at his nubs in turn. He felt Ben's fingers against his head, and he paused, not looking up, waiting to see if Ben would understand or if Gareth needed to remind him. Within seconds, the hands were gone, and Gareth continued. It wasn't that he didn't want Ben to touch him;

it was that he wanted Ben to learn that Gareth was in charge. His Daddy was in charge.

Gareth continued his ministrations until Ben was squirming beneath him once more, and he proceeded lower and lower. When he stopped above Ben's cock, there was a pool of precome waiting for Gareth on Ben's stomach. He lapped at it, groaning as the flavour burst across his tongue. He intended to drive Ben crazy while he prepared his ass for him, but that taste—Gareth wasn't sure if he would last without sending Ben over the edge so he could taste his release.

"Fuck, Ben. You're addictive."

"Please, Daddy!" he murmured.

Ben's words warmed Gareth's heart, but he didn't miss the way Ben's shaft jerked in response.

"I'll give you everything, Ben. Don't you worry."

Gareth licked up the underside of Ben's cock, swirling his tongue against the sensitive nerves beneath the tip before swiping across the head and gathering all the precome waiting for him. He was sure there would be plenty more for him as he continued.

He fumbled around on the bed for the lube while he played at seeing what noises he could drag from his boy. The tube opened easily enough, and he concentrated on Ben's cock as he slicked his fingers enough to start sending Ben higher. Lifting his head, he gazed at the pupil-blown, flushed face, and he smiled. "Ready?"

"Oh, god, please!" he whispered.

Ben's hands were still above his head, but they were clenched in the pillow with his arms cradling his head. A slight sheen of sweat was visible on his forehead, and his lower lip was red and swollen. Gareth reached for the bruised lip, brushing his finger gently across it.

"Stop hurting yourself," he murmured, eyes fixed on the puffy area until Ben licked his lips, catching the tip of Gareth's finger. Gareth stared at his boy, eyes narrowing when he glanced to the side and back again. Gareth tilted his head, wondering what the movement was about. He followed Ben's gaze and cursed. He rose, swiped his slicked hands on the covers and grabbed Ben's arm. On his biceps, there was a perfect outline of teeth marks depressed into the skin, the blush of the blood beneath having risen to the surface but not broken through.

"Why did you do that?" he asked as he climbed off the bed and strode for the bathroom. He ran the cold tap and wet a flannel, wringing it out, and brought it back to the bed. Returning to his position, he lay Ben's arm out to the side and applied the flannel to the area. He held it gently against the skin and stared at Ben. "Why?"

Tears glistened in Ben's eyes, and his nose wrinkled. "I..." He inhaled and swallowed, dropping his gaze.

Gareth covered Ben's body with his own, hoping their physical closeness would help centre him. "You can tell me anything, Ben. Anything."

Ben cleared his throat. "I didn't want to make too much noise. I'm used to hiding what I'm doing from my parents in case they enter my room without knocking. You were so good, and I could barely keep it in. It was the only way I could think of."

A swell of anger grew in the pit of his stomach, and not for the first time, he wished he could have words with Ben's parents.

"Oh, sweetheart." Gareth kissed him. "You don't ever have to keep quiet with me. Here, you're safe. We'll discuss the other part of that at a later time, but while you're here, you have nothing to worry about. Be as loud or quiet as you want to be, but don't hide from me, and certainly don't hurt yourself." Gareth winked. "That's my job."

Gareth kissed him again, soft and slow, and lifted his head to check the injury. It was red and inflamed but would be fine in a few days. He flipped the flannel over to the cooler side and glanced at Ben again.

"You're going to keep this arm like this while I finish what I started. The flannel needs to stay on, and if you move, it'll fall off. Do you think you can do that?"

"I don't know," Ben admitted.

"It's what I'm asking you to do, and you need to do your best, okay?"

"Yes, Daddy."

Gareth rewarded him with another soft kiss before moving down his body and resuming his position at Ben's cock. "This is going to be good." He grinned and lowered his head.

14

BEN

Ben couldn't contain his gasp when an electric current shot through him. His reward was an increase in suction, and despite wanting to close his eyes and revel in the sensation of it, he kept his eyes on the spectacle in front of him. A questing finger rubbed against his pucker, and he instinctively clenched. The simple act of massaging his ass relaxed him, and Gareth's fingertip slid inside with barely a hesitation. It might have had something to do with Gareth thrumming his tongue against his nerve endings at the same time. Ben's head spun, and this time, he had to close his eyes.

He'd never had this. Anyone he'd slept with before—which were few and far between—had been perfunctory and quick. This...attention to detail never happened. It could get highly addictive.

Ben moved his arm to grip the covers, but the flannel reminded him of Gareth's order. He snapped his eyes open, checked the flannel was still in place and glanced at Gareth, whose eyes were already on his, crinkled at the edges as if he knew what had almost happened. Ben's cheeks heated, and he chewed on his bottom lip again before Gareth narrowed his eyes, and Ben let it go again. That would take some remembering. He wasn't used to looking after himself in that way.

A particularly strong suck had his attention zeroing in on his groin, and he pushed his head back into the pillow. A second finger joined the first—at least he thought it was a second, it could be a third as out of his head as he had been—and he exhaled at the feeling of being full. He knew he would stretch further once Gareth himself slid inside, but it still felt amazing.

The thrust of Gareth's fingers intensified, and Ben's breathing increased. He swam towards release at a leisurely pace, but he could sense its impending arrival.

"Gar...Daddy?" He met Gareth's gaze, the raised eyebrows acknowledging he heard. "It's coming. *I'm* going to come soon."

Gareth sucked harder, swirling his tongue around and around. The sensations grew, and Ben rocked his head on the pillow, wanting to push it back. He didn't want it to end so soon. He wanted more of this. He wanted Gareth inside him when he came.

Ben realised what he had to do and swallowed hard before lifting his arm, the flannel dropping to the bed, all the while watching Gareth's face. Gareth narrowed his eyes...and lifted his head, pulling his fingers free. Ben's stomach clenched at the glint in Gareth's eyes and the empty sensation in his ass. His impending climax released him from its hold, but the humming heat in his groin remained.

"Hmm. Now, why did you do that, I wonder?" Gareth said, his voice gravelly and deep. "Is there something you want to tell me, Ben?" he asked, resting back on his knees, his cock pointing towards his stomach, hard and wanting.

Ben licked his lips, staring at it and wishing he could have it in his mouth.

"Ben?"

He flicked his gaze back to Gareth, the man's eyebrows raised in question. "I...uh, I don't want to come yet."

Gareth crossed his arms over his chest. "Why do you think that is *your* choice?"

Ben's stomach churned, and his mouth went dry. "I..." His vision went blurry, and he cursed his body's reaction to feeling overwhelmed. He wiped the tears away and said, "It's my body."

Gareth rubbed his chin. "You're right. It is. But you're my boy, and that means you follow my rules."

"You said we needed to discuss these things first," Ben said, lifting his chin slightly.

"We definitely do, but you're the one who brought it up. I was looking after you by asking you to keep the flannel on your arm. I didn't want it to hurt more than necessary. You agreed. That, to me, means we have an accord."

Ben blinked. Damn him. He was right. He closed his eyes and sighed. "I'm sorry. I wanted you to be inside me when we came, but it's not my choice, especially when I agreed to keep my arms where they were." He exhaled again. "I'm struggling to let go."

"I know, sweetheart. You need to trust me. In here." Gareth patted Ben's chest. "I know you want to, but you're just not quite there yet. And that's fine. I'll show you every single time until you believe it."

This time, he didn't wipe away the tears; he let them fall, staring at the ceiling so as not to see the disappointment he knew must show on Gareth's face.

"I'm sorry."

Gareth covered his body, cradling his head. "You don't need to be sorry. I thought it would be better if we figured out how we would do things as they cropped up, but maybe we should pause things and talk everything through first. What do you think?"

Ben shook his head. "Too much information at once will make me panic because I won't be able to get it all right at the same time—perfectionist that I am. Little and often works better. I *know* this, yet I'm still struggling." He stared at Gareth, cupping his face. "I hate disappointing you."

Gareth smiled. "I'm not disappointed. As far as I'm concerned, this is how we work. You push; I push back. It's a balance. This isn't supposed to be something that worries you. It should be natural. Be who you are, and nothing can go wrong between us."

"Yes, it can. I've ruined this." He waved his hand between them.

Gareth kissed him. "No, you haven't. Delayed it, maybe, but not ruined it." He canted his hips, pressing his still hard cock into Ben's groin. "See."

Ben's eyelids fluttered as heat bloomed. "Yes." He slid his arms around Gareth's neck. "Can we carry on?" He licked his lips.

Gareth grinned. "It would be a shame to waste that lube."

Ben laughed, the tension flowing from his body now he knew Gareth wasn't upset with him.

Gareth kissed him, slow and gentle but gaining momentum. Deeper, harder, faster. Ben's head spun, and he held on while Gareth showed him how much he cared. He could feel it. The way Gareth held him. The way he focused on him. The way he looked at him. Nothing had felt better, and Ben needed to remember this. Otherwise, he might lose it all.

When Gareth moved down his body once more, Ben sighed and laid his hands above his head as per Gareth's earlier instructions. He would try to keep them there, and this time, he wouldn't mask his noises. That was something he could give Gareth.

His cock plunged into something warm and wet, and Ben closed his eyes as his cock rose to fully erect in less than ten seconds. A click of the tube lid reached his ears, and he stared down his body at Gareth. As if he'd been waiting for that exact thing, Gareth smiled as best he could with his mouth full of Ben's dick and pushed a finger inside him.

"Hell, yes!" Ben moved his hips, trying to entice Gareth to go further. "Please, Daddy!"

Gareth ignored him and took his time, stretching him again. When Ben was almost delirious, his mouth babbling nonsense continuously, Gareth pulled from his cock and rose above him. He tore the condom packet with his teeth, rolling it down his length, and Ben vowed, once again, that he would have that shaft in his mouth as soon as possible.

"Slowly does it. I refuse to hurt you." Gareth stared at Ben until he nodded. Bracketing Ben with his forearms, he moved his hips, the head of his cock nudging against his entrance. Ben widened his legs, and Gareth pushed, slowly breaching the ring.

Ben panted, his hands fisting in the pillow. "Please, Daddy. Can I touch you? Please?"

"Yes."

Ben reached down and touched the heat of Gareth's back. He wrapped his legs around Gareth's waist and felt something inside him settle. He crossed his ankles, securing himself around his Daddy, as Gareth sank deep. When he was as deep as he could go, Ben lifted his head and kissed him, loving the feel of him inside him, filling him, heating him from the inside out.

"Good boy. You've taken me well." Gareth nudged his hips again. "Are you ready for me?"

Ben sighed. "Always, Daddy."

"Hold on." Ben tightened his hold, and Gareth chuckled. "You have to let me move, though."

Ben's cheeks heated, and he loosened his hold a little. "Sorry."

Gareth kissed him, ending whatever else he had planned to say, and withdrew before sliding home again. His hands slid beneath Ben and gripped his shoulders, holding him in place.

"Fuck, Ben. You grip me so well." His hips increased his speed, and soon, he pounded into him, and Ben loved every minute.

"Yes!"

Gareth pulled away and lifted onto his hands, changing the angle. Ben missed the warmth of him but held onto Gareth's forearms, keeping them joined at more than one point.

"Touch yourself," Gareth said. "I want to watch."

Ben bit his lip, but as embarrassed as he was, he refused to disobey. He circled his cock with his hand and hissed at the first stroke. He leaked precome generously, and he used it as a lubricant, slicking his way. Gareth grabbed Ben's hips, changing the angle once more, and Ben cried out as he hit exactly where Ben needed it. His hand flew over his cock, stroking himself faster as he tumbled towards the end.

"Daddy!" he shouted breathlessly. "Can I... Can I...?" He couldn't get his words out.

"Come for me, boy."

Ben keened and fell over the edge, wishing he'd held on a little longer so he could've seen Gareth come, but he lost himself in the bliss of release. The rhythmic clenching and releasing sucked his energy from him, and when he finally came back to earth, he slumped to the bed, unable to move. No, that was because Gareth covered him. They were both breathing heavily, sounding as if they had run a marathon in five minutes; they'd probably expelled the same amount of energy.

Gareth moved sooner than Ben wanted, and he ineffectively grabbed at Gareth's arms to keep him close.

"I'm just getting rid of the condom. I'll be back in a minute."

Ben made a noise of understanding, though he kept his eyes closed, his body and mind sated—for the moment.

"I'm going to clean you," Gareth said, and Ben was too worn out to even jump at the unexpected words.

Ben didn't respond but felt a warm, wet cloth wiping his stomach, chest and groin. He couldn't even drag up an ounce of embarrassment. Gareth had given him a release—in more ways than one. The bed dipped beside him, and a warmth cuddled into his side after the covers were pulled over them. Ben mustered the energy to roll to his side to snuggle into Gareth's arms, and Gareth rewarded him with a kiss on the forehead.

"How are you?" Gareth asked.

"Perfect," Ben murmured.

"You can have another hour's sleep if you want before you need to get to work?"

The reminder of reality woke Ben easier than anything else, and he smoothed his fingers across Gareth's chest, images of all the things that awaited him at the office going through his mind. "I don't want to go," he whispered.

Gareth squeezed him. "Understandable, but you have a job to do."

Ben exhaled, watching the hairs on Gareth's chest sway. He didn't hate his job, but he didn't enjoy it anymore, either. He told Gareth as such.

"Find something you do enjoy and transition."

"I can't."

"Why not?"

Ben sighed again. "My parents, for one."

Gareth was quiet for a moment. "What did you mean by your parents coming into your room without knocking?"

Ben stared across the room, the sunlight already shining through the closed curtains, despite their dark colour. It was enough to see everything around them in a hazy sort of way. How could he explain the eccentricities that made up his parents? How could he tell Gareth exactly how much control they had over him? The social status was just the tip of the iceberg.

"It doesn't matter what it is, Ben. I want to help, even if it's only to listen."

The simple acceptance rolled through him as it always did whenever Gareth was with him. It made him feel like nothing could touch him with Gareth there to protect him.

"My parents have the belief that the house is theirs; therefore, there is no room they cannot enter. No room is off-limits. No privacy is allowed. If they want into a room, they enter, regardless of the person, people, activities happening in it."

"Even the bathroom?"

"The bathrooms are the only rooms with locks. That's their one concession. It's why I excuse myself to the bathroom at dinner parties because I know I can have some peace for the amount of time I'm in there."

Gareth's hand continued the circles he rubbed on Ben's back. What was he thinking?

"What did you think of the properties we saw?"

Ben blinked at the change of subject. "Um, I liked the first one the most, but I'd need to get a bath put in."

"Why?"

Ben bit his lip and released it quickly. "I love having baths."

Gareth pressed his lips to Ben's temple. "Is that because you enjoy them or because it's the only place you can be alone?" he whispered against his skin.

Ben tensed, having never put two and two together before. "I'm not sure."

"It doesn't matter, but maybe you could see how you go with the shower first, and if you need a bath, put it in because you *want* to, not because you *need* to."

It was a good idea. Ben had a lot of learning to do when he moved out. He needed to figure out how to live by himself. How to look after himself. How to...live.

"Will you help me?" he mumbled.

Gareth tightened his hold. "I will be there every step of the way if you'll let me."

Ben rose above Gareth, blanketing him completely, and settled down again. "I'll let you."

"Thank you. We have a lot to learn about each other, but first, we need to discuss punishments because someone has one coming."

Ben's breath hitched, and his heart raced. What would Gareth do?

15

GARETH

Gareth felt Ben's chest expand and shudder as the air left him again, and he smiled into Ben's hair. He knew the best first punishment for him, but he needed to make sure Ben was on the same page.

"Do you remember why you need punishing?" he asked, running his hand up and down Ben's bare back.

"I was trying to force you to sleep with me yesterday."

"That was a minor infraction due to your inebriation. I can forgo that one. What else?"

He could almost hear Ben thinking in the seconds following his words. He waited, knowing the answer would come to him eventually.

"I drank too much."

Gareth chuckled. "Almost. It's not that you drank too much. I don't have a problem with you drinking, but what I do have an issue with is you not telling me how much you've had. I can't take care of you properly if I don't have all the information. If you sneak drinks between the ones I know about and fall ill, I won't be able to give doctors the correct answers, and they might treat you wrong. I would hate for that to happen. I need to make sure you're safe, too. What if someone put something in a drink you were given, and I wasn't there with you? Who would keep you safe?"

It was just some of the panic-inducing thoughts running rampant through his brain at any moment in time. As much of an optimist as he was, when it came to looking after someone, he was excessively narrow-minded about the potential outcomes of events.

"I'm sorry."

"Thank you for saying that. I need you to tell me if you've had something to drink other than what I've provided for you. Can you do that?"

"Yes, Daddy."

"Now, onto punishments. What do you think is a good punishment for you?" He wanted Ben to take the driving seat for his punishments, at least in the beginning. Gareth needed to see where Ben's head was at, and the best way to do that was to talk through some options.

"I don't know."

"You've done some research on Daddy relationships. What did you find out?"

He felt Ben swallow. "The boys would be spanked or denied orgasms."

"Anything else?" Ben's wandering hands were distracting but not enough to forgo this conversation. They didn't have much time.

"They would be put in time out or have something they enjoy taken away from them."

"Do you think any of those are a good way to help you remember this rule?"

Ben was silent, and Gareth allowed him the time. He was enjoying this closeness, this time for just them, without the outside world encroaching on them.

"I'm not sure. I don't know how I would react to any of them, and I don't know if they'd help me learn."

"Thank you for being honest. How about we do it this way? I'll choose a punishment that I feel is suitable, and we'll go from there. We can change things as we go if we find it's not right for you. Remember, everyone is different. How does that sound?"

"Good."

Gareth kissed his head. "I need you to get on your hands and knees on the bed."

Ben paused, then did as Gareth had asked. Gareth rose and pulled the covers free from Ben's body. "I'm going to spank you. Five on each side of your ass. I want you to count each one as I do it and repeat, 'I will remember to tell Daddy about my drinks.' Okay?"

"Yes, Daddy."

Gareth stepped close to the bed until he was beside Ben. He ran a hand over Ben's ass cheeks, warming them more than they were already. "Remember, this is a punishment. It's not supposed to be gentle." He waited until Ben agreed. "Ready?"

"Yes."

Gareth pulled his hand back and sent it forward, colliding with Ben's ass in a loud smack. His hand tingled as he rubbed across the exposed skin.

"One. I will remember to tell Daddy about my drinks," Ben said.

"Good boy." Gareth repeated the action on the other side.

"Two. I will remember to tell Daddy about my drinks."

They continued with Gareth gentling the area with his hand after every smack. Ben's head dropped between his trembling arms with his last words.

"Ten. I will remember to tell Daddy about my drinks."

"Well done, Ben. You did well."

"Daddy?" Ben gasped.

"Yes, sweetheart."

"I think I liked that too much."

Gareth tilted his head and grinned. Ben's cock was standing proud and red. Gareth checked the clock. They had enough time. He grabbed the lube and a condom from the bedside and climbed on behind Ben.

"Hold steady. This will be quick."

Gareth rolled the condom down his hard length immediately and slicked his fingers, preparing Ben as quickly as he could while making sure he was ready for him and that Gareth wouldn't hurt him.

"Please, Daddy!"

Gareth sank balls deep with the first long, deep thrust. "Push back against me as I move." He pulled back and slammed forward, Ben resisting being pushed towards the headboard and making their joining harder and louder. Gareth gripped Ben's hips and fucked him fast. They had little time, and he wanted Ben to come, remembering everything that had happened that morning. He sank one set of fingers into Ben's ass cheek, and Ben shouted. Ben had taken his punishment well, but by fucking him afterwards, it would, hopefully, instil it deeper in his head as a reminder of why he'd needed the punishment in the first place. Spanking might not be the best choice of punishment in the future, but he would figure that out as they continued.

Refocusing on his actions, he increased his speed. "Come for me, Ben. Come just for Daddy."

"Yes! Please!" Ben lowered his head to the bed and gripped the sheets. "Oh, fuck!"

The telltale sign of clenching began, squeezing Gareth's cock within the confines of Ben's channel. Gareth dug his fingers into Ben's ass as Gareth released into the condom with a groan.

"Jesus," he said, leaning his head on Ben's lower back while he recovered. He pulled out, holding the end of the condom as he did, and tied it off and threw it into the bin behind him. Ben had collapsed to the bed, and Gareth chuckled. "What did you learn from this?"

"I will definitely remember to tell Daddy about my drinks," Ben said.

Gareth laughed and bundled Ben into his arms. "Well done. Come on. Time for a shower."

He carried the lax boy into the shower, dropping his feet to the floor but keeping hold of his upper body, and switched on the spray. Waiting a minute to make sure it was warm, he stepped under, bringing Ben with him.

"Come on, sweetheart. Open your eyes for me and stand on your own two feet. I need to wash you."

Ben did, but with a tremendous sigh. "I'm too tired to go to work now. You've worn me out."

Gareth smiled. "You'll be fine." He washed Ben from head to toe, enjoying Ben's scent mixing with his own, but didn't drag the time out. If they weren't careful, Ben would be late.

They dried off, but Ben paused in the doorway to the bedroom. "I don't have another suit."

Gareth glanced at him. "I don't think my suit would fit you. You're more slender than I am." He tilted his head. "You could probably get away with one of my shirts. Could you wear that over your jeans?"

Ben grimaced. "I've never worn jeans to work before."

Gareth chuckled. "There's a first time for everything. No one will care, I'm sure."

Ben wrinkled his nose and sighed. "I don't have much of an option. I don't have a spare suit in my car because I used it the other day." Gareth narrowed his eyes, and Ben backpedalled and held out his hands. "It was before you told me not to sleep at work! It won't happen again."

"It better not."

Gareth fetched a white shirt from his wardrobe and watched Ben pull on his jeans. He held the shirt out for Ben to slide his arms into the sleeves and turned him around to button it. "You look good."

Ben smiled. "I feel good."

"Even your ass?" Gareth raised his eyebrow.

Ben bit his lip. "Even my ass."

"Hmm, spanking is definitely off your list of punishments. Although it's a good learning tool because you'll feel that all day and be reminded of your promise." Gareth squeezed his hands on Ben's ass, earning a gasp. "See?"

"That's going to make sitting down uncomfortable."

"But it'll remind you of me each time you move." Gareth pecked his lips. "Come on. Let's get you to your car. I need to get some work done while you're away."

They visited the kitchen, and Gareth gave Ben a wrapped croissant and some fruit to take with him to work for his breakfast.

Ben asked, "What work do you do?"

"I write a blog about the Daddy lifestyle. Just answering some questions and giving people a look at what it's like."

"What's it called? I might have read it when I was researching."

"It's not that popular, but it's called Boys, Daddies, Snuggles and More."

Ben inhaled audibly. "I did read that. You're DaddyG!"

For a moment, Gareth felt a frisson of embarrassment, but he pushed it aside. It wasn't often he admitted being the owner of the blog. It wasn't that he didn't want people to know, but he didn't want anyone to think he was stupid for doing it. As far as he was concerned, he was helping those who didn't know anything about the lifestyle. However, some people *within* the lifestyle didn't agree with learning from a website, but Gareth thought it was better than nothing at all.

"I am."

Ben wrapped his arms around him. "That's amazing. It's helpful. I got so much information from it. More than any other site."

"You don't have to say that."

Ben glared at him. "I'm not just saying that. It's the truth."

"Well, thank you. I'm glad it helped. I have the next post to write for it."

"I better let you get to work."

Gareth lowered his head, pausing before their lips met. "Same goes for you." He took the kiss they both wanted, letting it go on for far longer than he should have before pulling back. "Get to work. If you want to, come back here afterwards."

Ben's eyes lit up. "Really?"

"Of course. You're always welcome."

Ben rested his face in Gareth's neck and inhaled before stepping away. "I'll see you later."

"Do you have everything? Phone, wallet, keys, coat?"

"Yes, Daddy." Ben closed his eyes and clenched his fists.

"What's wrong?" Gareth moved closer.

"Nothing." Ben rolled his eyes. "Okay, it's just because I said the word. My dick twitched."

Gareth chuckled. "Remember who that belongs to."

"You," Ben whispered.

Gareth nodded. "Have a good day."

Ben smiled, and Gareth waited by the front door until Ben drove away with a wave. Gareth closed the door and leaned against it. All in all, their relationship was going well. Maybe fucking him straight after a punishment wasn't the best way to teach him, regardless of the excuses he came up with while he was doing it, but it was done now. They'd figure something out for the future.

Gareth entered the kitchen again, setting the kettle boiling for his first cup of tea of the day. He slid two slices of bread into the toaster and thought about his next topic for his blog. It was the only way he would be able to stop thinking about Ben every second he wasn't there. Maybe he could answer another question instead of creating a completely new post. His latest post went live the previous evening, and he needed to check how well received it was. He wouldn't want to change things if readers weren't interested in listening to his specific advice.

When his toast and tea were ready, he climbed the stairs to his office and set the plate and cup on the desk. Switching on his laptop, he ate while he waited for it to load, then checked his blog site. Several readers had already commented on it, which was good. He answered them and focused on his list of potential topics to use for his posts. Instead of answering another question, he continued on a similar topic to his last post. This time, though, it would be all about a Middle—rather apt considering his new relationship.

Boys, Daddies, Snuggles and More

What do you do as a Middle? by DaddyG

Following on from my last post about Age Play, I decided to go a little deeper into the potential options for each of the different ages. I would've usually started at the Little, but—guess what, readers? I'm in a new relationship!—I thought I would start with what I'm currently experiencing myself. Not the intricate details! Come on! I wouldn't do that. But because it's close to home for me now, I will explain what I see and hear and how different it can be for everyone involved.

As always, if you have any questions, post them below, and I'll reply as soon as I can.

So, right off the bat, a Middle can be a teen or pre-teen in temperament and/or actions. They might show unique characteristics, but as I always say to you, everyone is different for a reason. Ask, and you will receive all the information you need to make the right choices for you and your partner/s. Nothing is wrong. There are no boundaries other than the ones you put in your lives yourselves.

As for me, my boy is as feisty as they come. Used to having control in some areas of life and no control in others, he's finally learning to be himself. He's finally realising he can be himself. And that, readers, is the best reward any Daddy could ask for.

16

BEN

As it was Saturday, Ben was alone in the office because it was Lindsay's day off. It gave him far too much time to daydream about Gareth, though he couldn't find it in him to care. For the first time in a long time, he was content. He went through the motions of his job, completing forms, analysing data, sending reports to his bosses, and did it all with a smile on his face, despite his cock being semi-hard the entire time.

He picked up his phone and called the estate agent. "Good morning. I viewed a property yesterday. I would like to take on the lease, please."

After several minutes of confirming his details and arranging to visit to sign the tenancy agreement, Ben put his phone down, smiling. He would be in his own place by the end of the following week if everything went according to plan. Earlier if he could manage it. He considered calling Gareth to tell him what he'd done, but he chose to surprise him that evening. At least he would be able to see him when Ben finished work because Gareth didn't work on Saturdays.

He chewed his lip. That wouldn't always be the case, though, would it? When Ben would finish work, Gareth would already have started during the week. When would they get to see each other?

Squirming on the chair had him remembering what they'd done that morning. Gareth had been completely right about Ben's ass smarting every time he moved. The pleasant warming hum he felt kept his mood from plummeting in the direction of his thoughts. He needed to trust in their relationship. Trust in Gareth. Trust that they would be able to work everything out. He had to fight to keep that trust, but he would try his hardest because his Daddy was the first person to have his back.

Ben slumped in his chair and stared across the room. Was that true? Was Gareth the first person? Images of Lindsay, Ruby, Jane, Felix and other members of staff who saw, spoke and worked with him on a regular basis came to him. Did he have more people around him than he thought? Was *he* the ogre in this scenario?

His brain didn't want to quit with the soul searching, but he couldn't create coherent answers when everything was vying for his attention.

His phone rang, startling him from his musings. He smiled at Gareth's name.

"Hello."

"Hi, Ben. How are you doing?" Gareth said, and Ben could hear the smile in his voice.

He opened his mouth to say he was fine but paused, wanting to give his Daddy a proper answer, not his rote reply. "I have a lot going through my head at the moment."

"That's understandable. Is it anything I can help with?"

Again, he paused, his usual independent answer frozen on his tongue. "Maybe."

Gareth didn't press. He stayed quiet, giving Ben the time to work through what he wanted to say. "I was thinking about how you were the first person to have my back, but I started thinking about the people who were already around me that I hardly acknowledge. Like Lindsay. She's here for me every single weekday without fail, and I hardly give her any praise or encouragement. She must hate me."

"I doubt she hates you, Ben. She wouldn't be working for you if she hated you, I'm sure."

"But I'm not the easiest person to work for."

"No, but you're aware of that, and that's the first step in changing how you behave towards other people."

"What do you mean?"

"Well, you know you can be grumpy and short with people—I've told you this—and you can figure out the triggers for that. My guess is stress and the fact you don't like the job."

Ben opened his mouth to argue, but he couldn't. "I don't, but I like how it challenges me." He rested his head back against his chair and closed his eyes, pressing the phone closer to his ear as if it would bring Gareth closer.

"Is that a recent realisation?"

Ben hummed. "Yes. Literally, just now." He chuckled. "I always thought I'd been forced into this position, and maybe I was, but subconsciously, I must have known I would like it, which was why I didn't fight it."

"I don't know if you would've fought it anyway, but I understand what you're saying. I'm glad you realise you like the challenge. Maybe we could find something that challenges you somewhere else. Somewhere you would enjoy."

"That's an idea."

"Can I make one recommendation, though?"

Ben smiled, swaying his chair back and forth, and for once, he was able to ignore the squeak. "Of course. Always."

"Don't try to change too many things at once. You already have a new relationship, possibly a new apartment soon. You need to find your centre from where you are now."

"I know. I want to change everything now, but I know it's not a good idea. I do have some news." He decided to tell him now.

"What's that?"

"I've signed up for the apartment."

Gareth chuckled. "That's great news. I'm proud of you, Ben."

Ben teared up, his throat closing at the words that he hadn't realised he needed to hear. He scrunched his eyes tighter, not wanting the tears to escape, though he had a feeling he would lose the battle.

"Ben? Sweetheart?" Gareth paused. "Was that too much for you?" he asked quietly. "It's okay, Ben. You don't need to say anything. You've probably heard those words before but never believed them. I never say anything I don't mean, sweetheart. I *am* proud of you. So proud. You're so strong to take back your life, and I will be there every step of the way if you'll let me."

The simple faith in those words strengthened Ben more than any others ever had. Because he *knew* they were true. Coming from Gareth, who had never lied to him before, he believed them with his whole heart.

"Thank you," he croaked.

They stayed quiet, though Ben knew Gareth was still there, even without taking the phone from his ear. He took his time to gather himself, tears drying against his cheeks.

"Thank you, Daddy."

"You're more than welcome." He paused. "Do you have much more work to do?"

"I'm here for a few more hours. The assistant manager doesn't come in until five o'clock."

"Okay. Well, you know where I am if you need me. Just call. Anytime, okay?"

"I know. Thanks."

"Don't work too hard."

Ben chuckled. "I'll try not to. Bye."

With the deep certainty that he had made the right choice, both about Gareth and the apartment, he focused on his paperwork. He wouldn't be working the following day, but Gareth would in the evening, so he'd have most of the day to spend with him, and he'd have to face going to his parents' house—because it certainly wasn't home any longer—and figure out how to get his stuff out of the house without them figuring out what he was doing.

Pushing that thought aside, he dug in, wanting the time to fly until he could head back to his Daddy.

"Benjamin, where are you?" his mother asked through the speakers of his car, which was connected to his phone.

He hadn't considered who else it might be when he'd pressed the accept button on his steering wheel. He'd expected Gareth and, instead, got his mother.

"Benjamin!"

"Yes, Mother?"

"I asked you a question."

"I'm driving."

Alice gave an audible sigh. "I know that. I can tell by all that dreadful noise in the background. Why you connected your phone to the car, I do not know. Highly unprofessional."

He didn't mention that if he hadn't done it, she wouldn't have been able to contact him. He wasn't that brave, although thinking about it now, maybe he should undo it. Neither of them would be able to get through to him until he wanted them to. Something to consider.

"What can I do for you, Mother?"

"You can get yourself home, is what you can do. We expected you back yesterday, but you weren't there. Did you have a long meeting?"

Grabbing onto the idea, he said, "Yes, I did. I stayed over at the office to get an early start this morning." Obviously, it wasn't true, but he wasn't about to tell her the real reason. Or the location of the house he had just pulled up in front of.

"Admirable work ethic, Benjamin. We expect you home shortly. Henry and Martha are coming for dinner, and you need to talk to him about the party."

He gazed at the front door. "Yes, Mother." The phone call ended with a beep and not a single word of goodbye. Ben continued to stare, wishing he could go in but knowing he needed to go to his parents. The door opened, and Gareth appeared, leaning on the door frame and tilting his head to the side as if knowing Ben needed to make a decision. The longer his Daddy stood there, waiting for Ben to make up his mind, the more Ben knew his decision was the right one.

He switched off the engine, climbed out and ran up the path and into Gareth's arms, nuzzling his face into Gareth's neck as he wound his arms around Gareth's waist.

"Shh. It's okay. Everything's okay."

Gareth continued murmuring, but Ben let his mind float, losing himself in the security of those arms. He felt himself being guided through the house, and Gareth lowered them to the sofa—Ben could tell by the length of it when Gareth stretched them out and threaded their legs together. Ben sank into him, grateful for the quiet. He just needed to breathe, to recalibrate now he'd decided, with all certainty, that he wouldn't be doing his parents' bidding any longer. He wondered if he would be able to fetch any of his stuff or if it was all lost to him now. He didn't have much in the way of personal items. They bought most of it for him and was stuff he could easily replace, but there were a few items he would've liked to keep.

He didn't know how long they had laid there when he finally lifted his head and peered at Gareth. "Thank you."

Gareth smiled. "You don't need to thank me every time."

"Yes, I do. You deserve every thank you I give."

Gareth pecked his lips. "Is everything okay?"

Ben lowered his gaze to the buttons on Gareth's polo shirt and began playing them between his fingers. "Mother called." Ben sighed. "She wanted me home tonight for dinner with someone she believes is influential. Again."

"What did you say?"

"I said, 'Yes, Mother,' and she hung up the phone. I switched off the engine and came to you."

Gareth's arms tightened, and Ben closed his eyes, inhaling Gareth's scent. He knew Gareth would not be what his parents wanted for him in a partner, but it was no longer their decision. The moment Gareth's arms had held him close, he'd made his decision.

"Would you like to stay here until your apartment is ready for you?"

Ben smiled, another weight lifting from his shoulders. "That'd be great if you don't mind."

"I wouldn't have offered if I minded."

Ben scrunched his nose. "I need to fetch my things. Tonight."

"Why tonight?"

"Because the moment I don't show up for dinner, they'll know something's changed. I don't trust them not to go through my stuff."

Gareth sat them upright, setting Ben to the side but keeping his arms around him. "Let's go now."

"No, you can't come with me."

Gareth cupped his jaw. "Yes, I can. You're mine. I'll protect you from their words while you collect what you need."

Ben's eyelids closed, and tears spilled over. Gareth wiped them clear. "Thank—" Gareth stopped his words as he dipped his tongue inside Ben's mouth. Ben clung onto him, not wanting to part, but eventually, Gareth pulled back, putting their foreheads together.

"You're mine."

"Yours."

"And I'm yours."

Tears threatened again, but Ben kept hold of them this time. "Mine," he whispered.

"Let's go. I'll drive."

The journey went by quickly, and Ben became tenser the closer they got. He had no idea how his parents would react, but he expected fireworks and harsh words. Ben directed Gareth to park on the driveway, and Gareth manoeuvred the car so it was ready to drive straight out once they had what they needed.

"Quick exit." Gareth winked, easing Ben a little. "Come on. The quicker it's done, the faster you can relax."

Ben swallowed and exited the car, heading up the steps to the house. Before he reached the door, Gareth threaded his fingers through his. Ben almost pulled back, but Gareth squeezed his hand, and Ben found he couldn't. He needed that connection. Inhaling, he let them in and headed straight for the stairs. His mother called his name, but he ignored her, hoping he could get to his room before she cornered them.

They did get there, and Ben pulled his hand free, grabbing a bag from the top of his wardrobe. He left it open on his bed and started with his bedside table. There was a small wooden box, a couple of books and some toiletries—he coughed and slanted a look at Gareth when he threw them in. Gareth grinned, and Ben bit his lip. He grabbed a few items of clothing from his wardrobe and his chest of drawers, grateful Gareth hadn't offered to help, probably understanding Ben needed to do this himself. He nipped to the bathroom, grabbed a few things and raced back into the bedroom when he heard voices.

"Who are you?" his mother said.

Ben stepped into the room and paused. His mother had her hands on her hips and glared at Gareth, who stood in the same position he had been in the entire time they'd been there—relaxed and without a care in the world. Ben wished he was the same.

"Benjamin, who is this?"

He took a breath. "My boyfriend." He strode for the suitcase and threw in the items he'd collected.

"Don't be ridiculous, Benjamin. He's not worthy of someone with your status."

For the first time, Alice's posh way of talking irritated Ben. He spoke similarly, but he tried not to sound like he was looking down his nose at people, unlike her.

"You're wrong. It's the other way around, but he's willing to have me. I'm going."

"Going? Going where?"

"I'm leaving. You can live without me from now on."

The words were met by silence, then an almighty shriek sounded, and his mother glared at him, finger raised. "After everything we have done for you, this is how you repay us? You ungrateful brat!"

Gareth stepped forward, getting in her face. "I think you have that wrong, Mrs Mycroft. After everything *he* has done for *you*. You need to realise what you've done. You've lost an amazing man because you're spoilt and selfish. I will take care of him like he deserves to be taken care of."

Gareth held out his hand, and Ben zipped up the suitcase, casting one more glance around to check he had what he needed, and linked their hands and followed his Daddy from the house.

17

GARETH

Gareth was so proud of his boy. He didn't waiver on his decision, and they exited the house with Ben's mother screeching behind them. An older man met them at the bottom of the steps with raised eyebrows, looking as if he'd just arrived back, but he didn't try to stop them despite what the woman shouted at him.

Gareth put Ben's suitcase in the boot of the car and held the passenger door open for him. He gave Ben's hand a final squeeze before he let go and closed the door, glaring at the couple near the house while he rounded the car and climbed in. Without pause, he drove away from those people, grateful to have Ben away from them. He reached across the space and covered Ben's hands with his, unable to give him his full attention while he was driving but wanting to give him what he could. Was he overwhelmed? Did he want to talk about it or not? Why was Gareth suddenly second-guessing himself?

"Are you okay?" He glanced across at Ben, doing a double-take when he saw a wide smile on Ben's face. "What?"

"I'm free."

Gareth smiled himself at the sheer joy in Ben's voice. "You are."

He left Ben to his thoughts for the journey, knowing, no matter how happy he appeared, it would take some time for it to properly sink in that he only had himself to think about now. He was sure Ben wouldn't be unduly affected by the change of circumstances, but he would monitor him. His heart rate increased when he remembered that Ben was staying with him for several days. He was looking forward to being able to take care of him. Well, when they saw each other, that was. For the first time, he wished he had a different job, but he enjoyed working at Market Foods. They'd make it work.

He parked the car in front of his house and grabbed Ben's suitcase from the boot before Ben could. Ben's eyes dropped to the ground when Gareth looked at him, and his lip disappeared.

Gareth pulled it free with his thumb. "I'm going to have to start punishing you whenever you bite that lip. Even though a red, swollen lip looks divine on you, you're hurting yourself, and I won't stand for it."

Ben's eyes were wide, and Gareth smirked. He held Ben's hand and tugged him towards the front door. When the door closed behind them, Gareth led him towards the kitchen, leaving the suitcase at the bottom of the stairs when they passed it.

"I was thinking of an all-day breakfast for lunch. What do you think?" he asked, letting go of Ben after giving him a chaste kiss.

"Sounds good."

"Why don't you relax? Choose a film or something to watch while I cook?"

"Are you sure?"

"Definitely. I'll shout you when it's ready."

Ben wrung his hands together, staring at him for a long second, then pivoted and left the room. Gareth wanted to give him time to himself, and cooking for him would settle Gareth. He didn't want to throw himself at Ben when he was still unsure about things, no matter what his body told him to do. The man needed time to let what had happened sink in.

While Gareth got the sausages, bacon, eggs and beans cooking, he tried to remember if there was anything he still had to explain to Ben about the lifestyle. They'd done a pretty good job of getting everything on track, and the rest would need to be discussed as they came up rather than pre-empting them. Things might move a little quicker now that Ben and he were under the same roof, and Gareth needed to make sure he didn't push too hard.

He glanced at the clock. He had around six hours before he had to go to work, and Ben wouldn't be working that night—if he tried, Gareth would have words with him because he needed time away. He felt awful having to leave Ben at the house by himself on his first night there, but he would have time to get used to being there.

When the last of the food was cooking, he grabbed two lap trays and set a plate and some cutlery on each. He filled two glasses with lemonade and put them on there as well. He dished up the food, making sure Ben had plenty to eat. Once he was satisfied, he carried both trays—one in each hand, a trick he'd learnt one year as a waiter—to the living room and found Ben sitting on the window seat, staring out into the sunny day while the TV played.

Quietly, he set the trays on the coffee table and stepped closer. Not wanting to startle him, Gareth cleared his throat softly. Ben peered over his shoulder and smiled, tight though it was.

"Everything okay?" Gareth asked.

Ben nodded. "Yes."

Gareth sat opposite him, studying the truth of the words on Ben's face. He reached for the hands that were resting in Ben's lap but were clenched tightly into fists. "Are you sure?" he asked, rubbing his thumb over Ben's skin.

"I said I'm fine." Ben pulled his hands away and stood, pacing to the sofa and sitting down again. "Thank you for lunch."

Gareth let him get away with the denial, but he wouldn't let the defiance stand. "Remember who you're talking to, Ben," he murmured as he joined him on the sofa.

He settled the tray on his lap and dug into the food, entirely aware of Ben's sharp, silent movements beside him. Ben needed time to decompress, and Gareth was more than willing to give it to him, but he wouldn't tolerate disrespect, even when Gareth knew it was coming from Ben's sense of being thrown into a scenario he hadn't expected. Everything had changed in such a small amount of time, and Ben hadn't caught his breath. That was the only reason Gareth was giving him a breather, although the reminders were necessary to make sure Ben didn't overstep completely.

"Well done," he said when Ben had finished. "Would you like ice cream for pudding?"

Ben sighed. "I'm not five years old, you know. You don't have to handle me with kid gloves." He set the tray on the coffee table, and Gareth was pleased to see he did it carefully and didn't slam it down.

"I know you're not, but everyone likes ice cream. What's your favourite flavour?"

Ben slumped back, but his gaze was on the window again. Gareth didn't press, but eventually, Ben said, "Chunky Monkey."

Gareth grinned. "Aren't you sweet enough?" He chuckled at Ben's glare. "I like chocolate, but if you throw in a few chopped nuts, it's even better." He stood, holding his tray. "Come on. Time to clean up, and we can have a treat."

He didn't wait to see if Ben would follow him but instead went straight for the kitchen and began filling the sink with warm, soapy water. Household chores were something he would always insist on, no matter whether Ben stayed with him for a day or several months. He put the plates and cups into the sink to soak while he gathered all the pans he'd used for making lunch within easy reach.

Ben waited by the sink, tray in his hands, when Gareth turned back. "Thank you." He took the tray. "Can you wipe down the counters for me and help dry, please?"

Ben hovered as if he was going to say something but took the cloth and set about cleaning the counters. Gareth hid his smile and started washing the plates, settling them in the draining rack for when Ben was ready. He could feel the tension in the other man and knew it wouldn't be long before he blew. Gareth had been expecting it. He had seen how Ben reacted to things in the past and had a good idea of how he would deal with the fact that he was officially out from under his parents' thumb for the first time in his life. If Gareth wasn't mistaken, Ben would push and push to see what he could get away with. Not just with Gareth, but with other things, too, but Gareth needed to make sure he didn't push too far. Although Ben didn't like his job, he didn't need to be fired for unacceptable behaviour.

Gareth continued the washing, pointing out the tea towel when Ben joined him. They worked in silence for a few minutes before Gareth started talking.

"Mindless, everyday tasks are great for working through your thoughts. You don't have to think about what you're doing be-cause your body has muscle memory to get through the tasks. It gives you time to think about what's happened during the day." He put another dish on the draining board. "Take me, for instance. I'm standing here, washing these dishes, but my thoughts aren't on what I'm doing. They're reliving the events of the day so far. They're reliving how proud I was and am to see you stand up to those who beat you down. How your actions at your parents' house made me realise exactly how perfect you are for me."

Ben scoffed. "Yeah, perfectly weak and humiliated."

Gareth didn't reply to those words. "The images I recount are of a man standing tall while his mother tried to bend him to her will. A man choosing to live his own life instead of a life chosen by his parents. A man learning to live as the person he is, not what others think he should be."

"Easier said than done." Ben sighed.

"Choosing to change your entire life is like going through a grieving process. You're grieving what you believe you've lost, angry at those who stopped you from being who you want to be. You'll be angry at me for making you choose to upheave your life. You'll be angry at those you work with because they didn't see what you hid from them. But mostly, you'll be angry at yourself because you stood by and let it happen."

Gareth stopped there because he knew everything would be overwhelming for Ben. He finished the dishes in silence. Once he'd dried his hands, he left Ben to dry up and headed for the freezer, taking out the Chunky Monkey he just happened to have, thanks to it being Victor's favourite, too. Grabbing two bowls, he dished up the servings and put everything else away. He carried them out of the kitchen, calling over his shoulder, "When you've finished drying, your ice cream is waiting for you. As am I."

He settled on the sofa, crossing his legs at the ankles, though he didn't start eating. The TV's volume was low enough that he could hear Ben's movements. At least until it went quiet. It took everything in him to stay where he was and wait. Ben's response to Gareth's words would help Gareth learn more about him. As much as Gareth wanted to swaddle him in blankets and keep him safe from the world, it wasn't the best course of action for someone learning to stand on their own two feet. Yes, Gareth would be there every step of the way if Ben allowed him to be, but Ben needed to decide for himself.

The Chunky Monkey was halfway to melting by the time Ben appeared. He sank into the seat beside Gareth—as close as he could possibly get—and dropped his head to Gareth's shoulder. Gareth pressed a kiss to his head and rested a hand on Ben's thigh, giving it a squeeze.

"I hated you seeing me like that. So weak. It's humiliating." Ben exhaled, the heat wafting across Gareth's chest and through his shirt. "I hate feeling unsure like I don't know what I should be doing. Being a manager might not be my dream job, but I know what's expected of me. This—us—I love the idea of it, but I don't know what to expect, and it's making me nervous."

Gareth lifted his arm and slid it around Ben's shoulders, holding him closer. "Thank you for telling me that. First, you don't need to feel humiliated because all I saw there was a man who stood his ground. A strong man defending his right to choose for himself. As for feeling unsure, I'm here to support you. We can make up the rules ourselves. There is no right or wrong answer to how we live our lives. My job is to give you structure to make you feel secure. If I haven't done that yet, I'm sorry. That's part of my job as your Daddy." He sighed. "Okay, we're going to eat ice cream while we finish watching...whatever this is," He waved towards the TV, "and then we're going to bed. Once we're snuggled under the covers, we will talk. Properly."

"But it's the middle of the afternoon."

"Doesn't matter. I have to work later, and I want to spend the rest of today with you."

Eating one-handed was a novel experience, but Gareth made it work because he didn't want to take his arm from around Ben. He was upset with himself because he thought he'd done everything right, but if Ben was feeling uncertain, Gareth hadn't done his job properly. He was supposed to be a support network for him, and he'd obviously failed so far. It was time to change things up.

While the show continued, he thought about the rules they might need to put in place for Ben to feel happier with the situation. Chores, routines and fewer working hours were just a few they would discuss. Ben might not like them, but Gareth knew they would be a good starting point. He didn't want Ben to feel like he'd left one prison only to be locked in another, but structure was important to all boys and Daddies. It gave them reassurance of knowing what to expect and trusting the other person to give that. Because Gareth needed to trust Ben as much as Ben needed to trust him.

18

BEN

An hour later, they lay with Ben's head resting on Gareth's chest, their legs entwined beneath the sheets of Gareth's bed. They still wore their underwear, but they had discarded every other item of clothing. It made Ben feel more relaxed, for some reason. As if, because they didn't wear clothes, Gareth wouldn't suddenly disappear. Which was stupid, really.

Ben closed his eyes, soaking in not only the heat from Gareth's body but the closeness, the sense of belonging. He knew he was a difficult person to be with, but he couldn't seem to stop his mood swings. He never had been able to, but he was usually better at hiding them because his parents would have never stood for it.

Gareth's arms tightened around him, and Ben let out a sigh. "Finding the heart of what *you* want is the most important part of all of this," Gareth said. "If you jump into our relationship because you don't want to be alone, we won't last because you're not being true to yourself. I can tell you what I see, but unless you agree, my opinions mean nothing. And that's how it should be."

Ben frowned. "I don't want to be a horrible person."

"You're not. I believe, at the moment, you're balancing between two worlds. The world your parents created for you and the world you want to live in. Only you can choose where you want to go from here."

"I want to be with you. You make me feel...real. Like you can see me."

Gareth tipped Ben's chin up. "I can see you, and I love what I see." He let go again, and Ben snuggled close. "You need routines and structure to keep you from flying away like a balloon with no string. What I would like is for you to reduce the hours you work. Now, I know that might be difficult, but I'd like you to try. It's not good for your health—mental, physical or emotional—for you to work as many hours as you do."

Gareth's fingers drifted up and down Ben's back, sending tingles and goosebumps across his skin. "I worked that many hours because I didn't want to go home," he whispered.

A kiss landed on his head. "I know. Now, though, you don't have to, and we can work on reducing your hours. I think you'll find your moods will level out if you're not as stressed with everything."

Ben nodded against Gareth's chest and sighed. "I'll never get to see you because of your night shifts. When I'm working, you'll be sleeping, and when I'm sleeping, you'll be working."

Gareth chuckled. "That means you'll *have* to finish work at a reasonable time, won't it? If we work it out right, we can have breakfast and dinner together."

Ben rolled his eyes. "Yeah, like that's enough time."

Gareth dug his fingers into Ben's side, making him squeak. "Brat. I don't work weekends. We'll have Friday morning through to Sunday evening together, except when you have to work. We'll figure it out. It's all about compromise." Ben inhaled, closing his eyes again. At least until Gareth said, "You'll be punished if you don't follow my rules, Ben. I'm doing this for your benefit as well as my own."

"What punishments?"

"Well, we've found that you like spanking, so that's off the table. Time outs and doing chores you don't like can be what we start with, but we can learn what works best as we go along. Or maybe Victor has some ideas."

The last words were teasing, but Ben glared at him, relenting when Gareth laughed and pulled him closer. Ben felt like he could take on the world when Gareth's arms were around him. He could fight any opponent, win any argument as long as Gareth was by his side.

He woke when the bed jostled, blinking his eyes to clear the sluggishness of sleep from them. "What...?"

"It's okay, sweetheart. Go back to sleep if you want to. I have to get ready for work."

Gareth pressed a kiss to Ben's lips, smoothing his hand over his cheek, and disappeared into the bathroom. Ben heard the shower turn on, and he yawned, stretching his arms above his head and arching off the bed. He slumped back down again, smiling. He couldn't remember ever sleeping as well as he did whenever he was with Gareth. Another bonus point in his favour. While he lay there, he thought of what they'd done the other night, and his cock lengthened, not fully, but enough to start a gentle buzz of need racing through him. He scrunched his nose, jumped out of bed and slipped into the bathroom. Stepping into the shower in front of Gareth, who had his eyes closed, he dropped to his knees and took Gareth's cock between his lips.

Gareth jumped, his hands flailing out to the sides to keep him from falling. He narrowed his eyes at Ben, who blinked innocently at him and slid his mouth down his length.

"Punishment number one. You don't get to come until I say," Gareth said.

Ben didn't like the sound of that, but it was a small price to pay for being able to taste Gareth.

"Sit back on your heels," Gareth ordered. Ben frowned and did so, a mewl of protest leaving his lips when Gareth's cock slipped free. "Open your mouth and hold still." Heat flushed through Ben as he did as instructed.

Gareth slid his cock into Ben's mouth, and Ben's eyelids fluttered as the thick member glided across his tongue. Gareth withdrew and repeated the action several more times, sliding deeper each time until he was touching the back of Ben's throat, which he opened, wanting to take more. Gareth stepped closer, resting his hands on the sides of Ben's face, and slipped into Ben's throat. Ben's eyes watered even as he gazed at Gareth, a look of something akin to wonder in his expression. Gareth pulled free again, and Ben inhaled, the air reinvigorating him. He lifted his hands, gripping Gareth's thighs when Gareth dived forward.

He could feel Gareth pulse on his tongue and an answering hiss from above. Ben paused, expecting to taste his release, but Gareth pulled back until only the head was resting on Ben's lips. "Suck. Slowly."

Ben wrapped his mouth around the head, laving the underside and the slit with his tongue. He wanted to take Gareth over the edge, to taste his release, even more than he wanted a release of his own. His dick protested the thought, twitching when a stream of precome slid down his throat. It would take very little for Ben to come. Just a stroke or two, and he'd find the release he craved, but he wanted Gareth to lose himself in pleasure more. To lose himself in Ben.

The lines bracketing Gareth's mouth and eyes tightened, and his breathing increased. He skated forward, towards the back of Ben's throat. "Are you going to take my seed, Ben?"

Ben's cock jerked again. He blinked up at him, unable to vocalise his "Hell, yes." Gareth appeared to understand, though. He pulled back. "Deep breath."

Ben inhaled, widening his mouth when Gareth slid home. Gareth paused deep inside Ben, and Ben could feel the twitch of Gareth's cock as it readied for release. His air supply began dwindling, but Ben wouldn't stop. He wanted everything Gareth would give him.

"Swallow," Gareth growled.

Ben did, and Gareth groaned as his shaft pulsed its climax. Ben's nails dug into Gareth's thighs as he became lightheaded, feeling every beat of his heart loudly in his head as his air ran out. Suddenly, oxygen flooded his lungs, and he coughed, falling forward into Gareth's arms.

"Good boy. You're fucking perfect, didn't I tell you? Perfect."

Gareth held him tightly as awareness came back to him. He hadn't completely blacked out, but he'd been close, and fuck, did he want to do it again. Dropping his head back, he stared up at Gareth, a small smile on his face.

"When can we do that again?" he whispered, his throat a little sore from misuse.

Gareth chuckled. "Soon." He stood, helping Ben to his feet. "Let's get cleaned up."

His Daddy held him close as he washed him, even his cock, though it was perfunctory cleaning rather than sexy. Ben pouted, but Gareth just grinned and shook his head. Gareth switched off the showerhead, guiding Ben to climb out of the bathtub and dried him off before doing the same for himself.

"Now, Mr I-aim-to-misbehave," Gareth said once they were in the bedroom. Ben settled on the bed with the towel around his waist. "You are not allowed to touch yourself while I'm at work."

Ben gaped. "What? You worked me up in there! I'm hard as a rock!"

Gareth raised his eyebrows. "And who started it all?" Ben glared at him but said nothing. "Exactly. Your punishment is to wait until I say you can come. That could be later tonight. It could be tomorrow morning. It could be tomorrow night. But you will do as I said. Understood?"

Ben worked his jaw while he stared at the person who was supposed to be looking after him. He wouldn't call leaving him with an aching erection looking after him. He reluctantly agreed, not at all sure if he could do what Gareth asked. It was a long time to go without coming, especially when he was ready to blow already.

Ben ogled him as Gareth dressed in his work uniform. He made no moves to get dressed himself. Instead, he lay back on the bed, letting his towel fall open, as Gareth headed for the door.

"Daddy?" Ben said.

Gareth paused, glancing over his shoulder. "Yes, sweetheart?"

"If I promise not to come into work early tomorrow, will you come back and fuck me beforehand?" Ben bit his lip.

"It depends if you keep your promise tonight." Gareth pivoted and strode towards him, bracing himself over him when he reached the bed. "Be a good boy for your Daddy, and you might get a reward."

Gareth closed the distance between them and kissed him. Taking no prisoners as he devoured him. When he pulled back, Ben panted, even more aroused than he had been.

"Now, be good for Daddy. I'll see you in the morning."

He dropped a single peck and left, closing the bedroom door behind him. Ben stared at the ceiling, his mind foggy with lust. There was no way he would be able to last all night without wrapping his hand around his cock and sending his body into the stratosphere. No way.

He licked his lips and glared at his purple, straining cock. No way, but he would try.

❖

As the clock neared midnight, Ben gave up all pretence of ignoring his dick. He'd long ago given up wearing underwear because every slight shift sent desire coursing through him, and he'd removed them, hoping that leaving it free would help it calm the fuck down.

It hadn't.

Every hour Gareth stayed away weakened his order's power over Ben, and as the grandfather clock in the hallway chimed the middle of the night, Ben couldn't take it any longer.

He'd been sitting on the sofa, trying to watch a film, but he had no idea what was going on. Switching everything off, he ran up the stairs to the bedroom and lay on his back on the bed. He hadn't plucked up the courage to touch himself yet, but he closed his eyes and thought of all the different scenarios that could take him where he needed to go. Gareth wouldn't know. He was at work, and Ben would clean anything up that needed it before he got back.

When he still couldn't take hold of himself, he groaned and rolled onto his stomach, burying his face in the pillow and muffling his scream of frustration. As he did, his cock rubbed against the sheets, and his scream rolled into a moan. He paused, lifting his head and considering his options. Technically, he wasn't touching himself if he rutted against the sheets.

He experimentally thrust his hips, eyes rolling into the back of his head when his arousal rose. He'd never humped something to completion before, and the idea turned him on even more. Happy to have found a loophole, he braced on his elbows and lifted his hips a little, allowing the head of his cock to brush against the sheets. It wasn't as electric as if someone's hand or mouth was surrounding it, but it felt amazing, nonetheless.

He swivelled his hips in circles, the small creases in the fabric tugging against the underside. If only he could have someone ploughing into him as he did this. It would feel ten times better.

He moved one hand to reach one of his nipples and tweaked it, sending fire through his stomach and into his groin. His hips jolted forward, and his eyes closed as bliss settled over him.

The moment his eyelashes rested against his cheek, images of Gareth as he had taken Ben flitted through his mind. He imagined his Daddy kneeling behind him, preparing him for his cock. Ben's hips moved faster, electricity sparking down his spine as his orgasm rushed forward.

His phone rang, and Ben froze, eyes snapping open and staring at the bedside table where he'd placed it. There were only two people who could be calling him. One, he refused to speak to. The other, he wanted to speak to always, but maybe not at that precise moment. The phone went silent, but Ben didn't move, knowing if it was the second person, they'd call again. The phone rang, and Ben closed his eyes, breathing through his mouth as he reached for it.

"Hello?" he said, after clearing his throat and hoping his voice was neutral.

"Hey. I just wanted to check on you before you go to sleep. I didn't wake you, did I?" Gareth said.

"No." He cleared his throat. "I was just getting ready for bed when you called."

"Good. You need your sleep. Have you been okay on your own?"

Ben looked down his body to where his cock lay straining beneath him. "Yes. I watched a film."

Gareth was quiet, then said. "That's good. What was the film you watched?"

Ben racked his brain, trying to think of the name of it, but he'd been too distracted to take much notice. "It wasn't very good. I can't even remember the name of it now."

"Sweetheart, what are you doing right now?" Gareth asked slowly.

Ben winced. "I've just laid down under the covers." His stomach soured at the lie, and the arm he had braced on the bed trembled.

"Have you been touching what's mine?"

The growl sent a shiver of warning through Ben's body. "No. You told me I couldn't." It wasn't technically a lie.

The phone vibrated, and Ben took it from his ear to see Gareth had requested a video call. Ben swallowed hard.

Fuck.

19

GARETH

Gareth knew exactly what Ben was doing, regardless of what his words said. He could hear the arousal in his voice, even though he probably tried to suppress it. Gareth could've pretended not to hear it and allowed Ben to continue, but the boy needed to learn to listen to instructions. The freedom Ben was experiencing was a good thing, but not to the extent of ignoring Gareth's rules, and Gareth had specifically told him not to touch what was *his*.

He'd called, knowing Ben would still be awake but had been immediately suspicious at Ben's innocent tone. The moment Gareth had decided to exert his claim, he'd hit the video call button. It would allow him to see exactly what Ben was doing. Or trying to hide what he was doing.

A flushed face appeared on the screen, and Gareth settled back in his chair, thankful his back was to the wall, and no one else could see the image in front of him. A bare-chested Ben was not for anyone's eyes but his own, even though he was on his stomach and there wasn't much to see.

"I definitely told you that you couldn't, but I'm not sure I believe you haven't," Gareth said.

Ben's nose crinkled as it always did when he wasn't sure how to react or respond. It was cute, though he wouldn't tell Ben that. "I haven't touched!"

Gareth tilted his head, trying to suppress the chuckle forming in his throat while he studied the picture on the screen. Ben appeared the epitome of innocence, but there was something about his position that was bothering Gareth. He couldn't put his finger on it.

"I'm glad to hear that." He squinted at his boy, taking in the flushed face, the slight sheen to his skin and the fidgeting Ben couldn't seem to stop. Inwardly, Gareth laughed, even as a tingle of warmth spread through him. "Freeze," he warned, "Right now."

Ben's eyes widened, and his mouth tensed as he tried to stay still. A drop of sweat beaded on his forehead and slowly snaked its way down Ben's temple. The screen trembled, and Gareth assumed Ben's hand was shaking with the effort to stop humping the bed.

"When I say it's mine, I mean *mine*. You don't touch it, and you don't touch it with anything else. Your release is mine to command. *Mine*."

Ben's breath released audibly across the speaker. "I can't..." He cleared his throat, eyes fluttering closed. "I'm..."

Gareth glanced around the room, checking no one had entered without him realising and leaned closer to the screen, inhaling through his nose when his cock pressed against the zip of his trousers. "You've been a naughty boy, Ben," he murmured. "You need to stop. Right this minute. You won't like the result if you continue."

He watched Ben's expression, the furrowing of his forehead, the closing of his eyes, the licking of his dry lips. The screen shook, and Ben bit his lip and opened his eyes, spearing Gareth with a lust-filled gaze. Gareth's cock throbbed as need tore through him, but he tightened the grip on his control and narrowed his eyes on Ben.

"Ben," he warned.

Ben's mouth quirked up on one side, and Gareth knew he was going to disobey. Ben's eyelids fluttered again, his lips parting on an exhale as his body erupted into climax. Gareth quickly reduced the volume on his phone as Ben's cries of release drifted through the speaker.

It took everything in Gareth not to follow him over the edge because, despite disobeying, Ben was a vision when he was in the throes of orgasm. The almost painful expression on his face gave way to a peaceful relief as his arousal declined on the other side.

Gareth needed to remember to put his headphones in whenever he spoke to Ben in the future—he didn't want anyone to hear what was solely for his pleasure.

"Tut, tut, tut, Ben. I hope you like the consequences of that when I get home later," he said.

Ben blinked open his eyes, the pupils contracting slowly. His boy dropped his head to the bed, barely keeping the screen on himself, and Gareth shook his head.

"Go to bed. You will not come to work until I am home tomorrow because I need to give you your punishment. Do you understand?"

"Yes, Daddy," Ben whispered.

"Get some sleep."

"Night, Daddy."

Gareth sighed and gave a small smile. "Goodnight, sweet boy."

He ended the call and set the phone on the table, turning to stare out of the window with a chuckle. Ben needed a firm hand; otherwise, he could fly off the handle with the freedom he would experience now he was out from under his parents' thumbs. If Gareth could've lashed out at those "people"—he refused to call them parents any longer—he would have, but it wouldn't have been fair to Ben to see that happen. No matter how horrible they were to him, they were still his relatives.

"Penny for them."

Gareth snapped his head around, having not heard anyone come into the room. Felix stood at the edge of his table, holding a mug and a bag.

"Lunchtime already?" Gareth asked with a grin, draining his mug of lukewarm tea, even though it tasted disgusting.

Felix glanced at his bag and snorted. "Might as well get the food in while I can. You never know what the night will bring." He gestured to the seat across from Gareth.

"Go ahead." He checked his watch. "I only have another five minutes, anyway."

Felix settled into his seat, swallowing a healthy amount of his drink before placing it on the table. "I wanted to catch you." He opened his bag and took out a filled sandwich bag. "You've been here a few weeks now. How are you finding it?"

Gareth frowned at him. "Haven't we had this discussion already?"

Felix tilted his head from side to side as he removed his sandwich. "Yes and no."

Gareth leaned back in his chair. "Is there something I should be aware of?"

Felix had taken a mouthful of food, and there was a moment of silence before he spoke. "I'm going to be upfront with you because I'm like that with everyone." He paused. "Bar one person, anyway." Gareth could probably guess who that was. "People have noticed you and Ben together. Now, from my perspective, I don't give a damn as long as you do your job, but others don't seem as happy with it." He held up one hand. "This is nothing more than a 'you should know' conversation, Gareth. I'm not telling you how to live your life. I wanted you to be aware of it so you can fight it if it becomes necessary."

Gareth bit his tongue on the initial words he wanted to say. It was no one's business but their own, but they should be aware of the situation. As Felix had said, they would need to decide on a course of action should they need it. He'd speak to Ben about it in the morning—after his punishment.

"Thank you for letting me know. And just for *your* record, Ben and I are in a relationship. It's still in the early stages, which is why we've not announced it, but we'll probably rectify that sooner rather than later now."

Felix nodded while he chewed and swallowed. "Probably a good idea. Despite it being no one's concern, it's also everyone's gossip." He rolled his eyes, which looked hilarious on him. "But seriously, how are you finding the job? Or should we call it the balancing act?"

Gareth chuckled. "We're still learning how to balance. We'll get there, though. As for the job, I like it, as I've mentioned before. Being able to get on with the work and not have to worry about anything else is mind-numbingly perfect for me."

Felix snorted. "Mind-numbing is one word for it." He took a swig of drink. "Some of the night shift staff are going out in a couple of weeks. A comedy club, I'm told. I'm not going, but I said I'd let you know about it."

Gareth winced. "Not my kind of thing, but thanks."

Felix canted his head and studied him. "Be careful, Gareth. They can bite if they think you don't like them."

Gareth knew what "they" he was talking about. The younger-aged crowd—who were no doubt the ones organising this comedy club night—thought they ruled the roost, but they had yet to learn what the wisdom of age taught them. To be themselves and not force their actual personality into a fake one to please others. Every company had a group like them, and woah betide anyone who stood in their way. Gareth didn't give a damn, though, but he understood the warning.

"Thanks for the heads up." He stood. "Break time is over. Enjoy your food."

"I plan to. Make sure no one breaks anything until I get back."

Gareth laughed. "I'll try."

He wandered through the corridors until he arrived back on the shop floor, passing several staff members and giving them his normal smile of acknowledgement. He spent the rest of his shift in a waking dream of how he would punish his boy when he got home that morning.

Turns out, he had plenty of ideas, but one stood out as being the best choice for this scenario.

The moment he arrived home, he let himself in quietly, not wanting to wake Ben if he had slept in. There was no sign of him downstairs. Gareth climbed the stairs and aimed for his bedroom, silently opening the door to see Ben sitting on the bed with his legs crossed under the sheets and his hands clenched in his lap. His gaze snapped to the door when Gareth entered.

"Good morning, sweetheart," Gareth said.

"Morning, Daddy." Ben's voice was quiet.

Gareth drifted to the bed and leaned down, pressing a kiss to Ben's upturned lips. "Thank you for changing the sheets."

Ben's cheeks flushed, and his lip disappeared until Gareth pressed on it with his thumb to release it.

"I'm sorry, Daddy."

Gareth raised his eyebrows. "But are you? Can you tell me it wouldn't happen again?"

Ben opened his mouth but paused when Gareth raised his eyebrows. He closed his mouth so fast his teeth clacked together. "I don't know."

"Good answer."

Gareth rose and headed for the chest of drawers, the bottom of which held a variety of toys. He opened the drawer and looked over the contents, finally finding what he was looking for. Lifting it from the drawer, he held it in his grip and faced Ben.

"As far as punishments go, we've tried spanking, but you enjoyed that far too much for it to be an unpleasant reminder." He smirked. "I've tried orgasm denial—granted, only once—but it was an epic fail, as I'm sure my dirty bed sheets can attest." Ben dropped his gaze for a brief second. "We're now going to try something new. Lay down on your back and remove the sheet."

Gareth stepped closer as Ben hesitantly did as he'd asked. When he was beside him, he asked, "What did you do wrong, Ben?"

Ben's Adam's apple dropped and rose. "I touched what was yours."

"Correct. What else?"

Ben's forehead creased, and Gareth could see him thinking what else he'd done wrong. That, if anything, proved that Ben had only disobeyed this one order.

"I don't know."

"You disobeyed. After I repeatedly told you not to, you still made yourself come."

"Yes, Daddy."

"Now, you don't get to come until I say, and you also won't be able to make yourself come."

Ben's eyes widened when he saw what Gareth held up. Ben shook his head. "No, Daddy."

"Yes. Naughty boys get the cock cage, Ben. If I can't trust you to keep your dick under control, I will control it for you."

Gareth waited. He needed to make sure they were both on the same page and that Ben agreed to this. He knew what he had to say to make it stop, but Gareth didn't think he would. By the look of his cock straining towards his stomach, he liked the idea, but there would be no cage when he was hard.

He left the cage on the bed and beckoned Ben with his forefinger. "Come with me." He headed for the bathroom and switched on the shower. "Jump in and clean up. I'll be back in a minute."

Gareth entered the bedroom and grabbed the cage, putting it in his pocket, out of sight. There was only one surefire way—as far as Gareth was concerned—to quickly and efficiently cool an erection, and Ben wouldn't like it.

He went into the bathroom again and watched as Ben finished up. "All done?" he asked when Ben stared at him. Ben nodded. "Close your eyes." When he had, Gareth flicked the switch on the shower to cold water, dousing Ben.

"Holy shit!" Ben shouted, getting out of the spray's reach. "What was that for?"

"It did what I needed it to do. Come out and dry off." Gareth grabbed a towel and held it out for Ben, helping to dry him when Ben shivered. He knelt in front of Ben, grabbed some Vaseline from the cupboard and spread it across Ben's cock and balls. He had to work fast because if he spent too much time there, Ben's cock would get hard again, and they'd have to do this all over again. He took the cage from his pocket and placed the ring over Ben's cock, then he carefully fed his balls through the ring as well. When that was in place, Gareth slid Ben's cock into the spiral cage. It was a good fit because Gareth already had an idea of which size Ben needed, but if it had been wrong, Gareth had several more in different sizes.

By the time Gareth pinched the ring and the cage together and locked it, Ben was panting and leaning his hands on Gareth's shoulders for balance.

"Oh, my god!" Ben dropped his head forward and closed his eyes. "Why did I think this was a good thing?"

Gareth chuckled. "It is a good thing. It'll keep you from misbehaving when I can't be there to keep an eye on you. And it will remind you that you're mine." He stood abruptly, fusing their mouths and exploring every inch of Ben's mouth while his caged cock pressed against Gareth's groin. He pulled back and held up the key. "And this will be with me every minute of the day because you'll never know when I will let you take it off and when I won't. At least until you learn. Otherwise, you'll be wearing it forever."

"How can I go to work like this?" Ben said. "I'll never be able to concentrate."

Gareth grinned.

20

BEN

The cold shower should've been the first sign Ben's day wasn't going to go as planned. Gareth helped him to dress, but the cage was both wonderful and distracting. Or maybe wonderfully distracting. Or distractingly wonderful. Either way, Ben knew he wouldn't be able to work as easily, but he had no choice. He had two meetings today, and he had to go through the calendar with Lindsay beforehand. He doubted anyone would get much sense out of him, but he wouldn't change it for the world. It made him feel wanted, cared for.

"Remember to leave at a reasonable hour. You don't want to get dragged back into staying all hours of the day. Plus, you have me to come back to now." Gareth winked, handed him a lunch bag and kissed him before Ben left.

By the time he'd arrived at work, he both hated and loved the cage. Every movement brought attention to it, and sometimes, it wasn't comfortable because of how he had to sit or stand. People would probably look at him strangely if he stood with his legs apart all day.

He settled behind his desk, fidgeted until he found a comfortable position and switched on his laptop. Glancing at the clock made his heart pound. It was stupid, but he knew Gareth would be waiting for him when he arrived home that night, and he couldn't wait for the day to finish. His stomach fluttered at the possibility of being allowed to come that night before they swapped shifts.

A knock on his door had him jumping because he hadn't realised the time. He'd been lost in a daydream.

"Come in," he called.

Lindsay opened the door and smiled tentatively as she crossed the distance between them. "Good morning, Mr Mycroft."

"Please call me Ben." The words were out before he could stop them, but he didn't regret saying them. "Have a seat, Lindsay." When she did, he said, "I want to apologise. I'm a complete asshole to work for some days, but you never complain. You get on with your work and do a damn good job of it. Thank you for putting up with me."

Lindsay's mouth opened and closed several times before she said, "Um, you're not an...asshole per se. I know this job is stressful. I don't mind."

"You still shouldn't have to put up with that. I'll try to do better, but I want you to tell me when I'm behaving that way." Lindsay's eyes widened, and Ben laughed. "I give you full permission to call me an asshole when I deserve it."

She shook her head. "No, I couldn't do that."

"My boyfriend tells me I need to chill out, and it would help me—and him—out a lot if you could. We're trying to find the triggers. We know stress is one of them, but if there's anything else, we need to figure it out."

Lindsay frowned. "I don't know."

"Please consider it, at least."

She nodded. "I didn't know you had a boyfriend."

Ben beamed. "A recent thing. You might know him. Gareth?"

"Gareth? I don't know... Oh! From the night shift?"

He nodded. "Yes. It was a complete shock to me, and it just sort of happened."

Lindsay smiled. "I'm happy for you."

"Thanks. He's certainly keeping me in line. Or at least, trying to." He shifted, feeling the constraint on his cock. It sent a warmth flowing through him. "Can we start again?" he asked.

"We don't need to. We're good."

"Thank you." He inhaled, feeling a lightness in his chest. "Let's go through the calendar for this week."

Lindsay leaned forward, resting her paperwork on the opposite side of his desk as she had done many times before. This time, though, seemed more relaxed.

"Okay, you have two meetings today. The first is at midday with the area manager. It's supposed to last an hour, but last time, he was here for three hours." She raised her eyebrows.

"Do I have anything that needs doing between twelve and three o'clock?"

She ran her hand down the calendar. "Nothing essential. Your second meeting with the team leaders isn't until four o'clock."

"That should be a fairly quick one because I just need to let them know the latest updates from the area manager meeting. Are you able to complete the minutes for the team leader meeting?"

She nodded. "Yes, sir."

"Ben."

Her cheeks flushed. "Yes, Ben." She chuckled. "That's going to take some getting used to."

"I'm sorry. Despite what was going on in my personal life, I shouldn't have taken it out on everyone here."

She waved her hand. "It's done now. Don't worry."

"I have a lot of apologies to make."

She tilted her head. "Can I make a suggestion?"

"Of course."

"Just start treating them differently, and they'll see that you've changed. You don't need to make apologies for it."

Ben scrunched his nose. "I'll think about it. I feel like I should apologise. Maybe I should discuss it with Gareth first."

Lindsay smiled. "I can see he's good for you. I don't think I've ever seen you this..." She waved her hand in a circle in front of him.

"Happy?" he asked.

"Yeah."

The fluttering in his stomach intensified as images of Gareth and him together bombarded him. "I am."

"I'm glad."

They spent half an hour going through the rest of the week's appointments, then he settled himself in to complete the paperwork required for that day. He also needed to get some documents together for when he met with Anthony, the area manager. For once, he felt like he could weather that meeting without feeling insignificant and worthless. Anthony had always appeared much more put together than Ben did, and he had been a little jealous of that. Now, Ben felt on an even keel and like he could stand up for himself without being an asshole.

He ate the food Gareth had made for him at eleven-thirty because he didn't want to miss out on his lunch, and he wanted it to bolster his confidence before Anthony arrived. He was glad he had done it because Gareth had left a note for him.

Remember, you've got this. You're amazing. You could do this job in your sleep. Don't let anyone let you feel inferior because you're not. I'm standing right there behind you all the way. Eat all your food, and I'll see you soon.

Ben stared at the note the entire time he ate his food, wishing he could hear Gareth's voice before his meetings. He'd barely packed away his lunch bag when Lindsay knocked on his door.

"Mr Mycroft, Mr Devlin is here for your appointment."

Ben grinned at her use of his formal name again and rolled his eyes but nodded for her to let him in. He stood, withholding his groan as the cage pulled on him, when Anthony entered, rounding the desk and holding out his hand.

"Anthony. Nice to see you again."

The area manager's hand was strong but damp, as it had been every time, but it didn't stop Ben from offering the greeting.

"Afternoon. How are things?" Anthony settled into the sofa, and Ben grabbed some files from his desk before sitting on the armchair opposite.

"Good, thanks. Everything seems to be continuing in an upward trajectory, which is a good thing as far as I'm concerned."

Anthony nodded. "Yes, I'm pleased with the progress you've made. You've yet to have a dip in your sales numbers in all the time you've been here. It's impressive, to say the least."

Ben breathed easily, confident that he had the plans to keep that progress. "Thank you." He passed over a file, wincing when the cage pinched. "Here are the latest reports and also my plans for the last quarter of the year."

He discreetly checked his phone while Anthony looked over the paperwork, but still no messages. Relaxing against the chair back, a calmness came over him. He knew how to run this business, and he was damn good at it, but did he want to do it forever? It was something he would need to discuss with Gareth, although the ultimate decision would be his. There was a lightness in his body that he could only believe was because he had the confidence of a man he loved.

Ben froze. How had he fallen in love in the space of what, three weeks? How could he not, though? Gareth was an amazing man, an amazing Daddy, and Ben couldn't have wished for a better person who wanted to be with him as well.

When Anthony began talking, Ben had to work hard to get himself into the conversation and not get distracted by the revelation. The cage was not helping him focus, but he managed. Two hours later, he saw Anthony out and dropped back into the chair behind his desk, staring at the ceiling. He knew he had to write up what they'd discussed and transfer it to the team leaders later that afternoon, but he'd run out of energy already. Checking his phone still showed no message from Gareth, and Ben completely admitted to pouting.

He sat upright when he remembered Gareth should've posted on the blog that weekend. Ben hadn't read it yet. Typing in the blog address, he found his way to the latest article.

What do you do as a Middle? by DaddyG

Following on from my last post about Age Play, I decided to go a little deeper into the potential options for each of the different ages. I would've usually started at the Little, but—guess what, readers? I'm in a new relationship!—I thought I would start with what I'm currently experiencing myself.

Ben couldn't help the grin spreading across his face. Gareth had told everyone about him! He hadn't expected that. For some reason, it made everything seem more real. He read the rest of the post, taking on board the comments his Daddy had made about being a Middle. For once, Ben was honest with himself and could see a lot of himself in what Gareth had described. He chuckled when he read some of the comments.

"I'm so pleased you've met your boy. You deserve it after all this time. I wish I could find my boy. Everyone around me seems to be

able to find their forever except for me. Keep your fingers crossed, eh?" D-Mad79.

"You're basically giving me ideas on how to piss off my Daddy. I love it!" 1Cyclops1.

"Can you tell me how to find a Daddy? I have never been to a club or anything, and I don't know anyone who would come with me. I don't want to go to one by myself." Oh2Bs3xy.

Ben felt for the last guy, especially when his username was "Oh to be sexy." He'd have to mention it to Gareth and see if there was anything they could do about him. Depending on where he lived, maybe they could go with him. It would be awful to have to attend by yourself when he didn't know anyone.

He distracted himself by completing the paperwork he needed for the meeting, but his groin tingled with a quiet thrill of knowing what he wore and for who.

"Sir? Ben? It's time for your meeting," Lindsay said, popping her head into his office.

Ben rubbed his forehead. "Where did the time go? Okay. I'll be there in a minute."

Several minutes later, he entered the meeting room to see the group of fifteen team leaders. "Good afternoon, everyone. Thank you for coming. Do you have your drinks and snacks ready? If we can, I'd like to get this done within an hour," Ben said as he sat at the end of the long table, eyeing the other occupants.

Fifteen pairs of eyes stared back at him, several with mouths open, until Felix piped up, "I'm all set. Everyone else?"

Ben's confidence didn't waver, and he was determined to take Lindsay's suggestion on board and not apologise, just change the way he behaved from that point forward. "If we're all ready, let's go through last month's minutes to make sure we did everything that could be done."

Lindsay read off the action points from the previous meeting, and Ben was pleased to find that most of them had been completed. They went through the incomplete ones and added them to this month's actions.

"Now, onto this month. I met with the area manager today, and he had several areas he wanted us to focus on this month." He pulled out his papers and ran through the items Anthony had brought up with him. They discussed the possibilities, and Ben allowed everyone their opinions, taking on board what each person said. As far as meetings went, it was better than the previous ones.

"Mr Mycroft, can I ask a question?"

Ben lifted his head and glanced at one of the checkout team leaders. "Of course. What's up?"

The man leaned forward on his forearms, linking his fingers. "What's different? You're not the same person who was here last time."

Ben smiled, resting his pen on his files and leaning back in his chair. "I've recently had it brought to my attention that I could be a little more lenient with certain things. I'm trying it out for size."

"Are you going soft on us? Because from what I see, you don't seem to want to push us as much as you did before. I'm concerned it will make us less likely to follow your instructions."

Ben narrowed his eyes at the man. "If anyone doesn't follow the instructions, I'll deal with it. Nothing has changed. We still have the success of the company in mind, and I assure you that will not change. If anyone doesn't like that, it's something that needs to be discussed between myself and that person."

"I've heard rumours," the man continued.

Ben raised his eyebrows. "Rumours."

The man glanced around the room, and Ben followed his gaze, seeing several of them not looking at either of them and others nodding or shaking their heads, advertising their feelings on the subject.

"From what I've heard, you're seeing one of your employees."

Ben licked his lips, trying to stem the need to argue and defend himself, which his previous incarnation would've done. "It's not against the rules to date an employee."

"So you admit it?"

"I don't need to admit anything because it's not your business. But," he said, holding up his hand when the man tried to talk, "I will tell you that, yes, I am seeing an employee. As I said, though, it changes nothing. Apart from maybe my attitude."

"Exactly my point, Mr Mycroft. You were always bull-headed and forceful before. Now, you seem to have softened. Will the company achieve the same results when you've lost your fire?"

When other people began chiming in, Ben clenched his jaw. The employees had no right to speak to him like that, but were they right? Was it something to worry about?

21

GARETH

Gareth had slept like a baby after sending Ben off to work that morning. He'd expected to lie awake for hours, wondering how Ben was contending with the cage covering his cock, but he'd fallen straight to sleep. His alarm had woken him at four in the afternoon, and he'd taken a leisurely shower before starting on dinner. After checking on the supplies, he'd decided to make a chicken casserole. Something easy to prepare and able to be shoved in the oven to cook without having to think too hard because Gareth needed to decide what he was going to do with Ben when he arrived home.

Would he remove the cage and edge him until he went crazy? Or would he keep him locked away? Gareth enjoyed the idea of the edging and decided to go with that unless Ben opposed it—within reason.

His phone rang, and he answered without checking who it was. "Hello?"

"Gareth."

"Hey, Dad. How are things with Aunt Helen?"

"They're going okay. She's back home and causing mayhem by trying to take over when she knows she can't. All the usual stuff, really."

Gareth chuckled. "I can imagine. How are you managing?"

"Everything's under control. I was just calling because I'm going to be here for a few weeks rather than days. I'm going to stay and do some jobs she has, but I'm going to be helping her interview for helpers, too."

Gareth stirred the gravy he was using for the casserole as he spoke. "That sounds like a good idea. She always said she could manage on her own, but getting help would increase her business as well, I bet."

"Exactly my argument."

Gareth smiled. Despite their many differences, they were scarily similar in some ways. "Well, let me know when you're heading home. I've been checking on the house, and it's still in one piece."

"Glad to hear it. I'll be in touch."

They ended the call, and Gareth poured the gravy into the casserole dish, mixed everything together and left it on top of the oven to put in when Ben arrived home. He tidied up, checking the clock every few minutes when Ben hadn't arrived at the time they'd agreed upon that morning.

He was just wiping down the counters when the front door slammed shut. Showing no reaction, he finished the job, put the food in the oven and set the timer for one hour, then headed for the front of the house. Ben wasn't in the living room, and he climbed the stairs, hearing the muttering as soon as he stepped towards his bedroom.

"—gives them the right? They don't know me."

"Who doesn't?" Gareth asked, entering the room and crossing the distance between them. He didn't touch Ben, though. The man trembled enough that one wrong move or word would make him explode. Gareth had to calm him down before he could get him to lift the lid on his anger.

Ben whirled around, glaring at Gareth. "Don't worry about it." He unbuttoned his shirt and threw it on the bed, following it quickly with his trousers. "Can I get this off so I can shower?" he muttered, waving a hand at his groin.

Gareth stared at him, trying to figure out what had happened without asking. Unfortunately, he wasn't a mind-reader. He stepped closer, pulling the key from his pocket.

"Yes, but no touching other than to wash."

Ben glared at him but said nothing, standing stiffly while Gareth carefully unlocked the cage. "Thanks," Ben gritted out, stalking towards the bathroom.

Gareth watched after him, frowning. Had someone said something to him? It certainly seemed possible with the change of behaviour from this morning. He gave Ben some time to decompress in the shower, jogging down the stairs to switch off the oven, then returning and grabbing a few things he would need for when Ben came out. When the man finally emerged, he had a towel around his hips and a scowl on his face. He paused when he saw Gareth but continued towards the bag containing his clothes.

"Come get on the bed, sweetheart." Gareth purposefully made it an order, not a question.

Ben hesitated before rising to his full height and staring at Gareth. "Why?"

"Does it matter?" Gareth tilted his head.

Ben glared at him, but the tears pooling in his eyes ruined the angry look he had been going for. He strode over to the bed and climbed on, laying stiff as a board.

"Roll onto your stomach and get rid of the towel."

Ben huffed but obeyed, and Gareth rose to his knees beside him. He grabbed a bottle and tipped some liquid into his hands, rubbing to spread it around. When he was happy, he placed his hands on Ben's shoulders and massaged him. Ben's muscles were so tight that Gareth didn't think they would ever relax again, but eventually, Ben's shoulders moved away from his ears, and his body sank into the bed.

Gareth continued massaging the oil into Ben's back and sides, his ass cheeks, his thighs, his calves and, finally, his feet, where he found the man was ticklish. He helped Ben roll onto his back, so Gareth could continue on his front, avoiding the area that was severely aroused. He wasn't sure if Ben had fallen asleep, but he finished and moved between his legs. Ben's cock was standing proud, and Gareth fed the head into his mouth, closing his eyes as Ben's flavour burst over his tongue. Gareth had been spoilt over the last couple of days because he'd mostly had Ben to himself, and he missed having easy access to him, but tonight wasn't for sating Gareth's need—at least, not that one—it was for seeing how far Gareth could push Ben before he had no choice but to orgasm. Tonight was for Ben's first proper taste of edging.

Ben's hips lifted when Gareth's mouth left his cock, and a mewl of dissent left his lips. Gareth pushed against his hips until Ben rested them on the bed again. He rubbed his hands in circles over Ben's skin, similar to the massage but not as firm. When he reached Ben's nipples, he feathered his fingertips over the protruding tips and lowered his head again.

This time, he tongued the veins running up Ben's shaft, finding the places that made him twitch and spending time on those areas, especially the bundle of nerves on the underside beneath the head. Every man knew this area was sensitive and could elevate arousal and even make a man climax if it was played with enough. With this in mind, Gareth kept one hand on one nipple, strumming away, his tongue flicking at the nerves, and his other hand, he moved to Ben's balls.

"Fuck," Ben breathed, his eyelids fluttering closed and his back arching.

Gareth could see the wave of goosebumps as it coasted across Ben's skin, a ripple of small bumps and raised hair with a mind of its own. He rolled Ben's sac between his fingers, tugging gently and pressing against his taint while his mouth took the head of his cock into his mouth and sucked.

Ben's feet slid against the covers as he tried to get traction to thrust his hips. "Please!"

Gareth ignored him and slid his hand to the opposite nipple, continuing his ministrations. The hand holding his balls slid further back, teasing the path to his entrance. His fingers were still slippery from the oil, and he massaged around his pucker, eliciting incoherent mumbling from Ben. He glanced up the sweat-slicked abs to the heaving chest and to his face. Ben's mouth was open as he panted, and Gareth could see his hands clenched in the covers.

Gareth pressed harder against Ben's hole, gaining entry, and Ben's cock jerked, leaking precome. He lowered his head, taking more of Ben's shaft into his mouth while his finger slid deeper inside his channel. Moans filtered through the air, and Gareth pumped his finger in and out, causing more fluid to escape Ben's tip.

"Daddy!" Gareth lifted off and removed both his hands, letting the climax recede. "No!" Gareth's mouth curled at the fire burning in Ben's eyes. Ben's hand lifted, but Gareth grabbed it and stopped it from wrapping around his cock.

Gareth shook his head. "No. Hands above your head."

"Please?" Tears filled Ben's eyes.

"Not yet. You have to earn it." Gareth tilted his head, staring at him until he reached above him, gripping the headboard. "Good boy."

Gareth's hand encircled Ben's cock, and a sigh that sounded very much like relief left his boy. He slowly stroked him and, with his other hand, opened the bottle of oil, tipping some onto his palm. He closed his fist, spreading the oil around his fingers, and closed the bottle. His oiled hand pushed Ben's legs apart, exposing his ass.

"You're bloody perfect," he murmured, pressing one finger against his hole. It slid in easily, and he followed it with a second. He continued stroking both his cock and his ass while watching Ben for signs he was getting close. Crooking the fingers inside him, he searched for that certain spot destined to send his arousal higher.

"Fuck!" Ben shouted, slamming his head into the pillow and hissing out a breath. "Oh, please! Fucking please!"

Gareth continued, studying him, finding his weaknesses, testing his resolve. When Ben panted, Gareth slowed the movement on his cock and released his prostate but kept up the thrusting. He scissored his fingers, stretching his channel, and added a third finger. The tension in Ben's body had lowered, and Gareth increased his speed once more. He also added a twist of his wrist when he reached the nerves, rubbing over them and undoubtedly sending sparks through Ben's groin.

Inside him, Gareth curved his fingers again, caressing his prostate, and sent Ben higher, faster. Ben's keening cry alerted him to the impending orgasm, and Gareth gripped the back of his cock and froze.

"NO!" Ben's head thrashed on the pillow, trying to thrust his hips and reach for the release Gareth denied him. Sweat dripped off Ben's trembling body and soaked into the covers. Gareth mapped every inch of him, locking away the images for future needs.

When he was sure Ben wouldn't climax, he let go and climbed off the bed. He glanced at the clock, noting he had plenty of time, and undressed, crawling back into place when he was naked. His cock was hard and red, and he picked up a condom he'd thrown on the covers with the bottle and rolled it down his length. He slicked himself with lube and settled between Ben's thighs. Holding his cock at Ben's entrance, he smiled up at his boy.

"Ready?"

"Are you going to let me come?" Ben hissed.

Gareth raised his eyebrows. "Ready?" he repeated.

"Are you... Yes!" he shouted as Gareth slid inside him in one long, slow, continuous thrust.

He paused when he was balls deep, inhaling through his nose to keep his control. He refused to climax the second he was inside Ben, but it was a close call. Gripping Ben's hips, he held still, waiting for what he knew would come.

"Move! Fucking move!" Ben jolted his hips, and Gareth grinned, tightening his hold. "Move, godammit!"

Gareth didn't, but he wrapped his hand around Ben's cock, spreading the precome around for lubrication. Ben sighed and closed his eyes, and Gareth withheld his chuckle, knowing Ben wouldn't like where this was going. He began a gentle, circular grind against him, not withdrawing but pushing himself deeper and massaging him from the inside. He knew he would press against Ben's prostate, but not enough to make him come. Letting go of his cock, Gareth lay over Ben's body, sliding his arms beneath him and trapping his dick between their bodies. He latched onto Ben's nipple and sucked, nipped and flicked his tongue over it while continuing his circular movement with his hips.

He knew from experience that this would create a build-up towards a climax, but it would be frustratingly slow. Ben's legs came around his back, changing the position slightly, but it allowed Gareth to go deeper, opening Ben further for him.

"Yes. Please let me come, Daddy! Please." Ben still had his hands around the headboard, and as a reward, Gareth withdrew a little and thrust forward. "Yes! Oh, god, yes!" Gareth returned to the slow roll. "Noo!"

Gareth moved to the opposite nipple, repeating his actions, and thrust his hips again. Ben cried out. The length of Gareth's spine sparked with electricity as his orgasm raced towards him, and he let go of Ben and knelt upright, sliding his arms beneath

Ben's knees and opening him further. He braced his hands on the bed, bending Ben in half, and pushed himself into a push-up position. His hips snapped forward, spearing his cock inside Ben repeatedly. He wouldn't be able to hold the position long, but enough to get them close to the finish line, which he did.

The moment he felt a ball of fire begin in his groin, he stopped and dropped back to his knees.

"No, no! Please, god! Just let me come!" Ben begged.

Gareth chuckled. "Not yet."

Ben sobbed. "I could've come ten times already. This isn't fair."

"Trust me. You'll like the ending."

Gareth gripped Ben's hips and thrust in a steady rhythm. Ben was riding the edge, so Gareth had to be careful. One jolt too many, and Ben would orgasm, and he couldn't have that just yet. Ben rolled his lips inwards, keeping his mouth and his eyes closed, and Gareth knew he was trying to hide his responses. It wouldn't work, though, because Ben's body told all the tales he needed.

When Ben was on the brink again, Gareth paused and received many curses and insults. He smacked Ben's hand away when he tried to stroke his cock and slammed deep inside him. They'd both had enough by this point. Picking up his speed, he hammered his channel, the sounds of their bodies pounding together loud in the otherwise quiet room.

"Fuck, yes! Please, Daddy! Please let me come! Please!"

The begging continued, but Gareth wasn't going to stop this time. He settled himself further upright and held Ben's thighs, battering his hole and hitting his prostate with every thrust. His spine and groin tingled warmer and warmer until Ben's climax triggered his own. Gareth watched as Ben's release covered his chest and abs, and his mind was lost in the euphoria of orgasm.

22

BEN

Ben's brain misfired as everything centred on his groin. The climax speared through him, leaving him a brainless mush of trembling limbs. Sweat stung his eyes, and he tasted salt when he licked his dry lips.

"That...was..." he panted but couldn't finish.

Gareth withdrew from his ass, and Ben groaned at the drag along his sensitive channel. He felt empty when Gareth left like he needed him to stay inside him, but he couldn't stand the denial. He'd lost count of how many times Gareth had brought him to the edge and left him hanging. It wasn't nice at all.

But that release had certainly blown all others out of the water. Maybe there was something to be said about edging.

A warm cloth swept over his rapidly cooling skin, and he hummed a thank you, though he wasn't sure if it was audible. Hands rested against his own hands and gently pried his fingers from the grip they had on the headboard. He winced as he straightened them—he hadn't realised how hard he'd been holding on.

Blinking open his eyes, he watched and felt Gareth press a kiss to each finger and rub them to get the feeling back into them. Gareth smiled at him.

"How are you feeling?"

Ben gave a small smile. "Like a limp noodle."

"My mission was a success."

Ben chuckled. "Your mission was an evil one," he rasped.

"Let me help you sit up. You need a drink."

Gareth slid his arms beneath Ben's back and helped to sit him upright with pillows behind him. Ben's head was too heavy, and he rested it back against the headboard while Gareth held a glass of water to his lips. He sipped, to begin with, then gulped the entire glass.

"Thanks," he said when he finished.

"You're welcome." Gareth brushed a hand over his forehead, settling on the bed beside him. "Are you okay?"

"Perfect."

"I don't want to burst your post-climax bubble, but what happened today?"

Ben groaned and slid down the bed, pulling a pillow over his face. "Don't worry about it."

Gareth yanked the pillow away. "Of course, I worry. You went to work with a smile on your face and came home like someone had taken your strawberry milkshake away from you."

Ben chuckled and sighed, staring up at Gareth. "I had some comments about us. Well, not us specifically, but whether I can still do my job now that I'm loved up." He bit his lip, not having meant to say that last bit.

Gareth frowned. "I forgot to mention the conversation I had with Felix, but why would you not be able to do the job?"

"They think I'm going soft."

"What?"

Ben laughed at his expression. "Yeah. Apparently, my assholery ways are an indication that the business will continue to do well. If I soften too much, they don't have faith it will continue."

"That's bullshit!"

"What did Felix say to you?" he asked.

Gareth's forehead creased. "He mentioned everyone was gossiping about whether you and I were a couple. I think we need to go public, Ben. Not have an announcement or anything, but not hide. It will give the gossip mills nothing to feed on."

Ben shrugged. "It's fine with me. I'm more than happy to make sure everyone knows you're off-limits." He grinned when Gareth growled.

"Yes, well, how about I take you and pick you up tomorrow?"

Ben wrinkled his nose. "But I have my own car."

Gareth chuckled. "Yes, you do, but if we want to show everyone we're together without announcing it over the tannoy, we need to do something else. If I drop you off and pick you up, we'll be seen together."

Ben nodded. "All right." His stomach rumbled, and he placed a hand over it. "Sorry."

Gareth smiled. "I should've fed you before. Let's get you set up again, and we'll go get some food."

"Set up?" Gareth reached for the bedside table and held up the cock cage. "Not again!"

"You like it. Stop complaining."

Ben sighed. He wasn't wrong, though he tried to think of something else to stop Gareth throwing him in a cold shower again. Once was enough. He closed his eyes and thought about work as Gareth oiled his dick and locked it in the cage. He was puffing by the time he finished.

"Come on. We can watch TV while the casserole cooks, but I'm sure a small snack won't stop you from eating later," Gareth said, holding out his hands to help Ben to his feet.

Ben slipped into some joggers while Gareth put on the clothes he had worn before their...adventure. When they descended the stairs, Ben veered off to the living room and Gareth to the kitchen. Ben checked the clock. They only had just over an hour before Gareth had to leave, so a film was out of the question. Wanting something light-hearted, he chose a comedy programme they'd watched before and enjoyed. Gareth came in with a tray on which was a bowl of fruit and two mugs of tea.

"Thanks," he said when Gareth passed him the fruit.

"Is what the staff are saying bothering you?" Gareth asked.

Ben put a strawberry in his mouth to delay his answer and give him time to think. After he swallowed, he said, "It's not so much what they're saying. It's more my brain trying to figure out if they're right."

"If it's making you softer?"

Ben shook his head. "I know it is." He smiled at Gareth. "I don't have a problem with that. I'm wondering if they're right about me not being able to keep the company going without my assholery attitude."

Gareth snorted. "If that were true, every boss would be an asshole, and I know plenty who aren't, and their business is booming. I think you just need to find your new way of doing things. You're crazily intelligent, Ben. You've managed to drag your store up without knowing if your actions would work. Now, if you decide to continue with the job, you just need to figure it out again."

"Yeah." He popped a grape into his mouth. "I apologised to Lindsay today." He chuckled. "She didn't know what to do at first. I think she thought I'd lost my mind."

"Was she okay?"

"She's fine. I told her about us. She's happy for us." He laughed again. "She gave me a piece of advice. She told me not to apologise to anyone else, just change how I treat them from now on. I'm going to try it, although I think most of them will think I've knocked my head or something."

Gareth rolled his eyes. "As long as you're happy with who you are, no one else matters."

"Not even you?" Ben asked, smiling.

"Not even me."

Ben stared at him. "But you're encouraging me to be better. You punish me when I misbehave. Isn't that a contradiction?"

Gareth shifted until he faced Ben and rested an arm along the back of the sofa. "I'm not trying to change you. I'm trying to help you realise who you really are. If that is an asshole, so be it. But I think you put on that persona to stop people from getting close to you. To hide who you really are from those *relatives* of yours."

"I don't *want* to be an asshole," he murmured.

Gareth's fingers threaded into the hair at Ben's nape. "You're not. If you were, you would've given those employees an earful, and I don't think you did, did you?" Ben shook his head. "I will say one thing, though," Gareth said as he stood when the oven timer beeped, "You need to put your foot down with anyone who tries to keep you later than your home time."

"I won't let it happen again." Although the idea of being punished as he had been earlier was a delicious enticement. He felt his cock try to fill, but the cage pressed against it and stopped it. It was the first time he'd felt aroused enough for an erection to happen, and Ben had expected it to hurt, but it didn't. There was a tightness to it that stopped him from becoming hard, even though the low-level arousal was still strumming through him.

They ate dinner at the dining table in the kitchen, and Ben offered to clean up and let Gareth could get ready for work. As they placed their plates on the counter, Gareth pulled Ben into a kiss, exploring his mouth while Ben stood there and took it. He inhaled deeply when Gareth pulled back and strode out of the room. He was always stupefied after a kiss like that.

He washed the dishes and put the remaining casserole in a dish ready to put in the fridge and settled in front of the TV, flicking through the channels for something to watch before bed.

Arms slid around his neck, and he turned his head to see Gareth smiling at him. "I have to go. Are you going to be okay?"

Ben nodded towards the TV. "I'll be fine. I'll watch something and probably go to bed."

"I've left Victor and Preston's phone numbers on the fridge if you want some conversation or company."

Ben chuckled. "I'll be *fine*."

Gareth sighed. "I know. I just wish I could be here with you."

Ben stood, rounding the sofa to slip into Gareth's arms. "Me, too. But remember what you told me? It just means I need to work fewer hours. We'll have plenty of time to see each other."

"We will." Gareth pecked his forehead. "Okay, I'm going." He patted Ben's groin. "Be good," he said with raised eyebrows.

Ben smirked. "I don't have much choice about that now, do I?"

Gareth grinned and kissed him, then left, and the house sank into silence. Ben expected to feel lonely or stuck, but he didn't. For once, he didn't mind being alone. Was it because he was surrounded by Gareth's things? He didn't know, but he dropped onto the sofa and grinned.

When the film finished, Ben yawned. It was only ten o'clock at night, but he was exhausted. He switched off the TV and pottered around, trying to figure out which things Gareth turned off and which he left switched on overnight. He wasn't sure, so he left everything as it was, but he sent a message to him about it and also told him goodnight.

Gareth hadn't replied by the time Ben was ready for bed, but he knew it wasn't close to his break time yet. If there was a problem, he was sure Gareth would call him. He climbed into bed and switched off the lamp. Rolling to his side, he gathered Gareth's pillow to his chest and inhaled. If he couldn't have Gareth with him, at least he'd have his scent.

He was woken by a cool body sliding in beside him, and he froze for a singular beat before Gareth's voice eased him.

"Go back to sleep. You have time."

A kiss on the back of his neck was the last thing he remembered.

The next time he woke, it was more abrupt when his alarm went off. He blindly reached for it, not wanting to wake from the dream of having Gareth wrapped around him. The alarm stopped before he touched it, and he blinked open one eye.

"Rise and shine, sleepyhead."

"Is that going to be my usual morning wake-up now?"

Gareth smiled from his recline against the headboard. "Why not?"

"Hmm." He rolled to his back. "How come you're still awake?"

"I wasn't going to go to sleep and miss seeing you. I'll sleep when you have to leave." Gareth leaned over him, pressing their mouths together. "Good morning, sweetheart. Why don't you have a shower while I get some breakfast ready?"

"Deal."

Gareth covered his body with his own. "Do you think I need to get you a little dirtier beforehand?"

Ben laughed. "I wouldn't say no."

Gareth reached for the bedside table and grabbed the key to the cage, making a production of unlocking him. Ben was in hysterics by the time Gareth freed him and couldn't remember the last time he'd felt so...loved. He paused and stared at his Daddy.

"What's wrong, sweetheart?" Gareth asked, rising above him until they were face to face.

Ben smiled. "Absolutely nothing." He cupped Gareth's cheeks and inhaled, hoping he wasn't going to make a mistake. "I love you."

There was a brief second of "oh, shit, he's not going to say anything" before Gareth slammed their mouths together. This was a take no prisoners kiss, and Ben lost himself in the primal act. Their bodies clashed, their hands touching and gripping and holding wherever they could reach. Ben's lips felt raw, but he wouldn't change any part of the exchange. Their hips thrust a shaky rhythm, their cocks rubbing against each other, but neither of them letting go. Ben wanted Gareth to fuck him, but he was too far gone to ask. He wanted to remember every bit.

Ben's lip pulled away from his mouth when Gareth tugged it between his teeth. He nipped at it and released it before untangling himself and bodily throwing Ben onto his stomach. Ben was too far gone to care about decorum and foreplay and rose to his knees, pushing his ass backwards, wanting Gareth's cock inside him immediately. Gareth must've found some lube because when his shaft pressed against his entrance, it was slick. Ben bore down, needing Gareth to fill him, but he was too slow, and Ben slammed his hips back, sliding Gareth deep inside.

"Fucking hell, Ben! Did I hurt you?"

"No, now fuck me."

Ben dragged himself forward, feeling the cock leave his ass, then pressed back again, hissing when his ass stretched to accommodate him once more.

"Shit," Gareth muttered, gripping Ben's hips in a bruising hold and letting himself go.

All Ben could do was brace himself on the bed while Gareth rammed and hammered Ben's ass. It was everything Ben had ever needed. He dropped his chest to the bed, his arms unable to take his weight any longer. The change in position sent Gareth's dick straight into Ben's prostate, and without any further stimulation, he came in stomach-clenching waves. He may have lost consciousness at some point because he didn't remember hearing Gareth come, but when his brain fired up, Gareth was lying on top of him, panting against his back.

"Fucking hell, Ben. You're going to kill me."

"Not if you fuck me to death first," Ben muttered. "I definitely need a shower."

Gareth laughed, causing a vibrating sensation through where they were joined. Ben's cock gave a valiant attempt at rising but gave up when his energy crashed.

"This is one way to make sure I come home on time," Ben quipped.

Gareth pulled free and slapped his ass cheeks. "I'll remember that." He smacked his other cheek. "Now get up. We have to shower."

And didn't that make him late for work for the first time ever?

23

GARETH

"**N**o one will care that you're a little later arriving," Gareth said as he drove Ben towards Market Foods. "I bet most don't even know what time you usually get in."

It was probably the truth, but it didn't stop Ben from worrying about it. After the meeting the previous day, he was highly aware of his actions and how they could be perceived. And pulling up outside the supermarket in Gareth's car could appear weak to some, but that's just what he was doing.

Gareth stopped the car and covered Ben's hand with his own. "I'm not pushing you to do this, sweetheart. If you really don't want to, we won't. I can drop you here and bring your car to you later so you can drive home alone. It's your choice. I know I can be overbearing and controlling, but things like this need to be decided by you because it affects you when I'm not with you."

Ben studied him, the scratchy scruff that had grown through the night more prominent in the morning light. His hair, leaning more towards shaggy that morning, held a sprinkle of lighter strands that almost sparkled. But it was his features that held Ben transfixed. The hazel stare was understanding and supportive, and it gave Ben the confidence he needed.

"Let's do this. I'm not ashamed of who I am or who I'm with."

Gareth's answering smile was worth all the fluttering of his stomach. His Daddy pulled back out onto the road and, several minutes later, stopped in front of the supermarket. Ben inhaled and stared around them, seeing a couple of employees, but not many.

"Have a good day," Gareth said, taking Ben's attention from their surroundings. "I love you."

Ben stared at him, his mouth dropping open. "I wasn't sure you felt the same," he whispered finally.

Gareth smiled and grabbed his hand. "I didn't want to say it after a round of sex, sweetheart. I didn't think that would go over well."

Ben chewed his bottom lip as tears filled his eyes. He wiped at them with a chuckle. "Now, I'm going to go in there looking blotchy."

Gareth cupped his jaw. "You're beautiful. Inside and out. Never forget that."

"I love you."

Gareth kissed him, soft and sweet, and pulled back. "I love you. Now, go be bossy."

Ben laughed and climbed from the car, taking his hastily pre-pared lunch bag with him. Before he closed the door, he leaned down to ogle his boyfriend. "Get some sleep, Daddy. I want more of what we had this morning later."

He shut the passenger door on Gareth's laughter and strode into the supermarket with his head held high and a smile on his face. He greeted every employee he saw, noticing but not caring about the widening of their eyes and the gaping of their mouths. Jogging up the stairs to the offices, he stopped at Lindsay's desk.

"I apologise for being late. When you're ready, can we go through the day's plans, please?"

Lindsay smiled and held out his travel mug. "Of course. I made you some tea. It should still be warm."

"Thank you." He took the mug and sipped it while he settled behind his desk, closing his eyes as he recalled Gareth's words. Nothing else could've given him enough confidence to walk through the store without caring what people thought. Nothing else calmed him except for Gareth's trust and belief in him. It felt so freeing.

Lindsay knocked on the door and entered, closing it behind her. She started talking even before she had sat down. "Everything is the same today, except for one meeting, which had to be moved to a later time."

"Which is that?"

"The one about extending the warehouse. Mr Ward had a family emergency crop up this morning and requested a later time. I've moved that meeting to five o'clock." She winced. "Sorry."

Ben sighed and rubbed his head. "Don't worry. It can't be helped. At least it shouldn't be a long one, as we're only going through the plans and getting updates from them."

"I know you were trying to leave here earlier now, though."

Ben shrugged. "It's a pain, but it's okay. We won't need the minutes for it, I don't think. I'll try to take notes as best I can so we have some record of what we say. Although you know my note-taking skills are not the best." He chuckled, and Lindsay smiled before going serious.

"Please don't listen to the team leaders from yesterday," she said. "They have no say in your private life, whether or not it affects your work. I hope you're not considering going back to the way you were."

Ben shook his head. "I'm not planning on it. It's rare you find someone who loves you as you are and doesn't try to change you; therefore, I plan to hold tight to Gareth for as long as he'll let me."

"From what I've seen of him, he's a good man."

"He is."

The day went surprisingly fast. Ben had three meetings—two in person and one video call—and tons of paperwork, which he completed in between. He ate his lunch at his desk, along with a strawberry milkshake, and ordered a light meal of sandwiches and snack foods for the final meeting of the day.

Just as the meeting was due to start, his heart clenched, and he frantically grabbed his phone.

BEN: *I'm sorry. A meeting has been rescheduled to five o'clock. I'm going to be late home. I'm hoping it won't be more than an hour, but I'll try to keep you updated. Sorry.*

He didn't bother turning his phone to silent when he entered the meeting room because he wanted to know when Gareth replied. The other attendees were present by the time he arrived, and he apologised for being late. His phone chimed.

GARETH: *Don't let that meeting go longer than an hour. You need to rest. You've given them enough already. Don't give them any more of your time than absolutely necessary. I'll see you soon, sweetheart. Love you.*

Ben smiled and started the meeting by going through the items they'd mentioned in the last meeting, and so it continued.

Ben hadn't kept an eye on the time when a knock sounded.

"Come in!" he called, frowning.

Gareth poked his head through the door. "I'm sorry to interrupt. Mr Mycroft, there is something you need to deal with. It can't wait, I'm afraid."

Ben stared at him for a moment and cleared his throat. "I apologise, gentlemen. Please continue your discussion. I will be back momentarily."

Gareth stepped back, holding the door open for Ben to exit. As soon as the door was closed, Gareth took hold of Ben's elbow and guided him towards Ben's office, two doors down. Gareth opened the door, led him through and shut it behind them.

Gareth let go and rested back against the door, crossing his arms. "What did I tell you?"

Ben's heart raced as he glanced at the clock and realised it was past seven o'clock. He spread his hands. "I can't help it if a meeting goes long! I can't just tell them to get out!" Gareth raised his eyebrows. "I can't!"

"Bullshit." Gareth stalked towards him. "I told you the meeting should not last longer than an hour because you're tired. You need to rest. Those people in there don't care if you've had an hour of sleep or if you've had ten hours of sleep. They will drain you dry and spit you out! I told you an hour. For your own health." Gareth was breathing hard. "Bend over."

Ben folded his arms. "No."

Gareth raised his eyebrows again. "Say that again," he dared.

Ben swallowed but lifted his chin. "No. I have a meeting to get back to." He stomped to the door, but Gareth grabbed his arm and spun him towards the desk, pushing him face down over the edge, the papers going flying. He kept one hand between Ben's shoulder blades while the other slipped underneath him and unfastened his trousers.

"Stop!" Ben cried.

Gareth leaned harder on his back. "You know what to say to get this to stop, and it isn't 'stop.'" He unzipped Ben's trousers and pulled them over his ass, repeating the action with his boxers, leaving him bare. Gareth rubbed his hands over the exposed skin, his hand cool against Ben's ass.

Gareth stopped mauling him and paused, and Ben relaxed.

"Fuck!" Ben gasped when Gareth whipped his hand forward, laying a smack on his ass cheek. He bit off his words because of where they were.

Gareth smacked his other cheek, rubbing in circles after. He continued in the same vein until Ben's ass smarted.

"You have a lovely red glow on your ass."

Ben gritted his teeth despite wanting to sink into the feel of it. He had to remember where they were.

"I think that's enough of a reminder right now." Gareth let go of Ben's back, and his hands came into view as he braced himself on either side of him, leaning over until his mouth was next to Ben's ear. It caused Gareth's denim-covered groin to meet Ben's sensitive skin, which made Ben's breath hitch because it felt delicious. "What will you be saying when you enter that meeting room?" His hot breath wafted across Ben's face.

Ben cleared his throat, and Gareth rolled his hips, generating another gasp. "I'm sorry...but something...has come up. We'll need to...finish this another day."

"Good boy." Gareth canted his hips again, and because Ben loved the feeling, he pressed back, unable to resist the feel of being held beneath his Daddy, while his cage stopped him from showing his arousal. Gareth kissed his ear and tugged on the lobe with his teeth before rising.

He dragged Ben upright, pulling his boxers and trousers back into place. Gareth patted Ben's groin. "If you continue to be a good boy, we will work off all that frustration when I get home in the morning."

He spun Ben around and squeezed his ass, earning a gasp as he pushed him towards the door. "You have a meeting to end. I'll wait here for you."

"Yes, Daddy."

Ben was floating on air as he returned to the meeting and made his excuses. The attendees appeared grateful. "I'll get Lindsay to call you to rearrange."

As they filed out, Ben rested his head back against the chair for a moment. He seemed to feel relaxed and complacent whenever he'd been punished. It was a strange feeling, but one he would no longer deny.

"Are you ready?" Gareth asked from the door.

"I just need to grab my bag…" He trailed off when Gareth lifted the bag in question. "Nope. I'm ready." He hustled over to him and threw his arms around Gareth's neck. "Thank you."

Gareth encircled his arms around his waist and kissed him chastely. "Thank you for not hating me when I go all controlling on you."

"Never."

They wandered down to where Gareth had parked the car and headed home. Ben needed to stop thinking about it being home, though, because he had the apartment he'd be moving into in a couple of days.

"Victor called me earlier. He wanted to know if you wanted some company tonight?"

Ben smiled. "Sure. That'd be nice."

"Can you do me a favour?"

"Of course."

Gareth sighed. "I think he's feeling lonely and fed up. He's not been able to find a Daddy who wants more than one night, and it's grating on him. I had hoped you wouldn't mind keeping him company because I don't want him to withdraw into his shell. He's such a good man." Gareth shook his head with a sad smile. "It's not fair on him."

"I'll try to cheer him up. I don't mind spending time with either of your friends."

"They're your friends, too, you know."

Ben scrunched his nose. "I wouldn't say that. I'd like them to be, but we don't really know each other yet."

Gareth chuckled. "I think the amount of time you spent together at the club would be enough to make you friends. You and Victor are two peas in a pod." Gareth frowned. "Hmm, maybe I should get Preston to come round, too. He might be able to keep you two out of trouble."

"Hey!" Ben pouted, fake though it was. "I can be responsible."

Gareth raised his eyebrows at him. "While you're on your own? Yes. While Victor is with you? I don't have as much faith."

Ben backhanded his shoulder and laughed. "I can't disagree with you. There's no telling what Victor might make me do."

By the time they arrived home, Victor was already waiting on the sofa with the TV on and a bowl of popcorn at the ready.

"Are you psychic?" Ben asked, not sure if he was serious or not.

Victor grinned. "Nope. I just didn't want to be alone."

Ben sighed and joined him on the sofa. "I know."

Victor snuggled into Ben's side, surprising him, but he held him tightly, rubbing his back until Gareth entered with two big plates of food.

"Decent food before crappy food, please, boys," he said, placing the tray on the coffee table and holding out the plates of spaghetti bolognese.

Gareth rounded the table and leaned down to Ben. "I have to go. Make sure you rest, and I'll see you for breakfast." He kissed him, and Ben wanted more than what Gareth gave him, holding onto his polo shirt and holding him still. After a few minutes, they parted, and Gareth smiled. "I love you."

"Love you."

When the door closed behind his Daddy, Ben snapped his head around at a loud sob. He grabbed Victor's plate and put both of them on the table before wrapping Victor in his arms.

"Oh, Victor. We'll find you someone. I promise. There is someone out there for you. I promise we will find him."

A knock sounded, but Ben couldn't get up to answer. After a second, the front door opened, and a voice shouted, "It's Preston! Can I come in?"

"We're in the living room!" Ben called back and continued rocking Victor in his arms.

When Preston saw Victor, he dropped to his knees in front of him. "Oh, little one. We need to find you your Daddy."

Ben and Preston stared at one another, unable to do more than they were already doing to comfort the distraught little. It reminded him of the commenter on Gareth's blog, Oh2Bs3xy. Once they had all calmed down, he would talk everything through with them and figure out a game plan. There had to be a way to help all these people.

24

GARETH

Gareth had a few days to glimpse what the future could look like while Ben was living with him, but when he received the go-ahead to move into his apartment, Gareth struggled to keep his feelings hidden. He didn't want to push Ben into staying with him when he'd recently received the gift of freedom, but as his boyfriend and Daddy, Gareth didn't want to let him go. But he kept quiet and showed the right amount of excitement when Ben picked up the keys.

Ben had arranged for someone to cover him at work that Saturday, and they got settled into the fully furnished apartment, which was handy, as Ben only had the suitcase he'd left his previous home with. They invited Victor and Preston over for the evening. His boy had told him what had happened when he'd left Ben and Victor to cause trouble the other night, and he'd be glad he'd messaged Preston to keep them company. He had no doubt Ben could've coped, but with Preston as support, it had been easier on him.

When Gareth had returned home the following morning, Ben had been wide awake and eager to speak to him about an idea he'd had. An idea of using Gareth's blog to unite boys and Daddies, like a matchmaking service. After asking how it would work,

Ben brought out the notepad he'd been writing on and listed everything they might need and how they could get it to work. Ben was a planner if nothing else.

Gareth still wasn't sure if it would work, but he'd agreed to write a blog post about it and was currently waiting for it to go live. Soon, all the readers of Boys, Daddies, Snuggles and More would give their opinions on the matchmaking idea.

Ben was like an excitable puppy, which was why Gareth had invited their friends around. Anything to keep his boy from bouncing around the apartment any more than he already was.

"I'm glad we checked what we needed before I moved in. I wouldn't have been able to make any food without the pots and pans," Ben said as Gareth washed the new items and he dried and decided where to put them in the cupboards. "And I wouldn't have been able to have guests. No mugs are an issue for those tea drinkers among us." He chuckled, and Gareth's chest fluttered at the happiness coming from him. "I was also thinking about getting some toys. Then Victor could be little around here if he wanted to. What do you think?"

Gareth stared at him, the pots forgotten in the sink. How could anyone have thought this man was anything but the kind, gentle person he was?

"What?" Ben froze and wiped at his face. "Do I have something on my face?"

Gareth shook his hands, getting the excess water off, but he didn't dry his hands. He couldn't. He stepped forward, cupped Ben's cheeks and kissed him. Kissed him the way he'd haltingly told him he loved to be kissed. Deep, hard, passionate. When he couldn't take the lack of oxygen any longer, he pulled back, chest heaving for air.

"I fucking love you."

Ben stared at him, his eyes dilated and glassy, his hands gripping Gareth's wrists. "What did I do?" he mumbled, the words coming out as if he was drunk.

"You care so much about other people. Making them feel at home. Helping them. Doing whatever you can to ease their stresses. You're amazing."

There was much more Gareth could say, but he knew he wouldn't be able to explain it all in a way that would make Ben understand what a precious gift he was to the world.

Ben's lip disappeared, and Gareth chased after it with his mouth, dragging it out from his teeth. "Do we have time before—"

The doorbell rang.

Gareth rested their foreheads together. "Nope. We don't." He pecked him on the lips and headed for the door.

"Not fair!" Ben called after him.

It was a good job he was still in the cock cage because Gareth knew his hands would be down his trousers quicker than he could say "supermarket sweep."

"Hey. Come on in." He opened the door wider for Victor and Preston to enter.

"What's not fair?" Victor asked when Ben joined them.

Ben thumbed over his shoulder at Gareth. "Working me up and telling me we can't finish."

Victor laughed and dropped onto the sofa. "Isn't that your usual state?"

Ben threw a cushion at him and plopped down next to him. "Yes, but usually, when he works me up like *that*, I am allowed to come." He pouted and glared at Gareth.

Gareth held up his hands. "Why are you mad at me? I wasn't the one who arrived at the wrong time." The pouting didn't stop. He changed the subject. "What takeaway are we choosing? If we order it now, it should be here within the hour."

"Indian!"

"Chinese!"

"Chips!"

Gareth sighed. "You lot are impossible. Ben can choose because it's his house warming party."

Ben threw his fists in the air. "Indian, please, Daddy."

Gareth smiled as he took orders, loving the happiness that was radiating off Ben. He was different from when he had first met him. Ben hadn't changed; he'd just brought out the person he was inside. The person he'd been hiding from the world. Even the staff at work had mentioned how he'd mellowed.

He got them to choose a film while he placed the order, knowing it would take them a while to agree. Despite Preston not being a boy, he certainly had the temperament of one sometimes. Once he'd ordered, he joined them on the sofa and wrapped his arm around Ben's shoulders.

They were just arguing about whether Victor had seen a continuity error when the doorbell rang, and Ben jumped up. "Food!" He raced to the door. "He definitely didn't have a bow tie on before. You'll have to rewind it and see," he said as he flung open the door and froze.

Gareth couldn't see who it was, and he jumped up and joined his boy, seething when he saw Ben's "parents" on the other side. "What do you want?"

Martin, Ben's father, had the grace to look uneasy, but Alice stepped forward, brushing the threshold with the toes of her shoes. "Ben, you owe us rent money. We need it."

Gareth snorted and slipped a hand under Ben's T-shirt to rest against his skin. It seemed to bring Ben out of his frozen state. Ben pushed back against Gareth's hand, and Gareth moved closer.

"I don't owe you anything," Ben said.

Alice stepped into the apartment, trying to get around them, but Gareth moved into her path and stopped her from going more than two steps. Her mouth pursed as she looked him up and down, then ignored him and faced Ben again.

"You pay your rent in arrears, which means you owe us for August." She lifted her chin and glared at her son.

Gareth's hackles rose, his muscles clenching with the need to let his anger show. His heart pounded so hard that it surprised him that no one could hear it.

Ben inhaled. "No, I pay in advance. I always have. If anything, you owe me for ten days, but I'll let you keep that."

"Don't be ridiculous, Ben. You've left us in the lurch. We don't have enough money to cover your bills."

Ben scoffed. "*My* bills? You don't have to pay any of *my* bills. I brought them all with me. What you can't do without is the extra money I gave you." He shrugged. "Well, you'll have to find someone else to give you that now. Or go out and get a job."

Alice gasped, her hand flying to her mouth, and Gareth couldn't help the laugh that escaped him. God forbid they had to work for their money. He brushed his thumb across Ben's skin, trying to tell him how proud he was of him for standing up to them.

"How dare you? After everything we gave you."

"Everything Grandfather gave me, you mean."

"That old coot did nothing for us."

Ben huffed. "Nothing? He paid off the house, he left you money in his will, he left you the cars. If that was nothing..." He shook his head. "Do you know what? Enough. I don't want to hear it anymore. Goodbye, Father. Goodbye...Mum."

Ben crowded her out of the door and slammed it shut on her gasp of horror, throwing the lock for good measure. He faced Gareth, saying nothing for several seconds, before throwing himself into his arms. Gareth grabbed his thighs and lifted him, encouraging him to wrap his legs around him.

"I paid for the takeaway. We'll be back shortly," he told Victor and Preston, who whistled at them.

Gareth headed down the short hallway to the bedroom, kicking the door shut behind them. He dropped Ben to the bed, following him down. His hands unfastened Ben's jeans as quickly as he could.

"What are you doing?" Ben laughed, the spark back in his eyes.

"Taking your cage off."

"But why?" Ben frowned.

"Because I am so damn proud of you, Ben Mycroft. You deserve a treat."

Ben's eyes sparkled. "A treat?"

Gareth pulled the key from his pocket and, after yanking Ben's boxers down, unlocked the cage and set it aside. Without further warning, Gareth licked Ben's cock, and it sprang to attention. He lapped around the head, flicked the underside of nerves and took him into his mouth. He held the base, lifting and lowering his head in a fast rhythm, then sank until his lips touched Ben's groin. He swallowed and pulled off, grabbing Ben's hands and placing them on the back of his head.

"I can't..."

"Fuck my mouth, Ben. It's an order if you need it to be," Gareth said and sucked him down. He stayed down, swallowing repeatedly, running out of breath while he thought Ben wouldn't do it until his hands pulled at Gareth.

Gareth lifted his head, his saliva leaving Ben's cock nicely lubricated. Ben pressed against his head, and Gareth followed instructions. At first, it was a gentle up and down, then Ben got brave and held him down for a few seconds while Gareth swirled his tongue around. Each time it happened, Ben held him for longer.

"Fuck, Daddy. Oh, god, yes."

For a short time, Ben seemed to forget to direct him, and Gareth sucked at the head, pulling more and more precome from his boy. Ben pushed his head, and he lowered as far as he could, and Ben thrust his hips, making him gag.

"Sorry!"

But Gareth stayed where he was, swallowing and tonguing where he could until he needed to breathe.

"I want you to come down my throat, sweetheart. I mean it. Fuck my mouth. You don't know when you'll get the option again." Gareth winked.

He kissed the tip and lowered his head, bobbing up and down until Ben's hands threaded through his hair again. This time, his hands were more forceful. Gareth slid his hand to Ben's pucker and massaged the area. Ben moaned and jerked his hips. He did this over and over, his cries rising the closer he came. Gareth pushed against his rim, and Ben keened as he fell over the edge, releasing a long, steady flood of fluid into Gareth's waiting mouth. He licked him clean and moved to lie beside him. He threw an arm over Ben's waist and rested his head on his hand, looking down at his worn-out boy.

"Wow," Ben said.

Gareth chuckled and leaned down to kiss him. "We'll put the cage back on if you want it on, or we can leave it off for tonight?"

Ben's lip disappeared, something Gareth thought he would never curb him of, and he whispered, "I like it."

"Then on it shall go." He paused. "In a few minutes, when I have my energy back."

Ben chuckled. "Touché."

They lay in silence. Gareth loved that they seemed to be in sync with quiet times. Well, mostly anyway. Ben had his moments, especially when he was throwing a tantrum, but Gareth wouldn't have it any other way.

"Your food's getting cold!" Preston shouted.

Gareth chuckled. "I guess we better get sorted." He rose, pressing a kiss on Ben's shoulder before standing between his legs. "Are you ready for the cage again?"

"Yes, please." Ben bit his lip, and Gareth narrowed his eyes.

He grabbed the cage, fitting it more easily now they were both used to it, and locked it in place, sliding the key into his pocket. He helped Ben to stand and rearranged his clothes until he looked put together again.

"Ready?"

Ben grinned. "Always."

When they returned to the living area, Preston and Victor cheered. Ben threw a cushion at them and wandered to the breakfast bar where they'd left the takeaway. Gareth joined him, grabbed his food and settled on the sofa next to Ben. They had chosen to watch a comedy, and now more than ever, did they need the levity. They'd missed a bit, though.

"Well, I won't try to guess what you two were up to in there. I didn't hear the bed creaking, though, so you either have a fantastic bed, or you went for the down and dirty *blowjob*." Victor whispered the last word as if it were sacrilegious to say it.

"Does it matter?" Gareth asked with a grin.

Victor threw his head back and laughed. "No. I'm just curious about the bed thing. I'd love to find a decent bed that didn't creak with every move your body made. There has to be one out there somewhere." He sighed.

Preston patted his shoulder. "There, there, Victor. I'd suggest you search the internet, but I'm sure you've already done that."

"Does your bed creak?" Victor asked Preston.

"Nope." He winked. "But that's more likely because I've not seen any action lately. I hadn't paid much attention to it before that. I was kinda busy at the time."

"Researching is boring," Victor whined. "It's too grown up."

Gareth smiled at him. "I think someone needs some downtime." He glanced at Ben, who nodded. "Do you want to be little, Victor?"

He sighed again. "I do, but I don't want to put on any of you. I'll go to the club tomorrow night and find someone. Even a night is better than the nothing I'm doing now."

Gareth got up and crouched in front of his best friend. "Hey, we're here for you, little one. Let's get some rest tonight and have a playdate tomorrow. Ben said he wanted to play with you in his new apartment. We just need to grab a few things. Okay?" He bent his head to catch Victor's gaze. "Okay?" he said again.

"Okay. Thank you."

Gareth squeezed his knee and returned to Ben's side. He kissed Ben's temple, glad for the generous soul he'd been given. Between them, they should be able to keep Victor above water until his Daddy came along.

25

BEN

"You want to organise what?" Lindsay said, her tone advertising that she'd heard but couldn't believe he'd suggested it.

"A night out for the entire store."

"I thought that's what you said." She slumped in the visitor chair. "Can I ask why?"

Ben twiddled the pen he held and stared out of the window. "I want people to see I've changed, and what better way to do that than to have a party where I can let loose with everyone around to see it?" He peered at her again. "Do you think I'm nuts?"

Lindsay raised her eyebrows and shrugged. "Probably." She smiled. "But it's a good idea. I know we have one at Christmas, but if you want some quicker results, a night out would be good. What did you have in mind?"

"Well, I had a couple of possibilities. There's a hotel that offers their ballrooms or reception rooms, whatever they call them, for such gatherings. But I also know a pub that has enough space. They have DJs or live music, a bar—necessary for obvious reasons—and plenty of tables and chairs."

Lindsay finished writing on her notepad. "I like the idea of the pub. The hotel, I think, might be too formal. It's okay for a

Christmas party, but if you want to show them who you are, a pub might be better. Which pub is it?"

"The Pub." At Lindsay's yet again raised eyebrows, he laughed. "Yes, that's what it's called. Gareth told me about it. It's a regular haunt for him and his friends, and he knows the staff."

"I'd suggest checking it out to be sure it can hold the number of staff we have."

"I will. Shall we go with that if they can fit us in?" Lindsay nodded. "Okay, the other thing, when?"

Lindsay opened her diary, flicking through some pages. "We don't want it too close to Christmas because people will have other plans."

"I was hoping for something sooner."

Lindsay scrutinised him. "How soon?"

Ben winced. "Next month?"

She covered her face with her hands and groaned, then sat upright. "All right. In that case..." She flicked a few more pages, "Let's go with 1 October. It's a Saturday, so most staff will be able to attend. There will still be some who can't, but maybe we can do a brief get-together here for them afterwards?"

Ben nodded. "Good idea. I wondered how we were going to accommodate everyone."

"It's not possible. We have people covering all the hours of the week, and unless we shut the place down for a few hours, some people will miss out."

He rested his chin on his thumb, his forefinger rubbing his bottom lip. "I wonder if I could get permission for that?"

Lindsay scoffed. "I doubt it very much. And besides, the staff might want to drink. If they did, they wouldn't be able to work afterwards."

He nodded. "Okay. Stick with the original plan."

"This is a plan, is it?" She chuckled. "I can't decide if I prefer your set-in-your-ways self or this new one." She tapped the pen against her mouth. "Nah, this new one is much more polite."

Ben threw a crumpled piece of paper at her, laughing. "Be careful. I'll set Gareth on you."

"I'm not scared of him."

"You should be."

They sorted a few more details, and Lindsay disappeared to help make it happen. It was less than five weeks away, and it all depended on whether they could get the location. With that in mind, he messaged Gareth, asking him to call The Pub and see if they're available on that date. He wanted to call him, but he would be sleeping after his shift the night before.

They'd had a busy weekend. Ben loved his new apartment, although it didn't have the same cosy feeling he had when he was staying with Gareth. That house felt like a home, whereas his apartment was a shell of what it could be. Maybe he needed to spend some time making it cosier and "him."

The previous day had gone a long way to making it more so. Playing with Victor when he was a little was an eye-opening experience. Ben hadn't expected him to be an older little. For some reason, with Victor's demeanour and attitude, Ben had thought he was a younger little, interested in nappies and bottles. The man had surprised him, though. He wasn't sure what age he regressed to, but he enjoyed having books read to him and playing with Lego and board games. At times, Ben had seen behaviours that wouldn't have been out of place on a teen. Would Victor do well as a Middle? Ben had forgotten to ask Gareth that question because once Victor had come out of his little space, they'd given him his aftercare routine, and he'd gone home, Gareth had ravished Ben. A lot of things got missed that evening.

Ben smiled, sighed and focused on his paperwork. It was never-ending, but he was coming to believe he did actually enjoy the challenge of hitting targets and finding ways around things. For the moment, at least, he would stay where he was, but he didn't push aside the idea of finding a new job if he decided this wasn't for him.

❖

The five weeks passed in a flash. Ben spent half the week at Gareth's place and half at his apartment, but no matter where he was, Gareth came back to him every morning. They'd got into a routine, and Ben loved it. He'd never been so relaxed and happy in all his years. But now, he was a nervous wreck.

Lindsay had pulled out all the stops for the party, and Ben had persuaded the bosses to allocate some extra money towards it, despite it being unnecessary. He would gladly admit to selling it as a team-building exercise, but it was more than that. It was his chance to show them he wasn't the ogre he had been.

His behaviour change had not gone unnoticed throughout the store, and many staff had warmed to him, even going out of their way to greet him. He was pleased, but the comments of the team leaders had not been swayed. The last meeting, three days ago, held less hostility, but some were still concerned about his ability to lead them. Ben rolled his eyes, even though no one was with him. Some people were so set in their ways that they didn't like change. Even change for the better. He understood that now, but it was hard to accept he couldn't change their minds. Showing them, however, was the only way to get through to them, and that was what he was doing. Not only in holding this party but because he was working his ass off to show he could still hold the store to the height he had before.

The office was quiet with it being a Saturday, but he was still there doing his job before the party that night. A few minor problems had arisen on the shop floor, although he had rectified them easily enough. He was clock-watching because he wanted to go home and see Gareth, but he still had too many hours to go. He refocused on his laptop, getting everything ready for that quarter. With it being the first of the month, he had things from his bosses that needed to be implemented.

A knock on his door pulled him out of his work, and he smiled when he saw his Daddy.

"What are you doing here? I thought you were waiting for me at your place." He rounded the table and threw his arms around Gareth.

Gareth kissed him and said, "I knew you were likely to be climbing the walls, and I thought I'd spring you early."

"I can't leave yet. Felix won't be here for another two hours."

Another knock sounded. "Reporting for duty," Felix said.

Ben snapped his head to the side. "What are you doing here?"

Felix chuckled. "Gareth called and asked if I would be willing to start a couple of hours earlier." He shrugged. "No skin off my bones. I'm just as happy here as I am at home."

"Thank you." Ben hugged Felix, too, surprising the man. "Let me go through a few things with Felix, and we can go," he told Gareth.

"I'll grab a cuppa. Come find me when you're done." He held out his hand for Felix. "Thank you, Felix. I appreciate it."

"Might as well let you young 'uns get some socialising in. I'm too old for that."

"No, you're not!" Ben argued.

They argued for a couple of minutes longer before Felix told him to shut up or he'd be late for his own party. Twenty minutes later, he found Gareth in the staff room, talking to several people. He didn't interrupt, but Gareth pulled him to his side, sliding his arm around his waist. Ben fought to keep his face from heating. Not because he was embarrassed about being with Gareth, but because he'd never been one for PDAs before Gareth.

He tucked his hand into Gareth's back pocket and smiled at him as he cracked a joke. The others laughed with him, Gareth made their excuses, and they headed out.

"You're so good with everyone. There's no one you can't talk to," Ben said when they stopped beside his car.

"There are plenty of people who don't like me, but I'm just me. If they don't like me, that's up to them. I'm not going to change who I am ever again. What you see is what you get." Gareth held his arms wide.

"Don't change," Ben said, resting a palm on Gareth's chest. "You're perfect the way you are."

"As are you."

They kissed. Right there in the car park, for everyone to see. And Ben didn't care.

When they pulled back, Gareth held the car door open for him. "Wrong door." Ben chuckled.

"I'm driving."

"Didn't you bring your car?"

Gareth shook his head. "Felix picked me up."

Ben sighed. "What did I ever do to deserve you?"

"You lived."

Ben closed his eyes to stop the tears from escaping at such a simple statement. Gareth kissed his forehead, and Ben climbed into the car. By the time they arrived at Gareth's house, Ben had recovered and was brimming with energy about that night. He still had flutters in his stomach because he wasn't sure anyone would turn up, but no matter what, he'd tried. And if no one turned up, Bound was not far away. They could visit there instead.

"I forgot to mention, Caleb is almost finished with the beta version of the app," Gareth said.

Ben almost tripped on the stairs, but his Daddy steadied him. "He is? That didn't take him long."

"He said he made it simple to allow more people to access it. If you add too many variables to it, it not only gets complicated, but it gets more expensive, too."

"Did he say when people could start trying it?" Ben asked, sitting on the bed.

Gareth stood in front of him. "Maybe a week or so. We need to get people to sign up for the beta version to help us iron out the bugs."

"I'm sure you'll have plenty of volunteers."

Caleb Duncan was a computer genius. Gareth had hired him to create an app when his blog post about linking Daddies to boys went nuts. Well, hired was a loose word. Caleb was a Daddy himself, struggling, as many seemed to be, to find his boy. When he'd seen Gareth's post, he got in contact and offered his services free of charge. They met, and within days, Caleb had a basic app created. Over the past few weeks, they'd tweaked it, and now it was almost complete.

"Right, sweetheart. Time for a bath."

Ben's heart raced. This was one of his favourite activities. "Are you joining me?"

"Of course." Ben jumped up and ran to the bathroom, almost colliding with the door frame in his rush to get there. "Slow down!" Gareth followed him into the room, shaking his head. "You're going to injure yourself one of these days."

Ben grinned, already stripping out of his clothes. Gareth set the bath running, added a healthy amount of bubble bath and faced him. Ben latched on to Gareth's clothes, undoing buttons and zips, sliding items off his body until he was as naked as Ben was.

"I have a treat for you tonight," Gareth whispered against his lips.

Ben licked his lips, catching Gareth's in the process. "What?"

"Patience, my boy."

Ben lifted his chin, and Gareth obliged the unspoken request, closing the distance between them. He pushed Ben back, making him arch away from the cold tiles, and devoured him. Ben lost all sense of time as Gareth kissed him and kissed him and kissed him.

Finally, his Daddy lifted his head, smoothing his mouth across Ben's cheek to his ear, "Time for a bath."

Ben whimpered, not wanting to move when he was content where he was, but Gareth stepped back, and cold air rushed in his place. Ben shivered. Gareth crouched in front of him, producing the key for the cage from somewhere, freeing Ben from its constraints. The moment he was free, he began to fill, and Gareth chuckled.

"Always so eager."

Gareth held out his hand and helped Ben into the warm water. Ben stood in the water while Gareth settled in first, then Ben slipped between his legs, his back to Gareth's front. As his Daddy's arms and legs came around him, Ben closed his eyes and enjoyed every second of feeling cared for and loved.

Gareth's hands skimmed over his skin, highly sensitising it. He dribbled water over his nipples and collarbone, and Ben hummed as low-level arousal started in his stomach. Their baths always ended with a happy ending for them both, but each time, Gareth did something different, and Ben couldn't wait.

He dropped his head back onto Gareth's shoulder and sank into the feelings Gareth evoked. The hard cock at his lower back was evidence that his Daddy was not immune, and Ben writhed in the water, pressing back against him.

"Patience," Gareth murmured.

"Want you."

"And I you, but enjoy the ride."

26

GARETH

While Gareth distracted Ben with the water and his other hand, he reached for the water-friendly lube, squeezing some on his fingers. He rubbed his fingers together and slid his hand around Ben's front and between his legs, already spread by Gareth's legs. A gasp escaped from his boy when Gareth's fingers massaged his pucker and his nipples simultaneously. Ben's ass pressed against his cock, and he hissed, biting at Ben's earlobe.

The fingers at Ben's ass pressed inside, one at a time, stretching him for Gareth's shaft. He left little bite marks along Ben's neck and shoulder as he prepared him, and Ben's whimpering grew louder and louder. When Gareth deemed him ready, he moved both their legs so Ben could straddle him and fitted his cock head to his entrance.

"Ready, sweetheart?"

"Always," Ben cried.

Gareth sank deep, leaving no prisoners until he was sheathed entirely, and Ben's ass rested on his thighs. He pulled Ben back again, resting their bodies together, and gently rocked his hips. He wanted this to be a soft, slow climb to the top to rid Ben of all the tension he was holding.

"Close your eyes." When Ben did, Gareth reached for the treat—his shower toy. The hollow cylinder of silicone would wrap nicely around Ben's cock, and the dual sensations should send him higher.

He squeezed some more lube into his hand and encircled Ben's cock, spreading it all over. Ben's choked gasp had Gareth smiling. He couldn't wait to see what his reaction was to this because Gareth had not shown him the toy before now. Continuing to stroke him for a moment, he readied the toy and swapped his hand for it. The moment it enclosed Ben's cock, Ben arched his back and nearly headbutted him. Ben's fingernails dug into the skin of his sides when Gareth strummed his nipples again.

The reaction Ben had to the toy showed Gareth that this wouldn't be a slow climb like he wanted. Ben was already shaking with holding back, and his pleading words were merging into a long stream of incoherent babble. Gareth felt him tighten around his cock and groaned.

"Fuck, sweetheart. Do you like that? Huh? Being impaled and having something around your dick?"

Gareth increased the speed of his thrusts and his hands, trying to keep an eye on the water level as their movements created waves.

"Yes, Daddy! Oh, fuck, yes!" Ben kissed the underside of Gareth's jaw.

Gareth slid his hand between them, pressing against Ben's back. "Get onto your knees, boy. Take what you need."

Ben struggled to move, and in the end, he stood, turned to face Gareth and straddled him again. Gareth held his cock to his entrance, and Ben slid down, groaning all the way. When he was in place, Gareth slid the toy over Ben's cock again.

"That's it. Move. Take me," Gareth growled. He could see every-thing: Ben leaning back, his hands on Gareth's knees, Gareth's cock disappearing into his hole, the toy surrounding Ben's dick, the expression of bliss on Ben's face. Gareth's climax roared to the front, but he held on, barely. He wanted them to come as close together as they could.

"Come on, sweetheart. Come for me."

Ben's movements increased, and Gareth stopped caring about the water, which was sloshing over the sides of the bath now.

"Yes! Daddy, I'm coming!"

Squirts of come landed on Gareth's chest and face and sent him over the edge. He gripped Ben's thigh as he pulsed inside him, glad once more that they had got tested and decided to forgo condoms. Feeling him bare was an amazing sensation that wasn't diminished by a latex covering.

He continued stroking the toy up and down Ben's cock, the aftershocks of both their orgasms rocking through them until Ben hissed and flinched. Ben collapsed onto him, and Gareth threw the toy into the water at the other end of the bath and wrapped his arms around his boy.

They stayed there until the water grew cold, then Gareth helped Ben out of the bath and wrapped him in a large towel, swinging him up into his arms and carefully navigating across the wet floor to the bedroom. He tucked Ben into bed, towel and all, covered him with a duvet and strode back to the bathroom to clean up. He mopped the water up with towels. Luckily, it hadn't been as bad as he'd thought, but he needed a different plan for when they did this again.

Once it was as dry as he could get it, he wandered back into the bedroom and sat beside Ben.

"Are you okay?"

Ben blinked open his eyes. "Perfect, but I'm worn out now."

"That's okay. Sleep. I'll wake you in a little while."

"No, I have stuff to do." He tried to rise, but Gareth pressed him back down.

"Everything is under control. Sleep."

Ben sighed. "Don't let me sleep too long."

"I promise." It was a promise he would happily break because what Ben didn't know was that Lindsay had been at The Pub all afternoon getting things ready. Ben didn't have to be there until just before it started. Gareth owed their friends a lot.

He left Ben sleeping and pulled on some joggers and a T-shirt. Drifting down the hallway to his office, he decided to make a start on next week's blog post. In the time since he'd posted about connecting Daddies and boys together, he'd been inundated with emails and comments about it. He was glad to be able to give them an update, but it was still hard to believe it had all happened because Ben had begged him to help one of his readers. Oh2Bs3xy, whose real name was Toby, had caught Ben's attention, and he had promised to help him. They had become close, messaging and calling often, and Gareth was glad Ben had found someone else who could relate to his experiences. Toby would be one of the first ones they tried to help.

Boys, Daddies, Snuggles and More

Who wants to be a guinea pig? By DaddyG.

Good news! The app will be entering its beta stage, and we need some volunteers. At the bottom of this post is a form you'll need to complete if you're interested, but there's no guarantee you'll be picked for the beta testing version. As soon as the beta stage is complete, we will set the app free into the world.

I just wanted to take a quick minute to say thank you to everyone. Your support, both the blog and the app, means a lot to BB0y22 and me. As something we wished for on a whim, it has blown our minds to think it's a wish coming true, and not just for us. I hope this app does what real life has not been able to so far—bring you closer to your HEA.

When he finished the first draft of the blog post, he saved it and went to his comments. There were far too many to answer all at once, but he did as many as he could in the time he had. One caught his eye, and he couldn't help but respond.

DaddyG, why do we have to choose what age we want to be? That's like telling me I can only ever have chocolate ice cream for the rest of my life just because I chose it once. I'm not like that. My age depends on the circumstances surrounding me on that particular day or hour. I could be a little in the morning, and by the time the evening comes around, I'm a Middle. Finding a Daddy who can put up with that has been a no-go. Any ideas? D3m0nBoy666.

Gareth chuckled at his username, but it was a truly valid question.

D3m0nBoy666, you don't have to choose at all. You need to understand what your brain and your body are telling you and listen to it. Is it unusual? Yes, but not unheard of. The main thing I would tell you is to be upfront about your needs from the very beginning of any relationship. Don't hide part of yourself away because that won't help anyone, and your Daddy might think you were being dishonest. Play up to your strengths. You have a love for life of all kinds. You enjoy exploring the lifestyle. You are not beholden to a description of who you are. Any Daddy worth their time will give you their time.

Arms slid around his neck, startling him, but he kissed the backs of Ben's hands. "Did you sleep okay?"

"You let me sleep too long. I'm going to be late," Ben groused, but he laid his head on Gareth's shoulder with his eyes closed.

"No, you're not. Lindsay has everything under control. You needed to relax before the party."

"Hmm." He lifted his head. "What are you doing?"

"Just answering a few comments. Want to read this one?" He scooted the chair back and patted his lap. Ben sat and leaned forward, elbows resting on the desk while he read. It pushed his ass into Gareth's cock, and he perked up. There would be no more shenanigans before the party, though.

"He sounds like a wild child." Ben chuckled. "I love your re-sponse."

Gareth kissed Ben's head. "Time for dinner, and we'll need to get ready to go."

"Aren't we eating there?" Ben frowned.

"We can, but I would like you to have something before we go in case you get busy and don't have time to sit down. If you've not eaten, the drink will go straight to your head. The idea is to leave them with a positive impression, not a drunk one."

Ben grinned. "Why not both?"

"Because you'll be embarrassed if you're drunk."

Ben pouted. "Fine."

They worked side by side to make spaghetti carbonara, and after, Gareth sent Ben up for a shower. He'd have one afterwards; otherwise, they *would* end up being late. When they were dressed and ready to go, Ben hesitated.

"Is this a good idea, Daddy?" His voice was small and timid, completely unlike his usual self.

Gareth wrapped him in his arms. "This is a perfect idea to get to know everyone. You'll be amazing, and I'll be by your side the entire time."

By the time they arrived at The Pub, a few people were already there. Lindsay ran over and hugged Ben, much to his boy's de-light.

"I'm glad you're here. This is going to be so much fun!"

"Thank you for doing all this, Lindsay. I should've been here to help, but someone," he side-eyed Gareth, "wouldn't let me leave."

Lindsay waved away his words. "I wanted to do it. I love organising things. Why do you think I'm a PA?"

"I'm truly grateful because you are the best PA in the world. I swear it." Ben grinned and looked around. "Hopefully, more people will arrive soon."

"Everyone is always fashionably late, don't worry about it." Lindsay pulled on his arm. "Come on. Let's get a drink."

Gareth followed in their wake, smiling at the people he knew, nodding at the people he didn't. Most of them probably knew who he was because he was Ben's boyfriend. It wasn't a secret in the company, and it made for creative gossip.

Ben started with a soft drink, which was wise given that he needed to speak to his employees as they arrived. As people drifted towards them, Ben's hand found his, and Gareth squeezed it in reassurance.

"You can do this. I have faith," he whispered in his ear.

Ben exhaled heavily and smiled at the newcomers. "Hi! How are you?"

And so the night went. If Gareth wasn't mistaken, the entire store, bar the ones who still had to work, had come. Whether it was to see Ben, get a cheap night out, or just show their faces, he didn't care. What he cared about was the smile on Ben's face as he spoke to those who had said things behind his back when Gareth had first started working there. From what Gareth could see, those feelings had changed, and they were completely on board with the true Ben.

The live band played all night, drinks flowed, and food was eaten. As the night drew to a close, a man and a woman approached.

"Mr Mycroft," the man said, holding his glass close to his chest.

"Clive. Melissa. Thank you for coming."

Gareth could feel the tension in the air, and he moved a step closer to Ben.

"We want to give our apologies for how the team meetings have been recently," Melissa said. "It wasn't our intention to upset you. We care about the company as much as you do, but we need to remember that it's not just on your shoulders that this all rests. It's on everyone."

"Thank you for that. I won't say it's been an easy few weeks with the meetings, but I'm hoping to prove to you all that the company can still thrive without an ogre for a manager."

Melissa chuckled. "We know it can."

Gareth glanced at Clive, who hadn't said anything after the initial greeting. He didn't look like he was going to add anything until he opened his mouth. "I need to learn to look at the bigger picture, Mr Mycroft, not the smaller one."

"Please call me Ben. And it's fine. We start the next meeting with fresh eyes. See what we can achieve together. How about that?"

"Sounds good."

They said their goodbyes, and Ben blew out a breath. "That was bracing. I didn't know what to expect, but it wasn't that."

Gareth pulled him close. "Everyone can see that you're a good man, Ben. Even before, you were not an ogre. You had standards you had to live up to, and it made things difficult, but you're the same person, except the inside person is now on the outside for all to see how amazing he is."

Ben smiled and sniffed. "Don't make me cry."

Gareth chuckled. "Sorry."

"I think we can probably leave everyone to their night now. What do you think?"

"I don't know, Mr Mycroft. Do you have something else in mind?"

Ben wrapped his arms around Gareth's neck, surprising him with the public display, and kissed him for all to see. The crowd threw cheers and whistles their way, and they finished the kiss laughing. Ben hid his face in Gareth's chest and groaned.

"Right, everyone," Gareth called. "I'm taking your boss home. Don't do anything we wouldn't do, will you?"

"Doesn't leave much, I'm sure," Lindsay shouted.

Ben lifted his head and glared at her, and Gareth grinned. "I don't know. I'm sure we could come with a few things." Ben slapped his chest and tried to pull away, but Gareth wouldn't let him. "Be good."

Ben bit his lip, and Gareth grabbed his hand and tugged him towards the exit. They stopped to thank Lindsay and raced home. For the rest of the evening, Gareth showed Ben exactly what he meant to him. Several times over.

27

BEN

"Are you sure we have everything ready?" Ben asked, leaning over the counters and checking each plate. "I don't see the fruit bowls."

"That's because they're in the fridge, keeping cold," Gareth replied.

Ben sighed. "I want this to be perfect."

"It will be. You and Lindsay have everything planned. Nothing would dare go wrong." Gareth chuckled when Ben glared at him.

"There's nothing wrong with being organised." Ben folded his arms and pouted.

"I agree, but this is your Christmas Eve party as much as anyone's. You have to enjoy it as well."

Ben dropped his arms. "I know. I just want it all to go well."

Gareth enfolded Ben in his arms and held tightly. "It will. Relax."

The doorbell rang, and Ben raced to it with Gareth's laughter following him. He whipped open the door without checking to see who it was.

"Lindsay!"

"Happy Christmas Eve," she said, holding up several bags. "I brought the cinnamon rolls I said I would bake and the game."

Ben fist-bumped the air. "I get first dibs on the rolls."

"Are you going to let her come in, sweetheart?" Gareth's voice brought Ben out of his excited bubble, and he saw Lindsay was still standing on the porch.

"Ah, sorry. Come in, come in."

He pushed the door shut, but a foot landed in the way. "Don't shut us out."

Ben opened it again and saw Victor and Preston carrying two large boxes. "What have you brought?"

Preston rolled his eyes. "Gifts and beer."

"Then, by all means," Ben waved his arm, "come on in."

"Where do you want these going?" Preston asked.

"Beer in the kitchen, gifts in the living room, please," Ben called. "Lindsay, rolls in my tummy, please!"

Everyone laughed, and Ben danced into the kitchen, grabbing a roll from the plate Lindsay had just set up. He took a huge bite and groaned at the flaky cinnamon taste. "These are delicious. You should sell them."

"Nah. I just make them for fun. I wanted to open a bakery when I was younger, but I chose the monetary safety of organisation rather than the debt instability of opening my own business."

"You could do it in your spare time, though. Just take on what you want to do. A hobby or something like that," Ben said.

Gareth slid his arms around Ben's waist. "You just want her to keep you in sweet treats."

Ben grinned. "Maybe."

Gareth wiped a finger over Ben's chin and slid it into his own mouth. "Tasty." He winked, and Ben's cheeks heated.

"I've got our list, Ben. I'll just go through and check we have everything we said we wanted," Lindsay said, holding a clipboard.

"I'll help..." Ben started, but a voice calling his name stopped his offer. "Hold that thought."

He wandered into the living room and gasped at the number of gifts already piled high near the Christmas tree. "Are we going to have room for everything?" He wrinkled his nose and tapped his chin. "Maybe we could use the hallway if there's too many for in here."

The doorbell went again, and Gareth shouted, "I'll get it!"

Ben was still considering the options for the present pile when Toby came barrelling towards him for a hug.

"Ben! Happy Christmas!"

Ben returned the embrace and greeting. "Thank you for coming all this way."

Toby had recently found success on the Daddy's Boy app, and this was their first visit as a couple. Ben smiled at Toby's Daddy, Ollie.

"I'm glad you're both here."

"Wouldn't miss it for the world. I have plenty to be grateful for this year," Ollie said, smiling at Toby.

Ben's heart lifted at the obvious signs of a good match. He'd known the moment he'd seen them that they would be good together, and when the app matched them, Ben had been over-joyed. They had met for the first time at the beginning of December, when Ben and Gareth had accompanied Toby to the meeting for no other reason than he was nervous. They trusted Ollie, but someone had hurt Toby before, and they hadn't wanted him to be a no-show. He and Gareth had driven the fifty miles to where Toby lived to give him moral support. As soon as the couple had hit it off, Ben and Gareth said goodbye and spent the afternoon sightseeing.

The front door opened, and Richard shouted his presence. "I found two other people on the street. I thought I'd invite them in."

Ben gasped. "I might not have enough food for extra people." He hurried into the hallway, ready to welcome the strangers, but found Felix and Jane. Ben huffed and wagged a finger at Richard. "Not funny."

Richard chuckled. "A little funny." He patted Ben on the back and headed for the kitchen, where he knew he would find Gareth.

"Thank you for coming." Felix held out a bottle of wine. "Oh, you didn't have to bring anything, but thank you."

"I brought some fruit cake, too. I didn't want to come empty-handed," Jane said.

"Oh, thank you. Come on through. We're spread between the kitchen and the living room at the moment, so feel free to mingle. I'll introduce you to everyone."

"Who would like a drink?" Ben called, and everyone joined them in the kitchen. While he took orders, he introduced everyone to everyone else, making sure no one was left out. As Gareth handed out the drinks, Ben asked Lindsay to let everyone know the plan.

"Okay, we have a fun-filled day ahead of us. We're going to get the munchies going so that everyone can eat as it's near to lunchtime. After that, we will do the gift exchange. We have a charades challenge, and we need to vote for the film we're going to watch later."

"I think this is busier than when I go to work," Victor murmured to Preston, and Ben glared at him from his place on the other side of Preston.

Ben clapped his hands. "Everyone dig in. Plates are on the counter over there, along with the cutlery. You can see where the food is. Oh, Gareth, can you get the fruit out, please?"

"Sure."

"Before I forget—on purpose—Lindsay's cinnamon rolls are on the dining table with Jane's fruit cake. I want to keep them all for myself, but I suppose I should share. As it's Christmas."

While everyone filled their plates, Ben checked his phone, frowning when his message remained unanswered. He pushed the phone back into his pocket and smiled as he turned back to their guests.

"Find a seat wherever you can. We might fit better in the living room, but it's full of gifts, so even that I'm not sure of at the minute." He laughed.

As they ate, Jane regaled them with the story of Secret Santa at work. "Ben's idea was a good one, but from what I could gather, people were swapping names here, there and everywhere. I lost count of the people who came to me asking to swap. It would be safe to say that most of the names were not from the original people who pulled them. It was crazy. I loved my gift, though. So thoughtful."

"We had a Secret Santa, too," Preston said. "I got a dreamcatcher, a candle, a book of poetry and a scarf." He rolled his eyes. "Whoever got my name had no idea who I was."

Ben chuckled. "I don't know. The dreamcatcher and candle seem pretty good." He took another bite of food from the plate Gareth had made for him.

"The dreamcatcher was quite shiny, I suppose."

"Oooh, shiny," Victor said, making everyone laugh.

"You're like a magpie." Preston nudged Victor's arm.

"But it looks good on me!" Victor whined.

"Now, now, children," Gareth said, giving them "the look."

Richard cleared his throat. "I meant to ask how the app was going, Gareth. I know you said you had created one, but I never got the chance to ask what it was for."

Ben paused, staring at Gareth, who stared at his father. He had no idea how to field that question because Richard didn't know about Gareth's specific lifestyle. Before either of them had the chance to come up with something, Toby started gushing.

"The app is absolutely brilliant. It helped me find my Daddy after waiting so long and having too many disastrous dates. I don't know how it works, but we're perfect for each other, aren't we?" He glanced at Ollie with a huge smile on his face.

Ollie slid his arm around Toby's shoulders and, with a small wince in their direction—he'd obviously caught the undercurrent going on—said, "We are."

Richard tilted his head, forehead creased. "It's like a dating app?"

"Uh-huh, but for those who are struggling to find their Daddies or their boys. It happens a lot, I'm told," Toby continued, unaware of the undercurrent. "I'd been looking for a Daddy for five years with no luck. And for Ollie, I think it was longer."

"Eight years."

"I've been looking for eleven years," Victor mumbled. "And I'm still looking."

Richard glanced at Gareth. "And you're the Daddy in this relationship?" he asked his son. Ben watched Gareth swallow and nod. "Makes sense. You always were the caretaker. I know I left you alone a lot, and you had a lot on your shoulders. It kind of makes sense." He peered at Ben. "Bet you have your hands full with him."

That broke the tension because everyone chuckled at the honest response.

Ben stood and excused himself to get another drink. He pulled out his phone when he got to the kitchen, and there was still no reply. Gareth's arms came around him, and Ben let him take some of his weight.

"Don't let them upset you today. You tried, sweetheart. If they're not willing to get off their high horses, there's nothing you can do."

"I know, and I know how much they hurt me, but they're still my parents. I wanted to wish them a good Christmas."

"You don't need them." Richard's voice made him jump and whirl around. Gareth's father, in an unusual show of PDA, took Ben into his arms and hugged him tightly. "You have me. Now, I'm not the best of the best, but I won't let you down."

"You have me, too," Jane and Felix said from the doorway when Richard freed him. Their words were identical and said at the same time. They glanced at each other and smiled.

"Don't even think about it," Gareth warned as the three older generation left the room.

"But they'd be good together," Ben whined.

"Then let them find each other. Don't go butting your nose in."

Ben pouted. "It worked with Toby and Ollie."

"No, the app worked."

Ben sank into Gareth's arms again. "Why is it not working with Victor?"

Gareth sighed. "I have a feeling he's not being entirely truthful. With himself or the app."

"We need to help him, Daddy," Ben whispered. "Or we're going to lose him."

"I know, sweetheart. I know."

Lindsay popped her head around the door frame. "Time for the film vote."

"We'll be right there," Gareth said.

Ben closed his eyes and listened to his Daddy's heartbeat, the steady thrum centring him as it always did. Richard was right. He had everyone he needed right here in this house, and he wouldn't change it for the world.

"Are you okay?" Gareth asked.

Ben tilted his head up and smiled. "I am."

Gareth lowered his mouth and gently kissed him. Ben's eyelids fluttered closed as he lost himself in the soft caress. His cock made a gallant attempt at rising, but the cage, which he still wore daily, stopped it. It didn't stop him from rubbing against Gareth, who gripped his ass and held him still.

"Don't start something we can't finish, boy."

"And why can't we?" Ben asked, head still high in the clouds.

Gareth nibbled his earlobe. "Because someone invited a load of people over to the house."

"Party's over. They can all go home."

Gareth chuckled. "Come on. Let's go make our vote before we're out of luck."

Ben gasped and opened his eyes. "No! We don't want that one!" He raced into the living room, dropping to his original place on the floor like a ton of bricks. "I'm here."

Lindsay shook her head. "I could tell. It sounded like you brought a herd of elephants with you." Ben flushed. "Okay, here are your pieces of paper. These are the choices. Make your vote."

"Gareth! Quick!"

"I'm here, sweetheart. No need to shout."

"Sorry." Ben bit his lip, and Gareth winked at him.

Ben carefully wrote his choice on the paper and folded it. He threw it in the basket when Lindsay held it out, and she called them out one at a time. "One for *Nightmare Before Christmas*. One for *Miracle on 34th Street*. Another for *Nightmare Before Christmas*. One for *Love Actually...*" She went through all ten. "The winner is *Nightmare Before Christmas*."

Ben threw his arms in the air. "Yes!"

"Is that your favourite, Ben?" Felix asked.

"Yep. Favourite ever, ever, ever Christmas film."

"Not just Christmas, I might add," Gareth said.

Lindsay clapped her hands. "Okay, we have a choice now."

"Another one?" Preston groaned. "It's Christmas. We shouldn't have to make choices."

She ignored him and continued. "Do you want to play charades now or watch the film first? Hands up for the film." Ben put his hand up. "Film it is. Gareth, can you do the honours?"

"Sure." He reached for the remote and turned the TV on while everyone chatted. Ben wriggled across the floor until he was sitting between Gareth's legs, resting against the armchair his

Daddy was sitting in. As he looked around the room, he realised how much of a ragtag group they had, and he loved it. He stopped his gaze on Victor, who looked so dejected Ben knew he wouldn't stay the whole day. Frowning, he recalled Gareth's words from the kitchen earlier. *I have a feeling he's not being entirely truthful. With himself or the app.* What wasn't he being truthful about? He'd have to ask Gareth later because that might be the answer to finding someone perfect for Victor.

And as for Preston, who knew what to do to help him? From what they'd been able to get out of him, his boss was still engaged, still ignoring him at work, but had finally answered some messages. He didn't know the content of the messages, but he hoped Preston wouldn't fall for his charm again. It wasn't a good relationship for him, and Ben would say as much if he thought it would help.

Felix and Jane seemed to be getting along better than they had been, and Ben hoped they would go out on a date. He might sneakily try to help with that or get Lindsay involved.

Lindsay, however, wanted to stay single. She had told him she was happy being alone and not having to answer to anyone else, and Ben could see that. As far as he was concerned, as long as she was happy, so was he.

As the film started, he rested his head on his knees and smiled. He couldn't wait until tomorrow.

28

GARETH

Gareth kept himself awake by sheer force of will until he knew Ben was fast asleep. He crept out of bed and down the hallway to the spare bedroom. He was taking a chance on doing this because if Ben's answer tomorrow was no, Gareth would've wasted his time. Closing the door behind him, he began working as quietly as he could. Once he was done, he went downstairs and into the living room.

The gifts they had bought for each other sat beneath the tree, but although he didn't want to spoil Ben, he'd bought more that he hadn't put there until now. He didn't think it was fair that Ben's childhood memories were of such dreary content from what he'd told him. He wanted Ben's first proper Christmas to be magical. Propping the extra gifts around the tree, he smiled, thinking of Ben's expression when he saw them in the morning. Gareth couldn't wait.

Tasks completed, he returned to bed and wrapped himself around Ben's body.

A naughty boy nudged him awake by grinding his ass against his morning wood several hours later. Gareth pretended to ignore him for a short while and sank his teeth gently into Ben's shoulder when the sensation became too much.

Ben giggled. "Please, Daddy. Let's start the morning off right," he whispered.

"Grab the lube," Gareth croaked.

Ben reached for the bedside table and rummaged around without looking before holding up a tube. Gareth grabbed it and slicked his cock within seconds. Squeezing some more lube onto his fingers, he ordered Ben to pull his upper leg towards his chest, opening his ass. He pressed a finger against Ben's entrance, rubbing a circle around it before pushing inside. Under normal circumstances, he would've taken more time to prepare him, but between them both being eager and Ben taking his fingers easily, he didn't need to.

Gareth slotted himself into Ben's hole and thrust forward, burying himself inside. He grasped Ben's upper leg and lifted it over his own, opening his boy further. Then he started a punishing rhythm set to take them over the edge as quickly as he could.

"Daddy! The cage!"

Gareth didn't falter at Ben's words. "You can come with it on. I know you can."

"No, I can't! Please!"

"Come for me, boy. You can do it."

Gareth increased his speed, tilting his hips slightly to ensure he hit Ben's prostate. Ben keened his approval. Gareth's heart raced as his spine and groin tingled with the first signs of his impending orgasm. He panted and groaned, wanting to make Ben come first but unsure if he could with how turned on he was. Lifting a hand, he tweaked Ben's nipples alternately and raked his teeth over his shoulder.

"Come for me," he ordered.

His body clenched as his climax roared through him. He continued to thrust until he was too sensitive.

"Sorry, sweetheart. I'll unlock you and help you out," he murmured.

Ben sighed and relaxed in his arms. "No need, Daddy. I'm good."

Gareth withdrew and lifted to his elbow, peering at Ben's cock. The cage was covered in come. He chuckled. "I knew you could do it."

"It's a different sensation than a normal orgasm," Ben said. "I don't think I came as much as I do without it. It was more like a wave of warmth flowing over me."

"Did you not like it?"

Ben smiled lazily. "It was still great, just less powerful, I suppose."

Gareth rolled Ben to his back and kissed him. "I'll make it up to you later."

Ben hummed, returning the kiss. He pulled back with a start. "It's Christmas!"

Gareth chuckled. "It is. Merry Christmas, sweetheart."

"Merry Christmas, Daddy."

After another lengthy kissing session, he dragged Ben to the shower to wash off and clean the cage. Gareth had told Ben he could go without the cage that day, but Ben insisted on having it back on after his shower.

"I don't think this can be classed as a punishment anymore," Gareth huffed. "You like it too much."

Ben winked. "You'll just have to find something else to punish me with."

"I can think of several things we've yet to try."

Ben squeaked when Gareth pressed him against the tiles., the cold teasing his nipples and cock. "No, Daddy! I want to open the presents!"

Gareth sighed. "I guess Daddy's attention is not good enough when gifts are involved."

Ben giggled. "Not today."

Gareth slapped his ass. "Cheeky bugger. Get clean."

"Yes, Daddy."

Once they were clean, Gareth helped Ben into his new Christmas pyjamas, with himself following suit in a matching set. He threaded his fingers through Ben's and pulled him towards the stairs, his stomach churning. As much as he believed he knew what Ben's answer would be, there was always a chance he was wrong.

He walked into the living room first and stopped, sliding his arm around Ben's shoulder. "Merry Christmas."

Ben gasped, his hands covering his mouth as his eyes filled. "When did you... How... What!" He gaped at Gareth.

Gareth chuckled. "Santa must've left them."

Ben rolled his eyes and wandered over to the piles of presents. "I can't believe you hid them from me."

"That's what a surprise is, sweetheart." He settled onto the floor beside his boy, resting back against the sofa, and waved his hand. "Go for it."

Ben squealed and grabbed a box, checking first that it was for him before ripping the paper. He inhaled when he saw it.

"It's a milkshake maker. I know you like the thin milkshakes better than these, but it also makes smoothies and other stuff."

"I do like the thin ones better, but the thick ones are good, too. Thank you." Ben leaned forward and kissed him.

Gareth cupped his nape and held him when Ben would've pulled back. "Do I get a kiss for every present you open?" he murmured against his lips.

Ben snickered. "Maybe."

Gareth pulled back. "Next one."

"This one's from Victor." He tore off the paper. "Oh, my god!"

Gareth leaned forward. "What is it? He wouldn't tell me what he got you." He laughed when he saw it. "I shouldn't be surprised."

"I don't know what half that stuff is," Ben said, moving some of the sex toys around.

"I'd be happy to introduce you to some of them." He bit Ben's earlobe.

"That can be yours." He passed the box over, and Gareth put it aside.

"You'll like them. Trust me."

Ben grinned. "I do trust you." He kissed him.

They continued in the same vein until they'd opened all but one present. Gareth fidgeted and grabbed the last small box.

"This is something I've wanted to ask for a while, but I didn't want to push too hard." He swallowed hard and handed the box to Ben. Both their hands shook as Ben opened it to reveal a key nestled inside, along with a black ring. "First, I would like you to move back in. Permanently. And second, I would like you to consider the possibility of us getting married one day. I know it's quick, but I really believe—"

His words cut off when Ben silenced him with his mouth. Gareth clutched him when he felt tears on his face. He had no idea who they were coming from. They rested their foreheads together while he waited for Ben's answer.

"When I signed the tenancy on the apartment, I asked them to change something. Instead of signing up for a year, I only signed up for six months because I wanted to be back home. Here. This has felt more like home than anywhere else. I would love to move back in." Gareth tightened his hold. "As for the second thing, what was the question?"

Gareth snorted and shook his head. "You are a menace. You know that?" He rose to his knees and grabbed the ring. "Ben, my darling boy, would you agree to marry me at some point in the future?"

Tears streamed down Ben's face when he nodded. "Yes. Definitely, yes."

Gareth swallowed to keep hold of his emotions as he slid the ring onto Ben's finger. It fit perfectly, which uncurled another knot of uncertainty.

"How did you know it would fit?"

Gareth winked. "I measured your finger when you were sleeping one night."

Ben laughed and touched the ring. "I love it."

"Good. I have one more surprise."

"What! You've done enough."

"You're only getting this because you agreed to move in." He stood, pulling Ben up with him.

"Why wouldn't you have given it to me if I didn't move in?" Ben pouted. "That's bribery."

Gareth held up a finger. "No, it's only bribery if I told you that *before* I asked you to move in. I told you after." He tugged Ben towards the stairs. "Up we go."

"Why is it upstairs?"

Gareth tutted. "So impatient."

He led the way to the spare bedroom and invited Ben to open the door. Ben wrinkled his nose and turned the handle. They stepped into the newly furnished office, complete with everything Ben could need.

"I thought you could use this as a work-from-home place, or if you decide to change jobs, you'll have this space for you. Or just a space for you to hide away if you need a breather. Whatever. It's yours."

Ben stayed quiet as he wandered around the room, touching the desk, the shelves and the chairs, and Gareth worried he wasn't as enthusiastic as he'd hoped.

"You don't have to use it. We can always make it into something else if you don't want an office. It could be a library, or you could put a spare bed in it if you need space. It's your area to do whatever you want with it." Gareth was rambling, but he couldn't help it. He had actually been more nervous about this gift than asking him to move in or marry him.

Ben sauntered over to him, a neutral expression on his face. When he stopped in front of him, he said, "This is beautiful and thoughtful, and I love it."

Gareth's breath rushed out of him, and he felt light-headed. "Thank god."

"One question, though." Gareth raised his eyebrows. "Are you psychic?"

Gareth chuckled. "Not that I know of. Why?"

"Because I only decided a couple of days ago that I wanted to find a different job. As much as I have enjoyed the challenge at Market Foods, I don't want to keep doing it. I had thought..." His words drifted off, and he bit his lip.

Gareth freed it from its confines with his thumb. "You can tell me anything. What did you think?"

Ben inhaled. "I thought I could do something with the app. Organise some parties or something in the different areas around the country to allow Daddies and boys to meet in a less stressful way. I don't know. It's still just a brief idea floating around my head. I know I'd have to get a job in the meantime, but maybe something less stressful."

Gareth slid his arms around Ben's waist. "I love that idea. Have you asked Lindsay about it?"

Ben's cheeks flushed. "Yes. Sorry." Gareth smiled to show he wasn't upset. "I wanted her input, and I think she would be able to help."

"I agree. We'd have to think about how to make this feasible. We might have to make a membership fee or something to be able to pay for the upfront costs of hiring rooms and things."

"I don't know if I like the idea of making it so they have to pay."

"We could make it a tiered approach. That way, those who don't want to attend the parties or those who just want to try it can join for free. If they like it, they can pay for more benefits."

Ben wrapped his arms around Gareth's waist. "I like that idea." Ben sighed. "It wouldn't happen for a while, anyway. I want to make sure we're settled before I start a new venture."

"You're amazing, sweetheart. I wish you could see yourself as I see you. You have such a big heart."

"A heart that belongs to you."

Gareth pecked Ben's mouth and tucked his boy's head beneath his chin. Contentment sank into him as he held the most precious person in his arms. Despite having known Ben for less than five months, his entire being felt as if he'd known Ben for a lifetime. He couldn't wait to see what trouble the boy got up to next, especially if Victor was also involved.

Ben's stomach rumbled, and he giggled. "Sorry."

"No, I'm sorry. I should've made you breakfast before letting you get carried away with the presents." He took his hand and led him back downstairs, this time to the kitchen. He settled him into a chair and fixed him a strawberry milkshake. "What would you like for breakfast today?"

"Pancakes?" Ben asked, eyes wide.

Gareth chuckled. "Okay. As it's Christmas, I won't even make you have fruit with them today."

Ben threw a fist in the air. "Bonus!"

"Unless you want banoffee pancakes?" Gareth raised his eyebrows in question.

Ben scrunched up his face and pouted at the same time, making him look soft and squishy. "That's not fair. I love banoffee pancakes." He sighed. "All right. I'll have fruit with my pancakes today."

"I don't think you have to worry about them being too good for you. With the amount of sauce on them, it probably balances out the goodness."

"Even better. You can't eat healthy stuff on Christmas Day. You're supposed to fill yourself up with sweets and chocolate and cake and roast dinner and...and...lollipops!"

"Lollipops?"

"Yes."

"You don't even like lollipops." Ben huffed. "And anyway, stop letting Victor fill your head with nonsense. For example, roast dinners have vegetables in them."

"Yeah, covered in honey or gravy."

Gareth shook his head. "You're a menace."

"But a cute one." Ben put his hands under his chin and smiled sweetly.

"A deceptively cute one," Gareth agreed.

29

BEN

Six months later

"Welcome, guests. I hope you are all as excited as we are to hold this first Daddy's Boy Mixer event." Ben smiled at the cheers and waited for them to die down before continuing. "This event has been a long time coming. When DaddyG and I first thought up the idea of the app, we never believed how much it would blow up. How much you all needed it. Until we saw the results, we never truly realised how many people were affected by the same things those close to us were. We thought we were few and far between. But you gave voice to your struggles and your hopes and dreams. It was with that outpouring of emotion that we can stand where we are right now.

"Now, I may be the official spokesperson for this company, but we wouldn't have even started this journey without one special person. DaddyG."

The audience of around fifty men clapped and cheered for his Daddy, and Gareth hesitantly waved back before going back to hiding in the shadows.

"I won't detain you any longer. Have an amazing evening, and find a steward if you have any questions or problems. And if you see us around, feel free to say hello. I deem this Daddy's Boy Mixer open!"

The DJ set a horn blowing for a few seconds before the music took over. Ben stepped away from the podium and into Gareth's arms.

"Well done, sweetheart."

"Thank you, Daddy. It's so exciting. I hope at least one pair can find something long-lasting."

He glanced around the room, ecstatic with the way things turned out. He and Lindsay had spent many hours pouring over the details of what was and wasn't needed. They'd decided that each Daddy should wear a blue shirt or T-shirt, and each boy should wear a red one. It made them immediately identifiable on sight and would reduce the number of misunderstandings. They chose female stewards who wore white shirts with black waistcoats to make them identifiable, too. With the exception of him and Gareth, everyone else working there was female, as they had wanted the focus to be on those who had paid to be here, not on potential side-eyes on the staff.

They'd hired a ballroom at one of the local hotels, wanting to keep their first event close to home, and had been pleasantly surprised when people were willing to travel to attend. Lindsay had already used the data they'd accrued from the app to choose different locations across the country, the next of which was in the northeast of England.

Ben couldn't believe how much had changed in the year since he'd met Gareth. He would never have believed this was his life if anyone had told him what it would look like. Living with and engaged to an amazing man, a new business venture under his belt, a group of friends he loved dearly, and parental figures he wished he'd had all along.

"What's ticking around in that brain of yours?" Gareth asked, squeezing him tighter.

Ben closed his eyes and smiled. "Just thinking about how much has changed in a year."

"I wouldn't change anything that happened to me before because it brought you to me." Gareth kissed his temple. "The original Daddy's Boy."

Ben chuckled and batted him on the stomach. "I'm *your* boy. No one else's."

"I beg to differ. According to these people around us, you are *the* Daddy's Boy. The poster child for boys all over the country."

"He's right," Lindsay piped up as she joined them. "The stewards have already had several requests to meet you. You are the face of the company, remember?"

He groaned. "Why did I agree to that?"

"Because you have good people skills and amazing speech-making skills." She waved her hand towards the podium. "As you've just shown."

"Okay." He sighed. "Who's first on the list?"

"Andy Soloman, username andyplays231. Gareth answered his question on the blog last year, he tells me. He's a 'superfan.'"

Ben smiled. "Who else?"

"Damian Horsfall would like to meet Gareth."

Gareth frowned. "I don't recall a Damian."

"His username is DemonBoy666."

Gareth grinned. "Now that name I do remember. Sure, I'll speak to him. Do you want to come with me?"

Ben shook his head. "You meet Damian. I'll meet Andy, although I bet Andy would prefer to speak to you as you answered his question." He chuckled.

"Behave," Gareth said, pecking him on the lips.

Lindsay laughed. "Actually, he asked for you, Ben."

Ben raised his eyebrows. "Oh, okay. Lead the way."

Lindsay led them to where Damian waited, and Ben shook his hand before making his excuses to see Andy. When he was introduced to a blue-eyed, ginger-haired, muscular man, he'd masked his stereotypical response and inwardly cursed himself. Just because someone was tall and built like a rugby player didn't mean they couldn't be a boy.

"Andy, nice to meet you."

Andy smiled and shook Ben's hand. "Oh, I'm glad I got to meet you. DaddyG has, um, mentioned you many times in his blog, and, um, I'm in awe of you."

Ben flushed, not used to so much praise that didn't come from his Daddy. "Thank you. I'm glad the blog has been useful to you. I know Gareth answered your question last year. Did you figure things out?"

"Yes, and no. I, um, know I want to be a Middle because I've tried the younger age at a club near home, and it didn't appeal to me." Andy twisted his fingers together, and Ben could see he was nervous.

"Shall we grab a drink and find a seat, and we can chat?"

"Um, sure. Thanks."

Ben led the way to the bar, ordered their drinks after Andy haltingly told him what he wanted and headed for a table furthest away from the speakers. It would be easier to talk. When they settled, Ben said, "How have you been, Andy?"

Andy took a sip of his drink through the straw, staring at the table, and it was all Ben could do not to pull the man into his arms and hold him. He seemed uncertain, almost scared. He didn't push him. Ben sipped his own drink and let Andy gather his thoughts—or courage.

"I want to be like you," Andy said in a rush.

Ben frowned. "A Middle?"

"Yes, but, um, you're so confident. You can talk to people. Um, I get too nervous, and I struggle, um, to explain things. It makes, um, others misunderstand, and I don't know, um, how to change that."

All the while Andy was talking, his hands were twisting in his lap.

Ben crossed his legs and leaned forward, his elbows on his knees. "I'll let you in on a secret. I'm not as confident as I appear. Just ask Gareth. What you saw up there." He pointed to the podium. "That's all smoke and mirrors. Yes, I used to speak in front of people in a boardroom, but I didn't enjoy it. I was always nervous. More now because this event means so much to us." He rested his hand over Andy's, stilling his movement. "To find your confidence, you have to find yourself. You have to know, unflinchingly, what it is you want and need. As soon as you know, that certainty comes across." A thought crossed his mind. "I have to ask, but feel free to tell me to mind my own business, but have you always been this nervous, or did something happen to make you this way?"

Andy's whole body froze, and Ben's heart wept. He knew the answer before Andy even uttered a word.

"My first Daddy wasn't the nicest," he whispered, Ben barely able to hear him over the music.

"Oh, I'm sorry. As trite as it sounds, not all of them are like that."

Andy nodded. "I know. That's why I wanted to do this. I knew you wouldn't let people like that in."

"I can't even begin to imagine what you might have been through."

Andy gave a sad smile. "It wasn't as bad as you're probably thinking, but he had a very low opinion of me, and it filtered into our lives until I believed every word he said. Panic attacks, anxiety, nerves and every other word associated with those are just some of what I deal with now. But it hasn't stopped me from trying to find the right person for me."

It hadn't gone unnoticed by Ben that Andy's words were clearer and had less uncertainty the more he spoke.

"I'm glad, and that just goes to show how much confidence you already have inside you. You need to let it out."

Andy blew out a long breath. "I try, but I get intimidated by people easily. When people meet me, they assume I'm a big, brash, overbearing, larger-than-life person, and when they find out I'm not, their opinions go completely one-eighty."

"We can help you find the right person, Andy. It is now my personal mission."

Andy's eyes widened. "Oh! No, you don't have to do that! I wasn't asking to make you do some work. I just wanted some advice."

Ben chuckled and patted his hands. "I know, Andy. I know, but I've now decided you are my friend, and I want to help." He glanced around. "Have you seen any Daddies here you like the look or sound of?"

Andy's cheeks flushed, and Ben hid a smile. "There was one guy, but I didn't catch his name. He's taller than me, has jet black hair and was wearing purple Dr Martens." Andy bit his lip, trying to stop his smile if Ben was right.

"Purple Dr Martens. Well, that should narrow the scope. Let me talk to Lindsay and find out. Are you okay here for a minute, or do you want to come with me?"

"I'm okay here." Andy cupped his drink and smiled. "I need some time to get up my courage."

Ben patted his shoulder and weaved through the crowd to where he thought Lindsay's table was. "Hey, Lindsay. I have a strange request."

"Doesn't that sum you up lately," she murmured with a small smile.

"Hey!" He frowned, but she laughed at him. "Anyway, do you know a Daddy who is wearing purple Dr Martens?"

She blinked at him. "No," she said slowly, "because we did not request a mention of footwear on the forms."

"Damn. I had hoped you'd maybe noticed him or something. I need to find him."

"We could do an announcement?"

Ben shook his head immediately. "No, that'll just cause embarrassment." He studied the occupants. "It can't be that hard. I'll have to go around and check everyone."

"Why is it important?"

"You know you introduced me to Andy? Well, he struggles to meet people, and I've decided to help. He mentioned liking the look of the guy, and I wanted to find and talk to him."

"That's like looking for a needle in a haystack."

"It's only fifty-ish people. It can't be that hard."

Lindsay sighed. "You start looking. I'll go around the staff and see if anyone knows who he is and ask them to keep an eye out for him."

"Thanks, Lins. You're the best."

"That's why you bribed me to leave Market Foods." She grinned and disappeared before Ben could reply.

He went right through the middle of the crowd, looking at the floor—or rather people's feet—as he went. He found someone wearing purple trainers but nothing else. He changed directions when he reached the other side of the room, ending up bumping into someone.

"Oh, sorry!" he said, then grinned and slid his arms around Gareth's neck. "Hey, Daddy. I missed you."

"Missed you, too, sweetheart. You're on a mission, I'm told."

Ben nodded. "To find a guy with purple Dr Martens."

"We've done more with less, so let's go."

Gareth kissed him and threaded their fingers together, but before they moved off, someone tapped Ben on the shoulder.

"I hear you're looking for me?"

Ben glanced at the guy's feet, confirming the purple shoes, and grinned up at him. "I am. What's your name?"

"Scott Chambers."

"Okay, Scott. I have a boy who's interested in meeting you, but he's super shy and nervous. Something happened in a previous relationship, which I'll leave him to explain if he wants to. It's made him jumpy, to say the least."

"Is this, by any chance, the tall ginger-haired guy?" the man asked.

Ben nodded. "How did you know?"

"I tried to talk to him earlier, but he ran. I've been trying to find him."

Ben pressed a hand to his chest. "I'm glad I don't have to try to persuade you. He's amazing. Would you like me to introduce you?"

"Yes, please."

"Yes! Follow me."

Ben turned and bumped into Gareth again. He chuckled. "Sorry. It's not like you aren't big enough for me to see."

"You're distracted. It's fine. I'll leave you to your matchmaking."

"Do you not want to come with me?"

Gareth pecked him on the lips. "I think the two of you will be more than enough for your friend to deal with. I don't want to overwhelm him."

"You're right. I'll find you in a little while." He glanced over his shoulder, seeing Scott with a grin on his face. "What?"

"You two are perfect for each other."

Ben grinned. "We truly are. Come on."

He led the way through the crowds to where he'd left Andy, hoping the man hadn't moved. Luckily, he hadn't. Andy's eyes widened when he saw them coming towards him, and Ben rushed to him.

"Breathe, Andy. Breathe through this, and I'll introduce you. You don't have to say anything if you don't want to," Ben said, sliding an arm around his friend's shoulders and holding a finger up to Scott, asking for a minute.

"What if he, um, he, um, doesn't like me?"

"We find someone better matched. This is not a contract, Andy. It's a conversation, and if you want me to be, I will be beside you throughout the entire thing."

"Please." Andy nodded. "Stay."

"Okay. Shall I bring him over?"

Andy inhaled shakily. "Yes."

Ben tilted his head, indicating for Scott to join them. "Andy, this is Scott. Scott, I'd like you to meet Andy."

Scott crouched beside Andy on the opposite side to where Ben was. He didn't touch Andy or reach for him. He just smiled and said, "Nice to meet you, Andy. I've been looking for you."

"Looking for, um, me?"

Scott nodded. "I wanted to talk to you. See if we had anything in common. Would you like to do that?" Andy bobbed his head. "Perfect. Is it okay if I sit down?"

"Please."

Ben whispered to Andy, "Do you still want me to stay?"

Andy bit his lip, and Ben knew exactly how he felt. "No, it's okay." He inhaled. "I can do this," he said, more to himself than anyone.

"You can do this, Andy. I have faith in you. I'd really like to get to know you," Scott said.

Andy's cheeks reddened, and he dropped his head. Scott's hand lifted as he was going to reach for him, but he pulled back at the last second. As much as Ben would've loved to see Scott help Andy, he knew it was too soon.

"I'm going to the main desk. You know where you registered when you came in?" He waited for Andy to nod. "If you need anything, find me there, and if I'm not there, Lindsay will help."

"Thank you, Ben."

"Lastly, don't leave without saying goodbye. I want your phone number before you go." He winked.

Andy chuckled and bit his lip again. "I won't."

Ben glanced at Scott, whose focus was on Andy, which Ben believed it should be. He patted Andy's shoulder and left them to it, hoping fate did its thing for those two. If not, Ben would pick up the pieces.

"All sorted?"

Gareth's voice made him jump, and he backhanded his chest. "Don't do that!"

Gareth laughed. "Sorry." He slid his arms around him.

"Yes, they're talking. We'll see what happens." He rested his head against Gareth's shoulder. "How is everything else going?"

"Fine. Some Daddies and boys are pairing off, but only time will tell."

"I'm glad we did this. Even if we help just one couple, I'll be happy."

"I wouldn't worry about that. Toby and Ollie are still going strong. There's your one couple."

Ben sighed, a smile on his face. "True. If only everyone else was that easy."

Gareth snorted. "Nice try, sweetheart. Nothing is ever that easy." He kissed Ben's head. "Let's get something to eat."

"Lead the way."

"I always will."

30

GARETH

Three months later

Gareth stood in front of the mirror, adjusting his tie. Everyone kept asking him if he was nervous, but why should he be? Today was the day he was marrying the man he wanted to spend the rest of his life with. What was nerve-wracking about that? He knew Ben loved him, and barring any incidents, nothing would stop them from tying the knot.

Preston came into the room with two takeaway cups. Hopefully, Gareth's held tea and not the sludge-type coffee Preston drank sometimes.

"Here we go. Caffeine for the groom." Preston rolled his eyes. "Yes, it's tea."

Gareth accepted the cup and sipped it. He'd been told he wasn't allowed to sit down because it would crease his clothes, and he paced instead. Again, not because he was nervous, but because he wanted to get out there and get it done.

When Gareth had first asked Ben to marry him last Christmas, he hadn't expected Ben to want to seal the deal as quickly as he had. When he'd broached the subject of why Ben wanted to get married so fast, he'd made Ben cry. His boy had thought Gareth didn't want him, despite his words and actions to the contrary.

Finally, Gareth smacked his ass and told him to listen, explaining exactly what he meant by that. Ben had reassured him that he wanted to be Gareth's—as soon as possible—for no other reason than he wanted to be his.

And that was that. The next day, they began arranging things for the September wedding Ben wanted. Why so long when Ben wanted to get married quickly? His boy had a few ideas of how he wanted to celebrate, and those took time to organise.

But they were finally at the last hurdle. All he needed to do now was wait. Patience, as he so often told his boy.

"From what Victor told me, everything is nearly set up. By the time you finish your tea, we should be good to go," Preston said.

Gareth studied his best friend and smiled. The past year had been good to him after getting over the crappy situation he'd been in with his boss. He'd never seen Preston happier than he was, and it was all down to Preston himself. As for Victor, the man was still waiting for his Daddy, but that couldn't be helped. The man would come along when it was time and not before.

Gareth downed his tea, uncaring how hot it was, and threw the cup in the bin. "I'm ready."

Preston rolled his eyes and shook his head. "I'm now going to rephrase. When I finish *my* tea, we should be good to go."

Gareth chuckled and went over to the window, leaning against the frame and staring out at the gardens filled with varying colours of flowers, shrubs and overhanging trees. The hotel was as picturesque as the brochure had shown, and Ben had been over the moon with it. They'd used the hotel once for a Daddy's Boy event, and they planned to return in the future.

Daddy's Boy had picked up speed in the community and had over two thousand members now. They'd completed three events so far, one in the northeast, one in the southwest, and one in their home county. They had organised another five events that were all fully booked, and several more were pencilled in for the rest of the following year. Ben was in his element, and they found more pairings every time another event took place.

Gareth and Ben had taken on the business as a partnership, with contracts and everything, to ensure they were both protected should the unthinkable happen. The unthinkable was they split up. It wouldn't happen. Gareth was certain, but he'd wanted Ben protected in case Ben had a change of heart. Ben had kicked up a fuss, and it had been one of their biggest ever fights. In the end, though, Gareth had got his way.

"Time to go, lovebird."

Gareth showed Preston his middle finger and stepped towards the door. "About damn time."

They strode through the hallways until they entered the ballroom they were using for their reception dinner. They had placed the tables on either side, leaving an "aisle" for them to walk down and out into the garden area. That aisle funnelled into the actual aisle for the wedding.

Guests from Gareth's side of the family and all their friends and colleagues were waiting on seats on either side. He smiled and nodded at them as he passed, eager to get to his place at the front. He shook hands with a friend of his father, who happened to be ordained and had agreed to marry them. Ben loved the idea that they were keeping it within the family, as he called it.

Stepping into his spot at the front and to the right, he held his hands in front of him and stared at the hotel, waiting for the first glimpse of his soon-to-be-husband. Ben had insisted on Gareth not being allowed to see his outfit until that day, and as it made Ben happy, he'd agreed to go along with it.

He glanced at his father, sitting on the front row of seats, next to Felix and Jane, who were now a couple after fighting the attraction for many months. On the opposite side of the aisle were Lindsay, Toby and Ollie. Because of Ben's situation with his relatives, he hadn't wanted the usual one side for one family, the other side for the other family. Gareth had suggested that they just let people find a seat and sit in it. That way, they didn't need to worry about a seating arrangement for the wedding, only for the reception. Ben had given him a thank you blow job for that suggestion, which Gareth hadn't turned down, of course.

Preston touched his shoulder, and he glanced at him, receiving a nod in the hotel's direction. He whipped his head around as the music started, waiting to see his boy. At first, all he could see was the silhouette of two people walking through the ballroom—someone must've turned the lights off—and his heart pounded. He couldn't stop the smile that spread across his face as Ben stepped outside.

His boy wore an ivory suit with a check design. The jacket was one-buttoned, with peak lapels and a navy-blue edge around the pockets. The waistcoat matched the rest, but he wore a plain white shirt with a navy-blue tie that matched the colour of Gareth's suit. Gareth now understood why his tie was an ivory check design.

As Ben navigated the steps down to the main aisle, Gareth stayed where he was, although he wanted to run to Ben and lift him to the sky, spinning them around. But that could wait until after their "I do's."

He locked gazes with Ben and smiled, seeing the love shining through Ben's eyes and hoping his were the same. When they arrived, and Victor held out Ben's hand for Gareth to take, he couldn't resist and leaned forward to kiss him. Everyone behind them laughed, and someone shouted, "You're too early!"

He kept it quick and chaste but tagged on, "You're gorgeous," as he pulled back. Ben bit his lip and smiled. Gareth led him to their places in front of the minister.

"We are gathered here today to observe the joining of Gareth and Ben in matrimony, and I ask you all to stand witness for these two people."

Gareth squeezed Ben's hand, having never let it go, and Ben squeezed back.

"The love between two people is not to be taken lightly. It is to be treasured, to be adored, to be cherished. The giving of one person's love to another is a value above all else. Ben and Gareth have chosen to show you, their guests, that they hold the other half of their soul as close as they would if it were their own."

Gareth glanced at Ben, seeing his eyes brimming with tears already, and handed him his handkerchief. Ben sniffed and smiled.

"Now, Gareth, Ben, please face each other and repeat after me. I, Gareth Tremain, take you, Ben Mycroft, to be my husband, to hold, to love, to cherish, to care, to carry, to champion, to encourage and to provide from this day forward."

Gareth repeated the personalised vows with a firm voice, meaning every single word.

"Ben. I, Ben Mycroft, take you, Gareth Tremain, to be my husband, to hold, to love, to cherish, to comfort, to strengthen, to support and to provide from this day forward."

Ben repeated with a shaky voice but no less strong.

"I now ask of the witnesses; do you know of any reason this marriage should not take place?"

No one said a word. If Gareth was to hazard a guess, he would think no one was breathing.

"Then it is without further ado, my greatest pleasure to announce you as married. Guests, I give you Gareth and Ben Tremain. And although you've already done it, you can kiss."

Their guests stood and clapped, whistles and shouts abounding. Gareth took Ben into his arms and kissed him like his life depended on it. This was what they would share for the rest of their lives if fate permitted. When they pulled apart, Gareth gripped his hand, tucking Ben's arm under his, and began their walk back down the aisle to the waiting reception. Confetti flew, landing in their hair, but Gareth didn't care. All he cared about was that the man beside him was his.

As they stepped into the ballroom, Gareth pulled him in for another kiss and rested their heads together. "I love you."

Ben sniffed. "I love you."

"All right. Enough of the lovey-dovey," Preston said, pulling Ben away from him for a hug himself and doing the same for Gareth. "Congrats."

"Thanks."

"I'm going to grab a beer before my best man's speech."

Gareth groaned. "Why did I ever think having you as a best man was a good idea?"

"Because you love me, man."

"Shove off, Prez. Gimme a hug," Victor said, throwing his arms around Gareth. "I'm so happy for you."

Gareth grabbed Victor's chin. "Yours will be here soon," he whispered.

Victor smiled, dislodging a tear, which he discreetly wiped away. "I already have my speech prepared. We're all good."

Gareth sighed and faced Ben. "I think we're going to regret that tag team."

Ben chuckled. "Maybe, but if they drink enough, we can blame it on the alcohol."

As they greeted each of their guests as they entered the reception, Gareth realised he didn't care what his best friends said. Anyone could say anything, and it wouldn't change a thing.

He'd still have his husband by his side.

He'd still have his boy.

He'd still have Ben.

❖

Thank you so much for taking a chance on this book. I hope you enjoyed Gareth and Ben's story. Would you consider leaving a review, please?

We will be seeing more from this series but not until 2023. You can, however, pre-order Toby and Ollie's book, Trust Him, now.

If you'd like to be given regular updates and exclusive content, please sign up to my newsletter, where you'll also get some free short stories.

In the meantime, if you like Daddy books, I have a novella series you might be interested in. It starts with Love Me, Daddy.

ACKNOWLEDGMENTS

Thank you to Renee. You've believed in me through every step of this journey. I wouldn't be where I was today without you. Please don't go anywhere.

Maria, you've made all my work better because you know when to use a comma and when to use a semi-colon, something I can never seem to figure out when it comes to my own work.

To Emma, who has been my cheerleader and alpha reader, telling me when the storylines just don't cut it and making me laugh and cry with the comments you leave for me.

When I was writing this book, I needed the names for a pub and a club, and I have two people to thank: Anka, for coming up with 'The Pub,' and Heather, for naming the club 'Bound.'

About Elouise East

Elouise East writes sweet and steamy connections in gay romance. She also touches on taboo stories under the name Elouise R East.

Books that tell the stories where friendship and family are the focal point - be it blood family or chosen - are very important to her. That's why she includes a variety of personalities, talents, ages, situations and abilities as she believes a story or character needs. She wants her characters to be real, to be relatable, to be free to have whatever views they tell her they have. And trust her, most of the time, she does not have *any* say in the matter!

Her characters come to life on the page for her as well as her readers. Their stories unfold in front of her as she writes, and she has very little input into how they want to be shown. Just like real life, the lives of her characters change with every choice, every interaction and every conversation. And she wouldn't have it any other way.

She writes books that are emotionally realistic, even if liberties are taken with other aspects of the stories. She doesn't know any other way to write. It comes from deep inside.

Who is she? A single parent to two children living in the UK. An avid reader who still tries to devour every book she can get her hands on. A student of learning about any subject that takes her fancy. An author of books she would read herself. And a romantic at heart who loves anything cheesy.

Who's joining her on her journey?

Stalk her here... ;-)
Website : https://elouiseeast.com
Newsletter : https://readerlinks.com/l/2368814
All links : https://linktr.ee/elouiseeastauthor

BOOKS BY ELOUISE EAST

Boys, Daddies, Snuggles & More
Need Him
Trust Him

Daddy
Love Me, Daddy
Soothe Me, Daddy
Spoil Me, Daddy
The Complete Daddy Series

Club Royal
Rogue Royal
Secretive Royal
Grieving Royal
Disowned Royal
Trained Royal
Awakened Royal
Commanding Royal

Love in Flames
Out of the Frying Pan
Smokescreen
Breathing Fire

Crush
Love Conquers
First Kiss
Instant Desire
Primary Seduction
Deep Down
A Crush for Christmas
Life Support
Covert Strength
Love Scene
Lawful Attraction
Crush Box Set: Books 1-3
Crush Box Set: Books 4-6
Crush Box Set: Books 7-9

Just A Little Crush
He's Behind You
A Special Love
Three Thirds

Standalone
Treehouse Whispers
Star-Crossed
Protecting the Thief
Sizzling Chauffeur

Elouise R East (taboo)

Dark & Divergent
Forbidden Temptation
Too Many Secrets

Collide
When Fantasies Collide
When Dreams Collide
When Pleasures Collide